Yseyl blinked, looked into the innocent eyes. Zot had already people do to each other than any child should.

> *Holoas swooped at her, whispered in her ears: Watch the rape and murder of a nomad tribe. Harnke's Picture Palace has it all. See the secret orgies of the White Brothers. Harnke's Picture Palace has sensearound, you'll have every sensation as if it were you in the white robe. Learn what the Bond Sisters do in the heart of their Enclosure. Things so secret and perverse you won't believe your senses. Harnke's Picture Palace has group rooms or private viewing, whichever you prefer. Watch the torture and eating of an Impix anya. Bring a friend or meet a stranger with your tastes. Who knows what might come of it. . . .*

"There are things a lot worse than being bored, Zot. And if you go where you don't have friends, you're going to find them. Real fast."

Zot's eyes went wide, then she smiled.

It was easy enough to read what was going through her head.

> *Not me. Wouldn't happen to me. I been around, not like some dumb femlit never been out of the mountains.*

Yseyl shook her head, but said nothing. Pain and loathing were the only teachers for some lessons.

THE BURNING GROUND

THE SHADOWSONG TRILOGY #2

Jo Clayton

DAW BOOKS, INC.
DONALD A. WOLLHEIM, FOUNDER
375 Hudson Street, New York, NY 10014

ELIZABETH R. WOLLHEIM
SHEILA E. GILBERT
PUBLISHERS

First Printing, September 1995
1   2   3   4   5   6   7   8   9

Many thanks to Lynnell Luerding
for her generous help
working out the Tale Cards of the Pixa.

1

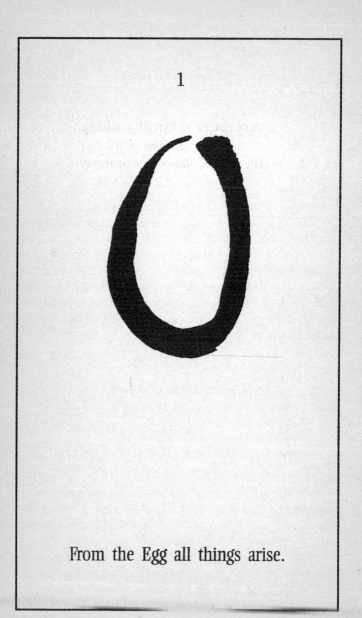

From the Egg all things arise.

Chapter 1

1. In the city Khokuhl

And now, for all you lovers out there, Bashar's Lament.

Isaho leaned her head against the radio so that her father's voice vibrated in the bone. Thann looked up from the sweater xe was knitting as xe's thinta picked up the child's reaction. Isaho didn't fuss, but since she'd seen her brother Keleen die, shot through the head by a sniper's pellet, she'd gone very quiet and clingy, worrying every time one of her parents went out without her. Hearing her father announcing the music assured her that he was still alive.

> *"Love in the daylight is sad, Ammery*
> *Oiling our passions when our anya is gone*
> *It is done, it is done, Ammery*
> *Where has xe run, our gold Amizad?*
> *Love in the darkness is sad, Ammery. . . ."*

When a shell from one of the mountain guns crashed through the hulk next door, Bazekiyl started and pricked her finger, jerking it away from the shirt she was sewing so the blood wouldn't stain the cloth.

Thann dropped the sweater and hurried to Isaho, taking her hand, whistling soft encouragement to her. To xe's fembond xe signed with her free hand using abbreviated gestures, +It didn't hit anyone this time.+

Bazekiyl shivered, wrapped her finger in a strip of rag. "You're sure, Thanny? Sometimes squatters . . ."

+I'm sure.+ Xe brushed the hair off Isaho's wide brow, sighed as the femlit cuddled against her. Xe'd been so frightened for so long, xe felt only a vague relief that the shell had missed their building, could barely sense a reaction in xe's family to the eerie whistle of the shells and the blast when they exploded.

There was a second crash-boom, a third, then silence and a plume of dust drifting past the window, past glass miraculously uncracked after years of near misses.

In the middle of the new silence there was a rhythmic rattle at the door. Isaho pulled away from Thann and rushed to push the bar out of its hooks. She jumped back as her father's shoulder shoved it open.

Mandall came in quickly, staggering under the weight of the sack he was carrying.

Thann shoved the door quickly shut, slapped the bar home, then turned and signed to Isaho to bring her father the homecoming water. Xe snugged against xe's malbond, basking in the waves of well-being that rolled off Mandall, the sudden burst of joy from Isaho, the quieter pleasure from Bazekiyl as she set the shirt aside and came to give Mandall a welcoming nuzzle. So much better. For the moment the war was pushed back and the family was almost whole again.

Isaho came from the room they'd set up as a kitchen, walking slowly, eyes intent on the glass she held with both hands. It had an inch of water in it, clear water without sediment, drawn carefully from the top of the cistern Mandall and his cousin had built from scraps of tin, salvaged lumber, and pipe when the water plant had fallen to the mountain guns and every drop had to be carried from the city springs.

"A glass for coming home, Baba." She glanced toward

Thann, who signed xe's approval, then smiled shyly up at her father.

He bowed with grave courtesy, sipped at the water. "Water shared is water blessed." He handed the glass to Bazekiyl.

"Water shared makes a home though there be no roof on it." She sipped, handed the glass to Thann.

Thann signed, +Water shared is a bond given by God.+ Xe passed the glass to Isaho.

The child drank the swallow left. "Water shared makes the circle whole."

Isaho sidled up to her Baba and leaned against him as he worked the knot loose and opened the sack. He patted her absently, went on talking as he worked. "Juwallan's oldest mallit Luzh stumbled across a way into an old grocery store when he was digging around for wood. Didn't want it to get out, so that's why Juwallan said it was a wood hunt when he called me at work. We got most of the food cleared out and stowed away before a scout from the Zendida Clan spotted us. More than food, too. I got some spools of thread and some needles for you, Bazhy, hammer and nails for me. Ahh, that does it."

He spread the mouth of the sack open, began taking out cans of fruit and vegetables, setting them on the floor. "Thann, if you and Shashi can trot these into the pantry. . . ."

Bazekiyl knelt, helped Isaho fill her arms. "That's enough for now, Shashi, you know where they go. Dall, the Zendidas . . . was there trouble?"

"No. We had the best of what was there already, so we left and let them have it." He grinned. "And I got this just for you, Bazhy."

Thann saw her face change as Mandall reached into the bag and pulled out a wide ribbon, so soft and smooth it seemed to cling to her fingers. It was a pale blue the exact shade of her eyes.

Xe touched the egg in xe's pouch, felt the babbit squirming and shifting about inside the leathery shell. *Maybe there'd be another to keep it company.* Xe liked the thought of that. The egg was nearly ready for hatching, which meant that all too soon xe'd lose the pouch bond and the comfort of that wriggling weight. Just as Isaho clung to her father now, so Thann saw xeself clinging to the egg and the suckling that would live in xe's pouch for another year, a tiny piece of joy and sanity in the chaos their lives had become. Xe watched and listened, one hand on the tiny bulge at xe's middle.

The moment shattered as a shell crashed outside, closer than the others. The floor and walls shook when it blew.

Isaho came running from the pantry and flung herself against her father. Bazekiyl reached out to draw Thann closer, and the four of them huddled in a tight knot waiting for the next shell.

The silence went on as the light coming through the still unbroken window panes darkened and the room filled with shadows. The mountain guns were mostly silent at night.

Bazekiyl stirred. "I think that's all for a while." She eased herself free from her bondmates, crawled to the window, and pulled down the blackout curtain. "They must have gotten a new supply of shells from the smugglers." She tugged the blind tight, clicked the hooks at the lower corners through the eyes screwed into the wood of the wall, then groped about for the candle lamp. "You know how wasteful they are when that happens." A flare from a match lit her face from below, then the candle was burning. She fitted the chimney down around it. "Shashi, bring me the other lamps, will you? Then we'll start fixing dinner."

✦ ✦ ✦

Thann gestured, and Isaho pushed her chair back as quietly as she could manage and stood to sing grace for the meal.

Before she was ready, a nightbird, a weh-weleh, sang its three note courting song. It was a good omen. Bazekiyl laughed and snapped thumb against forefinger, Mandall clapped his hands, and Thann whistled a soft breathy appreciation.

Isaho giggled. Then she crossed her hands over her heart and sang, "Part of the stream of all that lives/Part of the bounty the Living God gives/We come from earth, to earth we go/From God to God our lives do flow." She had a strong true voice that sounded older than her small count of years, eleven almost twelve.

Bazekiyl closed her hand tight about Thann's. Xe returned the pressure and swallowed a sigh at this reminder of what might have been before this God-cursed war began. If Isaho were trained, they both knew she would be one of the great singers. There was no chance of that. Not now. No teachers, no theaters, only the radio and maybe a chance of clandestine songwires passed from hand to hand, the promise in the voice, but unfulfilled. Back when Isaho was still in shell, they'd had a lot of dreams for her. No more. Staying alive was about all there was.

"Shashi and Thann and I went over to Cousin Fokoza's for tea." Bazekiyl slipped a kaslik on Isaho's plate, a thin pancake rolled around chopped up meat and greens in a cream sauce. "Want some fruit on it, Shashi? Cousin Mikil, you know, the one that bonded into Yiswayo Clan, anyway she was saying her malbond was caught by a seven mal phela out looking for ablebodies, they wanted to make up to nine and they wouldn't listen when he said his anyabond was bedbound and needed him, Dall, you be careful when you go out, I don't know what . . . what was I saying." She spooned fruit in thickened juice over the kaslik and moved around the table to Thann. "Oh. Yes. He slipped his leash after they'd been on the river a couple of days, he knew they wouldn't chase after him because there was this Pixa phela that was coming to river and they meant to ambush it and they didn't have a lot of time to get ready, anyway he came across this peddler on his way back here." She smoothed her hand along Thann's shoulder, smiled when Thann signed that xe didn't want any fruit; xe didn't like sweet things. "Peddler was telling him about the Holy City, said even the Pixa don't bother folk there. Said the peace was something you wouldn't believe." She finished serving Mandall, rubbed the back of her hand against his cheek, and carried the platter to her own place. "If you'll pour the tea, Dall."

Thann kept an eye on Isaho while xe listened to xe's bondmates chattering on about the day, playing dream-games about Linojin. Xe could see no way of crossing the whole continent to get there, not with Impix and Pixa phelas roaming about, hunting each other and killing anything that moved. But dreams were all they had right now and would have any time ahead as far as xe could see—xe and Bazekiyl and Mandall and Isaho and the nameless egg in xe's pouch.

And it was the same for all the Impix who lived out the wrecks of their lives in this wreck of a city. Whole families and broken families, traders twisting a dangerous living as they scurried through the shadows of war, Brothers of God who were supposed to be untouchable, but who died, too, even when they came to bless, as did the fem Sisters in Godbond who tried to mediate between the clans and the Anyas of Mercy who cared for the orphans and tended the sick and dying. Xe looked at the blue ribbon tied in Bazekiyl's fine black hair and sighed. *Small pleasures. Maybe they're enough.*

Isaho had finished all the fruit and the glass of canned

milk from Mandall's trove and had just a few bites of kaslik left; she was pushing them around with her fork, her eyes so heavy with sleep it was obvious she didn't know what she was doing.

Thann slipped from xe's chair, moved around the table. Xe tapped Isaho's arm, signed, +That's good enough, Shashi. Time for bed.+

Isaho's mouth moved and Thann thought for a moment she was going to protest, then she leaned heavily into the anya, yawned and murmured, "Carry me?"

+A big femlit like you+ Xe finished with the flutter of the fingers that was anya laughter. Then xe slid xe's arms under Isaho's legs and lifted her from the chair. It wouldn't be long before xe's baby was indeed too big for xe to carry and the thought pierced xe to the heart.

Isaho's pallet was in the pantry which had been a walk-in refrigerator before Mandall had taken the door off. It was the safest place in the apartment.

They lived on the second floor of a five-floor building that once had been a fancy hotel, most of which was rubble now; their rooms were in the back of the hotel's restaurant—one of the private dining rooms, a piece of the kitchen, a bathroom whose toilet still flushed when Mandall poured the dirty dishwasher or bathwater into the tank, the old refrigerator and the laundry room which Mandall, Bazekiyl, and Thann used as their bedroom.

There was a candle burning by the sink in the kitchen and another in the pantry. Thann settled Isaho on the straw pallet, fetched a basin with a bit of water, washed her face and hands. +Now+ she signed. +Get yourself undressed while I fetch your toothbrush.+

"Ahhh, Thannny, I'm sooo sleepy. I can brush in the morning."

Thann gave a short sharp whistle, then signed, +And all night little bugs will be digging at your teeth and when you're trying to smile at a mallit or an anyalit, all you'll have left are gums.+

"Mallits, hunh."

Thann tapped her cheek, grinned at her, and went out.

As xe got a glass of water and the toothbrush, xe could hear Bazekiyl and Mandall still talking. There was that in the sound of their voices that made body parts soften and swell. Xe glanced through the door.

Bazekiyl took the blue ribbon from her hair and passed it through her fingers . . . her head close to Mandall's, her cheeks flushed, a little smile on her face . . . winding the ribbon through and through her fingers. Thann's thinta heated with the feel of xe's fembond loving the silky slide against her skin. . . .

Xe hurried back to Isaho, impatient suddenly with the child's demands on xe.

While Isaho brushed her teeth, xe lit the nightlight, a slow burning candle in a glass bowl, and set it near the door. Xe took the brush, so Isaho could rinse her mouth and spit the foamy water into a waste water bowl. Xe dropped the brush in the bowl and set them aside, pulled the blankets up and tucked them around the child, touched her lips with a reminding forefinger, then touched hands with her as they went through the nightprayers they'd signed together since Isaho was old enough to learn what the signs meant.

As xe bent over the drowsy child to give her the night kiss, the floor shook under xe and there was a deafening explosion, then a rattle as the walls of their place fell in.

"Baba!" Isaho pulled away from Thann and scrambled to her feet. "Mam!"

Thann caught her, tried to push her back down on the pallet, but Isaho broke free again and ran from the pantry.

By the time Thann reached her again, she was digging frantically at the pile of bricks and debris just inside the dining room door, grunting, snuffling, crying, calling

Mam and Baba over and over, calling her dead brother, making the dust and bricks fly like a little chal digging in a mound of rock and earth for the mayomayo hiding there.

Thann stopped, stared through the door at the child, at the poufs of dust still floating in the air. A brick fell from the outside wall, smashed one of the windowpanes that ten years of war hadn't broken. Xe could see the sky, Phosis' fattening crescent visible through the veils of dust and the glowing wander of the Silkflower Road where stars were so thick the eye couldn't separate them. And the tail of the constellation called Mayomayo after the little beast that the first Isiging had chased into the Sky. A shadow glided past, a weh-weleh on the hunt, maybe even the one that prefaced Isaho's song . . .

They're dead. They're under all that. They're dead.

Xe looked down. Isaho's digging had uncovered a patch of blue.

Bazekiyl winding the ribbon through her fingers . . . round and round her long delicate fingers . . . Isaho mustn't see this. She mustn't. . . .

Thann caught hold of xe's daughter and pulled her away from her frantic digging. The child fought xe, but xe held her until she finally stopped struggling and started crying, her slight body shaking with the intensity of her sobs. Xe held the child tightly against xe—leaning against the wall because xe's legs wouldn't support xe—the inner wall, the one still standing—it shuddered against xe, almost like Isaho, as the pounding went on and on.

Isaho's ragged breathing steadied as exhaustion settled like a blanket over her.

When she dropped into a child's sudden sleep, Thann lifted her and carried her back to her pallet and laid her there while xe used the water in the spit cup to clean the dust and blood off her hands.

Xe tucked the blankets around her, then went back to

the dining room to continue Isaho's digging because there
was some faint chance that one or the other of xe's
bondmates was still alive, protected by the table or some
vagary of the falling walls.

Xe uncovered Bazekiyl's hand, flattened and broken
yet still lovely, pale gray-green, smooth as the bark of a
silk tree, almost as soft as Isaho's baby skin. Xe pulled
the ribbon free, knelt weeping and rolling it into a tight
cylinder. Because xe couldn't bear to dig any more, not
right then, xe took the ribbon to the old refrigerator, set it
on one of the shelves, and stood looking down at her
daughter. Xe was the last alive of xe's clan and everyone
xe knew had little room in their lives for anyone else. Xe
didn't know what to do.

Isaho's face was relaxed, her breathing slow and deep,
but she was crying as she slept, tears seeping past her
short thick lashes, sliding down the sides of her face to
wet her pillow.

Thann went back to digging.

When xe uncovered Mandall's head, xe's last hope
died. Xe bent and kissed the matted brown crest hair falling over his ear, the only place xe could bear to touch,
then began covering him again.

Xe'd almost finished when a sound brought xe swiveling around, a piece of broken brick in xe's hand.

Isaho. The ribbon was tied in her hair, a big awkward
ugly bow. She was looking out past the pile of rubble, not
seeing it because she was seeing something else, though
what it was Thann couldn't guess. Xe's thinta read anguish driven so deep it was almost not there—and over
the top of it was a frightening eagerness, a need that
reached out and covered over everything like the devouring iscabu weed that was eating Khokuhl almost as fast as
the shells were destroyed the city.

"Linojin," Isaho said suddenly, "Mom and Daba and

Keleen, they've gone to Linojin. We have to go find them, Anya meami. Soon as it gets light, we have to go."

2. In the Mountains of God

The Heka's Shawl drawn tight about her shoulders against the evening chill, Wintshikan sat on her leather cushion and watched the remnant of her ixis moving about the stopping ground, setting up tents, the mallits and femlits fetching down-wood and maphik droppings for the fires, hauling water for the maphiks that pulled the wagon and the three skinny milkers that was all they had left of the Shishim herd. Her anyabond Zell knelt beside her, elbow on her knee.

"When it started, I was fierce for the war," Wintshikan whispered.

+I know.+ Zell's hand traced out the signs on Wintshikan's thigh.

"The Impix were doing evil in God's sight, dirtying the land and air and water."

+Yes.+

"I thought we'd teach them the Right Way and with God and the Prophet guiding our hands, it would be soon over and things would be right again."

Zell sighed and stroked her hand along Wintshikan's thigh, xe's fingers eloquent in the gentleness of their touch.

Shishim Ixis was camped here, in the hills above Shaleywa, when word came of the Impix marching into the mountains to build their filthy smelters and claw away God's flesh in their hunt for iron ores that they might go on in their blasphemous ways, destroying One's body, stealing One's blessings from their own grandchildren. And there on the Meeting Ground of Shaleywa the Hekas of all the Ixin and the Elders of the Pixa came together to declare Holy War. The Heka Wintshikan was strong in her loathing and sure of her rightness, impatient with the doubters and proud beyond pride when her mate Ahhuhl was first among the swell of volunteers to take arms.

It was here, in the hills above Shaleywa, that Ahhuhl lay for the last time in the arms of Wintshikan and Zell, his bondmates.

He was dead before leaves fell in the first War Winter.

It was her habit, when the Shishim Round brought her back to this stopping place, to spend her days in thoughts of God and her nights in contemplation of the occurrences of War, mourning her malbond and her only son who followed his father to God's Arms the year after.

She heard Zell hiss, then lifted her head and saw Luca come strolling into camp, her face sullen, her bare feet filthy from tramping off-trail. "Bhosh! I wish I knew what got into that fem." She lifted her hands, cracked them together. "Luca, get over here. Now."

Luca was the youngest of the ixis fems, moody and secretive, refusing to keep the Right Way. She came late to Praise and stayed at the edge of the group, hovering there as if she were readying herself to run at the first break she got. She wouldn't learn the Sayings, wouldn't join her heart to the heart of the ixis, wouldn't take an anyabond though she lay with any mal who'd have her. She didn't come out and say she refused to give a child to the ixis, but it was in her eyes and in her deeds. She hunched her shoulders as she answered the Heka's summons, not quite daring—yet—to refuse to answer it.

"Why do you take your tent into the trees away from us when you've been told again and again that your place is in the heart?"

Luca shrugged, dug at the ground with the toe of her foot.

"If you find this ixis unbearable, though we would sorely miss you, Luca, I will speak at the Meeting Ground and find another for you."

Luca's mouth tightened, her throat worked as if the words she'd swallowed for months and yet more months were fighting to find a way out of her. In the end, she said only, "It doesn't matter, does it. They're all the same."

Wintshikan pressed her lips together; it was a moment before she could speak. "I'll think on that," she said. "In the meantime, raise your tent where it belongs, or we will do it for you."

She watched the fem stalk off, anger putting energy into her walk.

"Ah, Zell, do you see the world falling apart? I do. There's no joy left in the Way. It's like a shirt that's been washed too often, only a few threads holding it together."

"So sayeth the Prophet," Wintshikan sang as the Praise began. "Rejoice in the Land for it is God's Flesh given for your pleasure."

"Rejoice," the ixis sang back to her, the anyas whistling and signing—an uncertain thin sound with all the mals gone except Oldmal Yancik and Blind Bukh. Ten fems (it should have been eleven, but Luca wasn't there), seven anyas, two very young mallits and three femlits.

"So sayeth the Prophet," Wintshikan sang. "Touch the land lightly, for it is God's Flesh given for your sustenance."

"Lightly," the ixis sang back to her.

"So sayeth the. . . ." She broke off as a band of Pixa mals came gliding into the firelight, nine of them; they moved into the circle of fems, ignoring her and the Praise. A Pixa phela but no one she knew, led by a mal with a thumb missing and angry red scars on his face.

He set his hand on Xaca's shoulder. "Where's your tent?"

Wintshikan was shaking with anger. The phelas that had come by before had been perfunctory with pleasantries, but none so unrighteous as to break into a Praise or expect the ixis fems to spread their legs without the courtesy of choice. "You are unGodly," she said, her voice coming out strong and full, powered by the anger in her. "Step back and let us finish."

He stared at her a moment, and she grew frightened when she saw there was no soul behind his eyes. He turned his back on her. "You want it here," he told Xaca, " 's all right with me."

In the flickering firelight, Xaca's face drained of color. Trembling, she got to her feet. "No. I'm not an animal." Her voice shook as she said it, and she wouldn't look at him. She walked ahead of him to her tent at the edge of the trees and went inside, still without speaking. She gave him no blanket blessing, telling him without words that she was unwilling.

Nyen, Patal, all the fems except the missing Luca and old Yaposh went with varying degrees of reluctance into the tents with the mals of the Phela. The anyas huddled together around the children, holding them silent and still, silent themselves as always, shuddering under the waves of emotion amplified for them by the thinta that was their blessing and curse. Oldmal Yancik stared at the ground, and Blind Bukh waited with stolid patience for the Praise to go on.

Wintshikan closed her eyes a moment, tried to gather serenity around her like the Shawl, but she could not. *For the children,* she thought. *We have to finish for the children's sake.* She cleared her throat, managed a smile as Zell's fingers closed briefly round hers. "So sayeth the Prophet . . ." she sang.

When the phela had gone, Zell pushed the flap aside and ducked into the tent. Xe signed, +They are gone,+ then knelt beside Wintshikan and leaned on her thigh, looking down at the cards spread on the silk scarf, two in the top row, three in the middle, one on the bottom. +Change?+

Wintshikan sighed. "So it seems. I haven't tried the reading yet. Hold my hand and look with me."

She touched the bottom card with a fingertip, murmured, "From the Egg all things arise." The card was a stiff leather rectangle painted white with an oval drawn by one sweep of a brush, set inside a thin blackline box with the number glyph for one at the top, a saying from the Prophet printed at the bottom, the whole varnished with a clear shiny substance. "A new thing arises and only God can judge whether it is for good or ill."

She touched the first card in the second row. "Here are the determinants that mark the days ahead." Inside the blackline box was a thick jagged line with arrow points on both ends and the glyph for nine.

"Lightning is God's Fire, both joining and sundering, illuminating and destroying."

She touched the second card, an inverted U drawn with one quick sweep of the brush by the long dead painter who'd made the cards; at the top was the glyph for six. "Mountain and fem, nurture and life, stability and the handing on of the Right Way." The third card in this middle row showed an oval like the first, but this was one filled with black. Glyph twenty-four. "Death. The end and the beginning."

She contemplated the row for a moment, then she shook her head. "Each sign is a contradiction of the others. I see only confusion not direction."

Zell patted her thigh.

"Yes. Finish the first scan, then try to sort." She moved her finger to the lefthand card in the top row. "These are guides to direct us to the Right Path." Three vertical lines, the sign of the tribond, mal-fem-anya. Glyph three. "As God is All and In all things, so should the Three be one, cherishing difference and celebrating oneness. I feel this

as a rebuke. I have left the Right Path and must return. I
am Heka and have led my own astray."

Zell pinched her, shook xe's head, pointed at the last
card.

Wintshikan moved her finger, touched the card. Two
vertical strokes with a third across the top, joining them.
Posts and lintel. The Gateway. Glyph twelve. "The sign
in the middle that looks two ways."

She contemplated the layout for several more minutes,
finally shaking her own head. "All I can take from this is
that we are on the edge of something, walking the balance
between good and evil. And we must be wise in our
choices." She gathered the cards and folded the scarf
around them, replacing them in the bone box the Painter
had made for them.

+You think of going hohekil?+

"I helped stone Raxal when he went hohekil, I called
him a deserter and abandoned of God. I've cursed hohekil
at the Meeting Ground. I've roared with the others to
drown out their words. I never listened to them when they
tried to tell us all that we'd chosen the wrong road, that
this is not God's war, but ours." She rubbed her hands
across her face. "Why isn't anything clear and simple any
more? Yes. I'm very close to standing before the ixis, taking off the Heka's Shawl and saying to them 'stone me if
you must, but I turn my back on the war and walk
away.' "

+I am glad. My heart for this war died with our son.+

"You never said."

+What use are words? I could not leave you and I
didn't wish to add to your grief, Wintashi.+

"I. . . ."

A scream broke into the silence of the camp. Zell
paused to gather up the card box and slip it into xe's
pouch, then ducked past the tent flap.

Luca stood by the embers of the fire, wild-eyed and

panting. "Get away," she shrieked, "They're coming, Impix are coming, I saw them, they're following that phe . . ." There was a shot out of the dark behind her, a sudden leak of blood darkening her sleeve. She dived away, scrambled on hands and knees into the shadow under the trees.

Then there were Impixa everywhere, yelling and shooting. . . .

3. The thief

The thief stared at the smuggler she'd tried to kill.

Yseyl was small and slight, little larger than an anya and almost as dark. Her face was thin and the color of late year leaves, a mix of green and brown, her fine long hair also greenish brown; ordinarily it was braided tightly, but the smuggler had pulled it loose when he searched her for weapons.

She'd slipped all his traps but the last, was caught in a sticky web she couldn't see or fight; it moved with her when she moved, held her with an unrelenting gentleness that she found more frightening than threats or pain.

She watched the smuggler as he finished unloading his shipment of ammo for the mountain guns above Khokuhl, black thoughts surging through her head, despair chilling her. How many more dead, how much more destruction? She was Pixa, but it'd stopped mattering a long time ago which side killed the other. She no longer believed in God nor cared what the Prophet said. And she knew she was not exactly sane these days. That didn't matter. She'd stalked and killed nine smugglers before this one, and if she could figure a way to get at him, she'd add him to her list.

He was an odd creature, like nothing she'd seen before, not much taller than she was, with fur like sooty plush covering all visible parts of his body including his face, mobile round ears set high on his head, eyes like pools of melted silver with pointed pupils. His ship was like him, sleek and black, with something about the paint that made it hard to see even on such a bright day as this was turning out to be.

She tried again to gain some ease in the invisible web, looked up, and met that enigmatic silver gaze. Why was he keeping her alive? That niggled at her, disturbed her concentration. Anyone with a grain of sense and the firepower he controlled would have ashed her the minute she tripped the trap.

He set the flare to let the Pixa gunners know where to find the load, swung the crane around and dropped a net beside her. When he got close enough, she could hear him singing something that ached her ears with its scratchy falsetto. He lifted what looked like a small rock from a cairn beside three bushes, tossed it in the air, caught it, then tucked it in a pocket of the broad belt he wore about his narrow middle. He spread the net out, tipped her into it, pulled it tight around her.

A moment later the crane lifted her into the hold of the ship.

Alone in that dark place, drowning in a sea of sour smells, she felt a shudder, a slight pressure, then nothing—or rather, nothing but a Sound that vibrated in the center of her bones.

That stone. Whatever. That was the control. He set it in a niche by the door. Door. Sphincter. Shat him out of here. God curse ... focus, Yseyl ... feel it ... feel. . . . "Ah!"

The stone was a hot little bit of business, but she'd handled worse getting to the other smugglers. The only reason she'd fallen this time was the cleverness of the furman. He'd set out more obvious traps to herd her to this one and left it quiescent until it was triggered by the shutting down of the rest. It had her before she could identify the source. *If I manage to get out of this, I'll have to sniff around more....*

Yseyl shook off anger and began reading the forcelines in the control. It was slippery, shifting with every touch, like trying to pick up a bead of mercury. Someone knew about mind fingers and what they could do. The thought chilled her, but she pushed it away and concentrated on finding the force knot that marked the shutoff.

After a while that her heartbeat told her was almost an hour, she tweaked a fine hot line, twisted another, there was a small pop and a smell—and she was free—and falling over as her muscles spasmed.

As she got to her feet, lights came on in the hold and a voice with a lisp and drawn out vowels spoke to her. "Remarkable. Adelaris swore even the psi-talented couldn't defeat that web."

"What do you want? Why did you ... ?"

"Capture you instead of killing you? Come talk to me. I've got a proposition for you."

"Have I a choice?"

"Not really. If I can't get value for you one way, I will another. There are places that buy people like you and play with them."

"I would die first. After I kill you."

"Yes. I'm sure you would. Number ten on your list, hm? I'd rather not test your skills in that area if you don't mind. You don't like the war, do you?"

"I don't like arms dealers."

"Nor do I, sweet assassin. It's not a profession I'd have chosen if I had any choice in the matter. How'd you like to put holes in that Fence?"

"What do you think? And why trap me?"

A weary sigh. "Because I want out from under. I want to buy my contract. To do that I need a thief who can pass through security like a ghost. You."

"I see." Yseyl found that she believed him, primarily

because she could think of no other reason for what he'd done. "Vumah vumay, I'll listen."

"Follow the lights."

Yseyl stepped from twilight into brightness. The furman sat in a large armchair facing the door sphincter, a heavy weapon on his lap. She leaned against the wall, crossed her arms, fixed her eyes on him. "So. Explain."

"Heard about the others you got to the past three years. I knew two of that nine, and they weren't gullible or fools. Three more I knew by reputation. You were sliding through wards that would stop anything up to a battle beam, anything more tangible than a ghost. I mean, you offed old Vervin, he's snakier than Holdarn viper in a snit. Well, maybe this is wasting time, but I wanted you to know why I came up with this idea." He shifted the weapon as she changed her stance.

She forced herself to relax. "You mean you'll promise to ferry anyone I bring you across the Fence and over to Sigoxol?"

"Would you believe me? Hah, don't bother answering. Even I wouldn't believe me. No smuggler's going to chance taking passengers past the Fence, so chuff that out of your head. It's something else I'm offering."

"I'm waiting."

He lifted his lip, showing his tearing fangs; it might have been a smile, but she didn't think so. "Plenty of time, sweet assassin, before we get where we're going. Hm, you might reach out and grab hold of that loop beside you, in about half a breath. . . ."

Craziness. Like the time she'd smoked khu with Crazy Delelan. Chaos criscross, floating floors and gloating doors, melting and pouring, terror's musk, puffball dust. . . .

Then the floor was solid under her feet, the wall cold and firm behind her back.

"What. . . ."

"Shifting to 'split. Upsetting when you're not used to it."

"Where . . . ?"

"That's part of the tale, Ghost. Yes. That's what I'll call you. Ghost." He set the weapon aside, waved his hand at the other chair. "Sit down and relax."

Hand closed on the loop, Yseyl bent a knee experimentally, leaned out from the wall. The vertigo was gone, her legs seemed prepared to hold her, and the floor had stopped melting. She took a step, then another. A third step brought her to the empty chair. She swung it around and settled herself in it, facing the furman. "So why have you stopped being nervous?"

"Haven't, but I dnn't think you're stupid. Kill me," he reached around, tapped a sensor. The expanse of black glass across the front of the room went an iridescent gray with loops and swirls of pale color shifting in ways that woke nausea in her upper stomachs. "And that's where you'll spend the rest of your life."

"Hell?"

"Who knows." He leaned back in his chair, crossed his legs, and dropped his hands on the armrests. "I can tell you how to put holes in the Fence. Big enough to pass a boat through and slick enough that no warning gets to the Ptaks. You want to hear it?"

"What'll it cost me?"

"There's a . . . mm . . . drug . . . a group of drugs, actually . . . that can extend the number of a person's days approximately tenfold. Very very expensive. Very very desirable, hm?"

"So?"

"I want you to steal some for me."

The Knot is the heart
of all things hidden.
Never cut
what you can untie.

Chapter 2

1. Observations

"I have been instructed to cooperate with you, but you'll have to tell me what you want to know. I can't have outsiders wandering at will through my files."

Sunflower Lab's chief security exec, by name Rez Prehanet, was a man who'd used all the resources of Dr. Denton's Meat Chop to carve himself into his own idea of perfection. *You can see his taste on his skin,* Shadith thought, *Brrr. Digby said trust him only as far as his own interests run and never be sure you know what they are; he's not the idiot he looks. Hunh! Dig, I look at him and I want to giggle.*

The office was brushed steel and leather with accents in rare woods, all carefully sealed in preservative so nothing could mar their perfection. No way to smell the wood, the leather, to feel their textures—they might as well have been holoas. *What a waste of trees and skin.*

Autumn Rose's smile had something of the same artificiality. "Oh, you may be assured, Exec. We will only request what we actually need."

Shadith slouched in her pulochair, her passive receptors open, trying to wring as much information as she could from the blunted emotions behind the exec's facade. She'd *looked* at the chair before she sat, caught a flare of interest from the man and stopped immediately. *Psi detecs. Suspenders on his sox, hunh! No doubt he's got ticky little spytecs tasting every twitch we make. Which is interesting considering how someone strolled in and got away with a big piece of the lab's assets.*

The pulochair shifted shape and inclination as Autumn Rose leaned forward. "The reports we've seen are summaries only. This is not adequate. We'll need to know your security arrangements in the lab building." She straightened, relaxed slightly. "Don't get your back hair up, Exec. I know you've changed just about everything, you're no fool. I am not asking for nitter detail. Just an overview."

A mildly amused look on his perfect face, he glanced at the readouts on his desk, then at her. "Nor are you a fool, given Digby's rep. It would not be all that difficult to extrapolate the whole from even a limited amount of detail."

"Ah. Digby's rep. You must know he considers all client-gained data as strictly confidential. His integrity is ... well, I wouldn't say unquestioned, there are those who would question a god if they could catch him ... say rather it has been tested over the years and never found wanting." Rose crossed long slim legs and rested her hands on her knees.

Not coincidentally minimizing her contact with the chair, Shadith thought, *she suspects them, too. Must have done before she even got here. Spla! I wish she'd talk to me. It'd help a whole lot if I knew something about what she plans before she does it.*

This wasn't going to be an easy collaboration. She and Autumn Rose just didn't like each other. *Two primas trying to work in harness? I suppose that's some of it. Oy! that means I'm a prima.* She smiled at the thought, *felt* a surge of interest/annoyance, looked up and saw the exec staring at her.

His eyes shifted, and he went back to watching Autumn Rose without a change in expression.

"If we're obstructed in the job we were hired to do, we

will so inform the Directors and withdraw. The retainer deposited will be claimed as recompense for our effort and irritation." Autumn Rose let a smile soften the predatory angles of her face. "However, at the moment all this is hypothetical. There are several points that need clarification—points that don't impinge upon your security except peripherally. You said individuals returning to ships in the Tie-Down were discreetly checked by the OverSec of Marrat's Market and pronounced clean, but you gave no details. We would like a listing of all ships out of the Tie-Down during the theft window and just after, along with a list and image of every life-form on them. Also, as much data as you have about those life-forms. It would be better if we could have a listing of all ships for the three weeks centering about the event, but the Market being what it is, the OverSec would probably howl and deny, citing confidentiality of customers. We understand that. If possible, we would like to view the original flakes and make our own extracts. You could arrange that?"

Shadith watched him relax. *Interesting. Digby was right. Rose is perfect for this part of the business.* She's used to handling these types, he said, she knows the body language and can talk the talk. As for you, Shadow, every time his eyes pass by you, his nerves are going to twinge. You look like you should be sucking your thumb and hauling dolls about. Now now, I admit that you've put on a little age and may I say it sits well on you, but you're not the standard model, are you?

"That will take a while to arrange, but it will certainly be possible. In the meantime, is there anything else?"

"Yes. You can have one of your ops walk us through the actual procedures of getting in and out of the other building and guide us over the route the thief must have taken. Hm. That might not be clear. I don't mean on comsynth, but the actual route, out there in the building."

"Why? Comsynth can give you far more data than you'd get just looking at walls."

"We prefer to have a variety of sources and as many primary impressions as time and circumstances allow."

Prehanet stood. "I'll take you myself; that way there won't be difficulties about what you're to see. My aide can deal with OverSec."

Prehanet waved a hand at the shield that enclosed the large asteroid, pulled the hand around in a wide curve to take in the transfer tubes that led to the other asteroids that made up the Market. "As you see, this is a closed environment which can be separated from the other nodes at an instant's notice, one of the benefits of operating at Marrat's Market, along with a certain docility in the workforce and the opportunity to maintain control over the product until we're paid for it—though we are careful to guarantee our clients anonymity as well as safety and quality products. We have a quiet but considerable reputation in the realm of pharmaceuticals and the mechanisms by which they are delivered. I should tell you that it was my advice to the Directors to write off the stolen articles and replace them as quickly as possible. It's my opinion that this is a one-off operation, so we don't have to bother ourselves with notions of repetition." He turned. "The lab building."

The lab's facade was a trapezoid two stories tall, with a modified holoa playing across it, a field of sunflowers blowing in a gentle wind, swaying against a deep blue sky; the entrance was concealed until someone on the slidewalk was within arm's reach of it. Behind them, the administration building where Prehanet had his office was a more conventional four-story structure of matte black stone and black glass windows; the kephalos that controlled both buildings was buried in the bedstone of the asteroid beneath Admin.

"Ordinarily, clients are not permitted in this area except when taking delivery; I doubt any of those involved discussed the arrangements with outsiders."

"You can never be sure," Rose murmured. "People do the most idiotic things. You might like to know that Digby echoed what you said when he spoke to the Director who hired us. That it would be a difficult, perhaps impossible, and certainly expensive business to locate the thief, and the possibility of recovering what was stolen is somewhat remote. There was one item the Director was very … mmm … anxious to reclaim."

"Yes, well, we won't discuss that out here." Prehanet stepped onto the slideway. "We don't issue passes to the labs. Unless someone is with me or with a designated op, they have been deepscanned and a template made. Every individual who presents himself has to match one of those templates, otherwise the door won't open. Anyone out of his, her, or its area or off the designated route to a workstation will trigger first a vocalized warning, then an alarm every time he or she passes a checkpoint without proper authorization. So this cannot be a matter of someone working here."

"No doubt you occasionally have a false alarms when someone's strayed."

"One or two every few months. Mostly the more independent workers cause them, lab techs on a looser rein than the contract labor. They seldom do so twice. We have a few prima donnas …" He stepped from the slidewalk, took Rose's arm to help her into the entrance alcove. Shadith he left to hop down on her own. "… who are at present too valuable to discipline," he finished. "They are always causing trouble. No alarms any time during the theft window, however. Stand there, please. A moment." He waved Shadith back. "If you'll wait. We'll set your temporary template next. May I remind both of you that the template is wiped the moment you leave the building. This is a one-time pass-through."

The corridor they stepped into was provided with demiholoas of sunflowers mixed with other scenes to give a sense of airiness and expansiveness at first glance, though Shadith wondered what seeing the same thing for months if not years could do to the perceptions of the people working down here. A slidewalk ran down the center, but the exec ignored it and led them to the right, his boots silent on the springy flooring.

"The storage space for the ananiles is in the first sub-floor. There's a lock on the door, but that's more to keep down pilferage than for any actual security reasons. The ampoules are packed in numbered, standardized lots, sealed in ceolplas wrapping. Inventory control is very strict and we have almost no leakage." He stopped at the mouth to the dropshaft, frowned as Shadith tapped his arm. "What is it?"

"Are dropshafts the only method of moving from floor to floor?"

"You have a problem?" He eased back so her hand fell away.

"No." She gave him one of her most ingenuous smiles. "The Director didn't include a schematic for this building in the packet he passed to Digby, so I was just wondering if there were alternate routes. You know, like emergency ladders if the power goes for some reason."

"I see. There is such a ladder. The doors are locked, however, and those locks will only open if the power fails. Any attempt to interfere with any lock will activate alarms and send security 'bots to that location. Even if there are no alarms, the kephalos checks the locks period-ically. They were, of course, also checked the moment the thefts were discovered, found untouched and intact. Hm. There's also the cleaner's lift, but that is limited to one specific female and her cleaning 'bots. There are no other routes."

"Thank you, despoi' Prehanet."

They stepped into a corridor much like the one on the floor above. Two turns later they were in a tunnel rather than a corridor, the rock of the asteroid given a perfunctory polish and fitted with strip lighting; the walls were interrupted at short intervals by doors of gray plasteel with numbers shoulder-high in the center. He stopped in front of 22, flattened his hand on the palmplate, then stepped aside as the door slid open and a light came on in the cubicle beyond.

"As you can see, we have refilled this order. The buyer will be here tomorrow to pick up his goods. To increase the security we have installed EYEs in the storeroom and along the corridor. An unnecessary expense, but whatever helps the Directors sleep soundly will be done. They know my opinion, in case you're wondering."

Shadith moved past him and stood in the center of the cubicle looking around. *No dust.* "Was the due date pushed back at all?"

"Yes. We informed the buyer that there was an accidental contamination of the Phase Three drugs, that they would have to be replaced."

"The former due date?"

"The morning after the theft. Why?"

"Do buyers inspect the merchandise before it's loaded?"

"Sometimes."

"Do you always clean the cubicles before the person arrives?"

"It depends upon the individual. This particular buyer, yes. There is an aversion to dust or any other signs of uncleanliness. The cubicle and every container in the shipment is cleaned thoroughly on at least three nights before it is to be inspected. But if you're interested in the cleaner, you'll get no joy there. She has passed a thorough probing and has no connection with the theft. And there is only one breather involved, the rest are 'bots."

"I see. Nonetheless I'd like a schedule of her movements on a typical cleaning pass. Rose?"

"If you're done, then I am."

The laboratory where the object had been stored looked open and airy despite being on the sixth level below ground; it was also quite empty. They'd passed a number of men, women, and others moving along the slideways and looking intently thoughtful or filled with purpose as soon as they caught sight of Prehanet. The only voices Shadith heard were those coming round corners; it seemed that the exec induced a zone of silence around him as he moved.

As they entered the lab, for the first time he had a shadow of a natural expression on his face, a crisscross of tiny wrinkles marring the skin about the eyes and mouth. "Several of the techs working on this project tried to refuse probe, but this is outside the reach of such conventions. They had reason, been running their mouths as if they had no off-switch in places with lots of ears. They have been disciplined. It is to be hoped Digby's people are more prudent."

Autumn Rose smiled. "It's part of the service. Proprietary information is restricted to those who need to know."

Ignoring this exchange, Shadith drifted about the room. It was a squat rectangle with smaller rooms opening out from three of the walls. The lock box where the gadget had been kept when it wasn't being worked on was set into the floor in the room most distant from the corridor.

She knelt, brushing her fingers across the face of the lock, a palmlock like that on the door of the storage cubicle. It was, after all, a working lab and the techs employed here would need to get into the thing without too much trouble. *I could do it easy as spit and not jiggle a flake in that kephalos. Only problem is getting into the building. No way of faking it I know of. Inside job? Our pretty Exec says no and I'm inclined to believe him. Otherwise the Directors would have the thief and Digby would never have been brought in.*

She got to her feet and looked around. Spotless as before. Impossible that it should be the cleaner, but who else went everywhere? *These techphiles ... depend on their instruments too much ... I beat a probe once ... different circumstances, still. . . .* "I want to talk with the cleaner, do her rounds with her tonight."

"That is not possible."

The answer came so fast she knew he hadn't even considered the question, reinforcing her impression of his rigidity. "Why?" she said. "You operate on a diurnal schedule with most things shut down during the assigned night hours."

"The schedule is to conserve trained workers; it costs less than finding adequate replacements and importing them. And it only applies to the subcategories. The Researchers come and go as they please, work to their own rhythms with such assistants as they consider necessary. They demand privacy and we ensure that they get it."

"I see. Have you considered a Researcher as the thief?"

"We have considered everything. The Researchers were not probed, but none of them were here alone at any time during the window and the assistants were tested thoroughly. Their evidence and that from the overlooks provide reasonable proof that none of the Researchers on this level or any of the others could have accessed both this lab and the storage cubicle without being seen. And probing gave further evidence that the assistants were not involved. We have also investigated the lives of all employees back for several months, which is not difficult given the conditions here. All interactions with outsiders or even with other Houses in the Market have been explored; none of them involved anything remotely connected to the theft."

Shadith strolled about, inspecting the instrumentation and making Prehanet very nervous. Looked a whole helluva lot like the lab was trying some back engineering. *No wonder they're so antsy to retrieve their gadget. Bet a year off my life they stole it themselves. Well, that's not our business as the esteemed employer would say. Wish I had a clue how the thief got in. . . .* "I've seen enough here. Walk us through the night security posts, please."

2. Itchy feet, itchy mind

The ottotel was a wart at the edge of the Marratorium, Marrat's version of a Pit Stop. Their rooms were standard nonluxe, what they'd find anywhere along the tradelanes. Shadith sat on the bed in her room, staring at the door, feeling that peculiar disorientation that plunging into a new place seemed to be bringing her these days—maybe this time because her harp was sealed in the ship and she'd nothing to do with her hands and her head was empty of words, so making a song or a poem was not possible. Or maybe it was because she was working to another person's rhythms. Autumn Rose was calling this one as long as they were here at Marrat's, Digby had made that quite clear. *I trust your skills, but not your instincts,* he said.

Her skin itched. Her brain itched. She wanted to be out and doing. But Rose said let it lay, so there it was, a corpse stretched out beneath her feet. *The cleaner's the key. I'm sure of that. She passed the probe. Contract labor with barely sufficient intelligence to manage a dust mop. But the only one who could wander unchallenged anywhere once she's in. So if it isn't her, it's someone who fooled the kephalos. And the Blurdslang overseer. How to get in, though? How to take her place? I. . . .* The musical chime of the announcer broke into her thoughts.

She got to her feet and sauntered across to the door, expecting another chime, but it didn't come. She tapped the announcer alive, saw Autumn Rose standing in the hall, her face calm, her hands still. *She's not one to fidget, no, not our Rose. That would be a weakness.* She opened the door and stepped back.

Autumn Rose nodded at her, walked to the small round table in the middle of the room, and flipped on the block. She beckoned, and Shadith joined her.

"Did you get anything definite or was that tour mostly for irritating Prehanet?"

Shadith rubbed her thumb across her chin, frowned at the wall. "Mostly I kept remembering Kikun."

"That noseeum of his wouldn't pass a template test or mask him from the kephalos."

"I know. But if you believe prettyface Prehanet, either there's someone who can beat a probe, or there's a ghost who can walk through walls. As it were."

"Hm. Assume a ghost and let him worry about how it got in. Find the ship it arrived on and trace that. There's a lot of traffic through here, but we should be able to eliminate some of it once we get the flakes."

"If we get them."

"I think it's likely. Sunflower really wants its gadget back."

"Wonder what it is." Shadith wrinkled her nose. "Very tightmouthed, our client. I think that lot stole it themselves and they don't want word getting out."

"Probably. Marrat's is definitely Gray Market. Prehanet just sent this over by messenger." Rose tossed a flake case on the table. "It's a list with visuals of all those who went in and out of the building on the night in question. Including your pet, the cleaning lady. Run this through a few times tonight, Shadow; Prettyface—apt name, by the way—he was snickering under his breath when he called to tell me the flake was coming. I suspect he's run the two lists through the kephalos and come up blank. Be interesting if you can tease out something he missed." She got to her feet. "We've an appointment with OverSec an hour after noon tomorrow. I'm going to find a game. Want to come along?"

"Thanks, but the circles you game in are so rarified I'd lose my breath before I started. I might see if there's any interesting music about."

Autumn Rose smiled, an urchin's grin that abolished her usual dignity. "And I'd be snoring before two notes were played. Enjoy, young Shadow. I won't play Mama and issue any warnings. From what Digby said, they'd be entirely misplaced."

Shadith blinked as the door closed. "Well, that was a surprise. Maybe we can cobble a team out of the pair of us."

She set the flake reader down, rubbing at her eyes. "Enough! Swarda was right. Better to play a little and let the overheated brain have a rest." Quale. Still hard to think of Swardheld by the name he'd adopted. A dozen years or so in the body didn't weigh very heavily against the millennia they'd spent together as concatenations of forces within the diadem.

I've got my house, he said. I've got my crew. I've got my ship. I'm happy with all that, Shadow. But there are times when life goes flat and the sun turns black on me and I don't know whether breathing is worth the effort it takes.

And then he looked around and smiled. He was building chairs now. There was one on the bench, lovely in the sunlight, its wood glowing with the rubbing he'd given it,

*taking in the light and sucking it deep down so it almost
seemed to breathe with the air that blew across it.*

*You found the right world, she told him, with all this
wood about.*

*Your music isn't enough? he asked her, then answered
himself. No. It isn't, is it? It's a grace, but it doesn't fill
the days. You're right to go with Digby. For a while, anyway. But don't let your songs and your playing slide. You
need both.*

"And that's the truth." She got to her feet, ran a comb
through her curls, then went out to find herself some song
and maybe a pinch of trouble to make the long night pass.

The Marratorium was crowded: ship's crews, servants,
and aides of the Meat Market patrons; labor from the fac-
tories; off duty guards; buyers and sellers; slummers;
players of all kinds; gamblers; scammers; thieves; smugglers; gun runners; druggies and druggers. Everyone who
had occasion to visit a gray market and had a bit of credit
to spare was out in the 'Torium hunting for pleasure.
Cousins of every sort; Bawangs stilting along, their heads
high over everyone else; Blurdslangs trundling about in
their nutrient dishes; Clovel Matriarchs and their cloned
attendants, little herds of chattering Jajes; Caan smugglers
with their velvety fur and the minimal leather strapping
they used for clothes; leathery Pa'ao Teely with eyes like
ice and half their merchandise on their bodies, those
weapons peace-sealed, a gesture to the peace of mind of
the rest of the swirling mix; Ptica-Pterri mostly in molt
though several had their mating plumage in full glory;
Xenagoa acrobats; gauze-wrapped Nayids, arachnoid
Menaviddans dressed mainly in stiff black hair and loops
of the shimmering monofilament that was their chief
wealth. A small group of Dyslaera moved into view, but
she didn't know them, and they passed her without a
glance.

She let a surge of strollers carry her into the casino, eased free of them and drifted past glitter-chitter games with dancing colors programmed to lure and half-hypnotize the watcher into playing, past games so ancient they might have been born rules and all with the universe itself, past dealers and shills, lingering a moment to listen to a flowerlike creature singing an eerie croon, moving on when the song was done. Autumn Rose was there somewhere, but she didn't see her. Probably in a private room away from this chaos, settled down with serious players.

This was the outer room where riff rubbed against raff, where the games were glitz and small change, the service by 'droid and 'bot, the music, such as it was, riffing off a dendron in the vast kephalos that ran the whole Marratorium. Where mezzanines were cantilevered from the walls and tables floated free with seatbelts and catchment basins for those who couldn't hold their drinks. Where hired men whispered suggestions to anybeing remotely mammalian, and hired women fluttered their lashes and suggested much the same without words, and hired others did what others did.

Shadith watched the avid faces of the assortment of life-forms crowded about the games, curiously alike despite the variety of species. It was one way of walking the edge, but losing money didn't thrill her much and winning would mean even less. No meaning to it, nothing to engage her beyond a moment's zazz.

The continual ripple and tremble of lights, the saturated color, and the tension in the gamblers started her head aching and she moved on, following wisps of music that drifted in whenever someone pushed through the silver membrane that slashed the whole length of one wall from ground level to the ceiling ten stories up. The casino's chief extravagance was the throwaway space. On their collection of enclosed asteroids such expansiveness was a luxury most structures didn't have.

Shadith shook her head at a man and pushed a woman's hand away, then followed the bits of music through the membrane.

The room on the other side was nearly as immense, a ballroom of sorts with tables in floating bubbles that drifted dreamily in and out of shadow, spiraling to a ceiling lost in smoke and mist, drifting down again. There were dance platforms that floated among the tables, flat ovals in their own environments that clicked home in sockets in the wall when the tiket-time was exhausted. All round the base floor, there were dressing rooms with costumes for rent if that was to your taste, costumes for every species and culture that came through the Marratorium.

The band on the main floor was an eclectic mix of acoustic instruments, a two-necked guitar from Komugit, a sha-horn from Sonchéren, an eight-string banjjer from Hikkerie, two fiddles from Somewhere Else, and an assortment of drums assembled from half a dozen worlds. The music they played was filled with an energy that invaded her body and set her feet to fidgeting.

A man's hand on her arm, a man's voice in her ear, "Dance, 'Spinnerie?"

Shadith started to pull away, then thought *watth'hell, I want to MOVE!* With caution's last dregs, she said, "What's your price?"

He chuckled. She felt it more as warm breath tickling her ear than as sound. "A gelder an hour, fifty the night, a la carte for the rest. First dance is free, just for the pleasure of it."

Her words breathless and fast, she said, "Convince me, hired man. Dance, and we'll see how you read me and go on from there."

He was a small man, a trifle shorter than her with a sharp face, pointed ears, and laughter in his black eyes as he swept her into the swirl of dancers.

At first his dancing was competent, even exciting, but there was an impersonal quality to it that muted her enjoyment, her extra senses reading his detachment, cooling her down to match his chill. Then—change. His pale face flushed as he opened himself more deeply into the music and the moving, reading her body as if his nerves were joined to hers. By the time the set was done and the dancing stopped, she knew she wanted this to go on.

She leaned against him, watched while the band fiddled with some minor retuning. "Tell me what I want."

"Music. Dancing. Talk. Danger. Sex."

"Then let's go find them."

3. Morning after

Head throbbing in sync with the caller chimes, Shadith groaned and groped until she found the shutoff and the wake-up call went silent. She lay a moment, her face buried in the pillow, flickers of memory running through her head. *Did I really strip to the skin in that cheechirrie dump and dance with a pack of rats I 'ticed from the conduits? Oh, Spla Ha!*

She moved her legs over the edge of the bed and pushed up till she was sitting with her head in her hands.

Her mouth felt like the tail of an old jack's ragship.

She straightened her back, sucked in a long breath. Mistake. The stink of sex and smoke and stale drink and who knew what else churned her stomach into instant rebellion.

She lunged up and reached the fresher just in time.

When she joined Autumn Rose in the lobby of the ottotel, she was neat and clean and ready for business. Rose smiled at the dark blotches under bloodshot eyes, but said nothing, just moved out with a brisk beat of her boot heels on the pavement. Shadith closed her eyes a moment, then grimly followed after her.

* * *

Marrat's OverSec was an ancient Blurdslang; his three rheumy eyes were set so deep in warty folds of tissue that an occasional gleam was the only evidence he was awake and alert. His nutrient dish was larger than most and closed in, his tentacles rested on the cover in contemplative loops. Around him, shut into cubicles of sound-proofed glass, much younger Blurdslangs worked over sensor boards or watched plates, the hair-fine fingerlets at the end of their handling tentacles busy at notation and half a dozen other tasks; the Blurdslang mind was more than capable of doing several things at once.

The Elder's age and status made him unwilling to attempt the usual approximation of interlingue most Blurdslang spoke. Instead he held a voice cube in one of his manipulators, the fingerlets wriggling like a nest of worms over the surface sensors, producing words in a sweetly musical voice that seemed to amuse him; when the cube spoke, his horny lips flexed and shifted in the silent dance of Blurdslang laughter. "You will make your copies here, and we will review them before they leave our hands. It is only because of Digby's reputation for magisterial silence that we have bowed to Sunflower's pressure and allowed this. We ask that you destroy the flakes once you have no more use for them." He paused and waved a tentacle tip at Autumn Rose.

"It will be done."

"Good. The room is prepared, access to the hours in question has been arranged, there is a supply of blank flakes in a recorder. Any questions?"

"The reviewing of the flakes can be accomplished in the room assigned?"

"Ah. That was not envisaged, but certainly can be arranged while the two of you are viewing the originals."

"Then we need to get started."

4. Eureka?

"I think this is the one." Shadith tapped a sensor and an image bloomed on the forescreen—a Caan smuggler and a slight androgenous figure whose species was as problematic as its sex.

They'd moved to the ship Digby'd provided and were working in a shielded cabin, having run the flakes from the day's work through a WatchDog to strip away any little surprises OverSec might have coded into them. It was a tedious job, checking names and putative worlds of origin of the seven hundred ninety-one entities who had left Marrat's Market within or shortly after the theft window, ten hours in all. A surprising number in so short a time, but this was a busy place.

"Why?"

"One. Because the little one is a fair match in size and build to the cleaner." She brought up the image of the cleaner from the flake Prehanet had provided. "As you see. Two. I don't recognize the species. What with one thing and another I've come across quite a good percentage of the star-hopping kinds, Cousin and nonCousin, at least those in reasonable reach of the Market. To get into that building you need a specialized ghost; Kikun's the only one I know who'd come close to that description. Certainly none of those others. Three. The registry of the Caan's ship. Mavet-Shi. That's one of Sabato's Mask Companies. You know the Caan and what they think of arms dealers. Just how happy would he be," she waggled a finger at the screen, "running on Sabato's lead? The gadget would be hard to sell without specs and provenance, but high-grade ananiles would go anywhere for top prices. What odds our Caan's looking to buy himself loose?"

"Hm. I've heard of Sabato. How did you discover his connection with Mavet-Shi? I doubt even Digby knows that."

"Ran across him on Avosing. Selling armaments for the Ajin's rebellion. I had a very odd and informative acquaintance who told me more than I wanted to know about a lot of things."

"I see."

Shadith wrinkled her nose. "Of course, the thief could be hunkered down somewhere in the Market, waiting for the noise to fade, and all this logic is angel counting."

"I doubt it. A world he could get lost on. Marrat's is too limited and too controlled." Autumn Rose examined the two images. "Make one last check. Set search parameters for height, weight, and body profile. Scrap the rest. Seems to me I remember a few that might be almost as good a match."

The ship's kephalos found two. One was a rather ambiguous figure in the crew of a Clovel Matriarch, the second a Cousin arriving in a small, battered merchanter, who claimed Spotchalls as world-of-origin and proclaimed himself a jewel trader.

"Hm. Given that Prehanet's security is as effective as he thinks, given that your reasoning holds about the cleaner, given that size is the determining factor, your first choice is by far the most likely. Matriarchs are so deep into control that clone must have about as much free will as an industrial 'bot. The other . . . we can drone his specs to Digby with the report. He just might be smarter than he looks. Hm." Rose rubbed at the faint creases at the edge of her eye. "There's something familiar about your pet. Something I've seen recently . . . in passing, I think, not interesting enough to command attention . . . doesn't matter, if I've seen it, Digby will have it. Let's get out of here before the local paranoia takes hold and makes life strange."

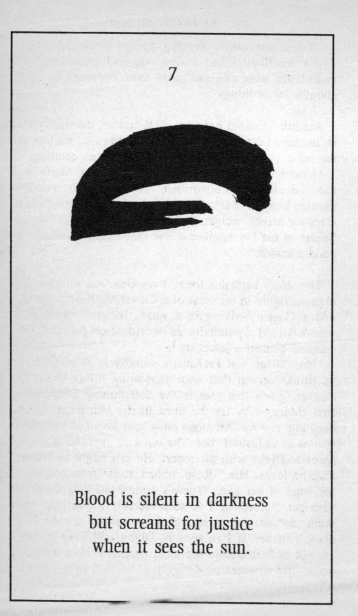

7

Blood is silent in darkness
but screams for justice
when it sees the sun.

Chapter 3

1. Runaway once, runaway twice

Thann huddled in the corner where a section of house wall still stood while the sniper in the hills sprayed pellets along the street; xe could feel Isaho getting farther and farther away, picture her scurrying like a mayomayo pup along the ruined streets. At least she was still alive.

Silence.

Thann crept from xe's corner and started on. Xe'd been careless before, too focused on Isaho and frightened for her to remember line-of-sight; the pellet burn across xe's shoulder was painful reminder that kept xe from forgetting pain. Bent over, black braid falling past xe's ears to tickle xe's chin, xe quickened xe's pace to an awkward trot, scuttling from shadow to shadow along the battered street.

Shots ahead. A squeal and a blast of pain and fear from Isaho.

Mouth working soundlessly in xe's distress, Thann straightened and raced toward xe's daughter.

Xe saw her finally, a small figure with a dangling arm, trotting by an open space as pellets rattled round her. Xe held xe's breath until Isaho was swallowed by a wall's shadow, then plunged across the gap and pinned her to the bricks with xe's body.

Isaho started struggling, whimpering, "Thanny, Anyameami, Linojin, I have to go to Linojin. Mam and Baba and Keleen, they're waiting for me."

By the time Thann quieted her, the sniper had stopped shooting and the big guns were silent. It was near sundown, the shadows were long and thick, the wind rising, whipping grit and debris against them, against the walls, scouring down the streets between the hulks still standing.

"Thanny, I've got to go to Linojin. Nobody listens. I've got to go."

Thann patted her. +When you're healed, Shashi. I promise you, we'll go together.+ Wincing at the pain in xe's shoulder, xe slipped xe's arms under xe's daughter and grunted back onto xe's feet. Xe lumbered across the open space, then began working xe's way back to the shelter they were sharing with Cousin Mikil.

Her shoulders rounded, her face weary, nothing in her eyes but fatigue, Mikil watched while Thann bandaged the pellet wound on Isaho's arm. She turned her head at a weak whistle from the other room, but she didn't move.

Thann cupped xe's hand across Isaho's brow, sighed. "Fever?"

Thann got to xe's feet. +A little,+ xe signed. +The wound is clean now, and she's strong; I doubt there'll be trouble.+

"What about you?"

+It's just a burn, barely broke the skin.+

Mikil rubbed at her eyes, then reached out, touched Thann's arm. "I don't. . . ."

Thann lifted a hand, stopped her. +I know,+ xe signed. +As soon as my baby's well, we'll find another place.+

Mikil started to speak, then shifted to signing after another glance over her shoulder. +It's Ankalan who's fussing. He says you're not his clan, so why should he have to give you room and feed you. When he hears about this . . . he told me if that femlit runs off once more and makes fusses for us, she goes. And our anya . . . + She quivered her hand in a "what-can-I-do" gesture. +Seeing you reminds xe too painfully of what xe has lost.+

+I know, Mika. These are hard times and they make for hard choices.+

Thann bent over Isaho, bathed her face and arms, got her to drink some bitter halaba tea, tucked her in again, and sat beside her trying to decide what they should do. More and more even the clan-bond was being broken. The people in Khokuhl were turning into scavenger gangs picking over the dead city, chancing death each time they left their holes to forage. How long before they were feeding on each other?

Would it really be worse to leave the city and try to reach Linojin? At least Isaho would be happier. And if they had just a little luck and were very, very careful. . . . Xe slid xe's fingers into xe's shirt, touched the flesh about the pellet burn. A little heat. Not bad, though. Maybe stiffness in the morning.

Isaho muttered in her sleep. Thann smoothed xe's hand over the child's hair, brushed back a curl that had crept across her eyes, left xe's hand tucked up against xe's daughter's face while xe whistled very softly an old lullaby.

2. Farewell to all we knew

As she huddled among boulders deep in a thicket of thornbush, Wintshikan tried to ignore the horror below, but the breeze climbing the mountains from the ixis camp brought her the smell of roasting meat and screams from one of the women they'd caught, brought Impix laughter and broken bits of words.

Zell was shaking all over, xe's tears hot as they touched her arm. She freed the arm, laid it about xe's shoulders and pulled xe close, wrapping the Shawl about xe to keep

away the sounds and as much of the smell as she could.
She couldn't do anything about Zell's thinta and tried not
to think about the emotions Zell shared with the dying
anyas.

The awful thing whispered by her sister Hekan was
true. Impix phelas ate Pixa anyas. Ate their flesh as the
flesh of a beast, not with honor and sorrow at a funeral
feast. Butchered them and ate them. She thought about
the empty eyes of the Pixa leader and it came to her that
Pixa phelas were no better, that they also ate anyas when
they could. Her mouth flooded, her stomach heaved, but
she clamped her lips shut, swallowed hard, and barely
breathed as she waited for this terrible night to end.

The Impix phela left before dawn.

They were so noisy in their departure that Wintshikan
was afraid of ambush and clutched Zell tight when the
anya tried to get to xe's feet. "Wait," she whispered.
"Wait till I'm sure they're gone."

The sky grayed in the east, a line of pink touched the
bit of peak Wintshikan could see through the tangle of
branches and vines. Below, at the stopping ground, a sicul
whistled and chirruped, then half a dozen others joined
in. In the distance a wild chal barked, then ran yipping
from something big enough to scare it but too slow to
catch it.

The light strengthened.

Shadows crept along the ground.

+It is time.+

Weary to the bone and sick at what she knew she was
going to see, Wintshikan put her hand on the boulder she
crouched against and levered herself onto her feet. "Zell,
stay here."

The anya shook xe's head, but xe stayed very close to
Wintshikan as the Heka worked through the thornbush
onto the more open slope under the muweh trees. The

growing light wasn't kind to xe, putting hollows in xe's cheeks and deepening the lines in xe's dark and gracile face.

The tents lay in rags. Everything the Impix couldn't carry off that could be broken was shattered; what they couldn't destroy, they urinated and defecated on. Eggs were stomped into smears, the embryos inside unrecognizable as anything but a scribble on the ground. Anya bones were scattered about, broken, the marrow sucked from them. All mixed together. Who could tell how many were gone. Seven of the Ixis women were sprawled on the trail, stakes driven through them. They'd died hard, but not from the stakes. Blind Bukh and Oldmal Yancik were tossed in a heap with three smaller bodies, the two mallits and one femlit who couldn't run fast enough but were too big to carry. Throats cut.

Zell thrust xe's fingers in xe's mouth, curled xe's tongue and let out the loud warbling whistle which was the emergency summons that was supposed to bring the ixis together.

One by one those still alive came back. Four women— Xaca, Nyen, Luca, Patal. Two anyas—Wann and Hidan, neither of them in egg nor yet in bond. Two young femlits, the last of the ixis children—Kanilli who was Xaca's daughter and Zaro whose mother had a stake through her heart, whose anya was bones with the others.

They came separately from under the trees but stood huddled together near the blackened spot where the Praise fire had been. They were silent, even Luca, standing with eyes down, looking uncertain, fear stronger than grief.

Wintshikan left the pile of the dead and came to stand with her arm about Zell's shoulders. She drew in a breath, let it out. "Xaca, see if you can find a knife, a pot that's usable. We need to bless the dead."

Luca lifted her head. "We've got to get out of here, they're going to come back this way. You know that. You have to know that."

"We will keep as much hold on the decencies as we can, Luca. You did well to warn us before. Would you keep watch for us again?"

Luca brushed at the hair falling across her face; it was as if she brushed a shadow away. She nodded and trotted off, vanishing up the trail in the direction the Impix had taken when they left.

"Nyen, Patal, help me carry the dead into the trees and lay them out. The rest of you, bring wood for the Eating Fire and look through what's left of the tents, see what we can still use."

Wintshikan lifted the small bowl that Kanilli had found among the rubble, a twisty line of steam rising from the bits of brain and marrow inside it. "The Prophet says the body is borrowed from earth and returns to earth when the spirit departs. Brother, Sister, Anya, we call you into ourselves, into the Remnant of Shishim."

She lowered the bowl, dipped into it with thumb and forefinger. "Blind Bukh, you were a good mal and true, following the Right Way with a whole heart and a good head." She ate the bit of brain, passed the bowl to Zell, who dipped and signed Praise for another of the dead, and so it went, round the small circle till all the dead were remembered and the remnants consumed.

The bodies and fragments of the dead were laid out in the forest, the possessions of the ixis that were unusable were burned or left to rot like the dead, away from the camp and the trail; what remained was sorted into piles for cleaning and dividing up among the living.

Zell's whistle brought the ixis together an hour after the ritual eating. Even Luca came running.

* * *

Wintshikan stroked her hand along the Shawl; then, to the gasps of the others she took it from her shoulders, folded it, and set it on the ground before her feet. She straightened, lifted her head. It was a moment before she could force the words out. "I am not fit to be Heka. I am hohekil. I find this war unGodly, and I will no longer be a part of it."

Xaca snapped her fingers and leaped across the ground to stand beside Wintshikan. "I, too. Him who took me to my tent, took me like I was nothing, gave no heed to my needs or my joy, only pleasured himself. And are the others any different, Imp or Pixa, does it matter any more? When did this change? When did we become less than a hole in the ground?"

Luca stepped from the shadows. "They knew they were followed. I heard them talking when they left. That's why I watched. Heka Wintshikan, did the Phelmal warn you about this? Did any of that phela warn anyone that there was danger? I see they didn't. They didn't care what happened to us. No, it's worse. They used us to give them time to get away. They knew the Impix would do what they did. They had to know."

Nyen came forward, lifted the Shawl, shook it free of leaves and twigs and held it out to Wintshikan. "Don't walk away from us, Heka. We need you. Tell us what to do."

Wann and Hidan whistled distress, signed agreement with large emphatic gestures.

Kanilli and Zaro ran to Xaca, stood beside her.

Patal was the last. She looked around at the camp; it was clean now, the bodies gone, even the bloodstains were brushed away. "It's hard," she said. "You throw away a thousand years when you leave the Round. I can't do it. I'm not as strong as the rest of you. I wish you well. I think you're wrong. In the morning I'll go down the mountain to Shaleywa. It's Meeting Time, there'll be others there. I ... wish I could stay with you, you're my family. I can't."

Wintshikan sighed, took the Shawl and snapped it round her shoulders. "We'll go north to Linojin. Peddlers say there's peace there still. Not even the unGodly touch the quiet of the Holy City. Patal, I won't force another's truth to match my own. God keep you safe and well."

3. Back with the goods

Cerex slid his ship into the shadow of the moon and settled to wait for night to slide across the landing site he'd chosen for putting Yseyl onto her homeground.

He swung his chair around and contemplated her. "You're clear about how to use that?"

She nodded, laid the disruptor into its case and closed the lid.

"Mind a little advice?"

"From an expert slider? Why not."

"They watch you, the Ptaks. And they've got paid agents working both sides. They're going to notice you when you start siphoning people out through the Fence, so you haven't got long. Maybe a couple months. And you're not going to be able to sneak a few through at a time, the Ptaks will just pick them up and toss them back. Hm. How're you going to get people to listen to you?"

"I've ... done some thinking about that."

"Why go back into that mess? One person, it's like spitting in that sea down there, sea won't even notice you. Come along with me. Once I buy my contract, there's a thousand and a thousand stars to visit and each of them with something worth stealing. A ghost like you and me with my ship and contacts, we'd have a real good thing."

Yseyl shook her head. "I can't. You kept your word, brought me back. I appreciate that. But I couldn't just go away. Not and live with myself."

Cerex shrugged. "It's easier than you think, dreamer. But I won't argue with you."

Yseyl managed a wavery smile. "Maybe after I finish this job. I ..." she paused, shivered. "I did enjoy very much playing the game back there. Walking the edge with nothing on line but me. No! I can't forget. . . . No. Just set me down where we planned. The mountains north of Linojin."

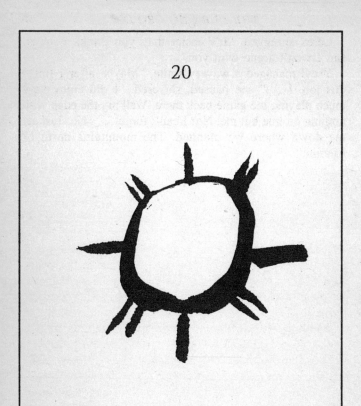

Fortune, enlightenment, joy
Such is the promise of the Sun.
Danger and excess
Such is the threat of the Sun.

Chapter 4

1. Digby spins a tale

> *The dancer on the highwire spun and leaped,*
> *feet light as feelers,*
> *flying the taut burn of the wire. . . .*

Shadith looked at what she'd written, wrinkled her nose. The image still wasn't right. Apt enough but overused. She struck out the word *dancer,* held the stylo above the sheet of paper and stared at the words, trying to force a new form out of the black lines. . . .

"Shadow, drone's just in from Digby, come on up."

She made a face at the speaker, snapped the stylo into its slot, slid the paper into the drawer of the foldout desk, and shoved the desk into the wall. "On my way, Rose."

Shadith put out a hand to steady herself as the ship seemed to hiccup, then steadied. "Course shift?"

Autumn Rose swung her chair round. "Right. As per Digby's instructions, I've switched the ship's internal ID to one of his Face Companies and we're now heading for a world the locals call Ambela. He's identified your little oddity. And agrees with your conclusions. A medkit came with the flakes, tailored to the ghost's species. First you catch her—and it is a her—then you tickle her lifestory out of her." She swung back as Shadith crossed the small bridge to the Co chair, tapped on the feed to the screen. "He's now set to lecture us on his conclusions."

* * *

Digby's simulacrum was in full professor mode, the tassel to the fez bobbing with every move of the image's head. He folded his legs in his favorite sit-in-the-middle-of-the-air stance, rested his virtual hands on his virtual knees, and smiled at them.

"Splendid work, my children." He lifted his hands, set fingertip to fingertip. "As a treat I'm going to tell you exactly what the gadget is our little ghost has lifted."

Autumn Rose sighed. "Dear Digby, if you didn't pay so well. . . ."

Shadith snorted.

"I see that your curiosity has been tormenting you." He paused, stroked the pointed beard he'd assumed for the occasion, and dropped his hands to his knees again.

"It is an opener of ways," he said. "A thief's wet-dream. An instrument for merging with a forcefield and insinuating a hole into it without informing the incorporated sensors that something drastic is happening. Among themselves our friends at Sunflower call it a disruptor, though that is an entirely inappropriate name. Inappropriate or not, disruptor we shall call it." He coughed and tilted his head to get the tassel out of his eyes. "Your supposition was quite correct, Shadow. Sunflower bought themselves some tempting loot of dubious ownership. And you will be interested in the source. Omphalos Institute."

"Tsah!"

Having paused for the expected reaction, Digby went on, "Yes, indeed. Our old friends, the Omphalites. Which brings up a point. I think none of us are happy with the thought of an Omphalos op walking through walls wherever he feels an urge to roam. We are contracted to return the disruptor to Sunflower, but I wouldn't be too disturbed if it were . . . mmm . . . damaged in the process. My source tells me the being who led the team that developed the gadget poisoned his aides, wiped the test data and specs from the lab kephalos, and went off with the only prototype. Before he sold it to Sunflower, he was careful to let nothing out of his head. Which is the major source of their agitation since he was killed very shortly after turning over the prototype and before he could dictate the specs. Probably Omphalos, but not necessarily. Which is why we were hired to get their toy back to them. Me, I'm seriously pissed because they didn't bother telling me Omphalos was involved. Maybe they didn't know, but I wouldn't bet on it." He tapped his nose, nodded, and paused to let them comment if they had a mind to.

Shadith chuckled, met Autumn Rose's eyes, and said, "You're a gambler, Rose. How much would you wager that even if we do retrieve the gadget intact, it has an accident on the way to Sunflower?"

"There's little pleasure betting on sure things."

Digby's image cleared its throat, the small sound meant to reclaim their attention. "The inclusion of the disruptor in the theft gives strong support to your first choice of thieves, Shadow. Which I will explain in a moment, after I've dealt with the other two possibilities.

"The Matriarch's crew person is most unlikely. They're too paranoid to buy stolen drugs and would be most upset by the presence of the disruptor on their world. Something that could bore silent holes in the shielding of all those little interlocking enclaves? No way, children. And no one they took off planet will have anything like free will.

"As for the mouse who calls himself a jeweler, he has more blotches on his record than freckles on a lass from Vallon and no evidence of any unusual abilities beyond a fast mouth and faster fingers. He steals things immediately salable, mostly gems, and wouldn't go within light-years of anything touching on Omphalos.

"Shadow, I knew about Sabato, of course, and have a list of his Face Companies which I thought was complete, but Mavet-Shi wasn't on it. When you get back, I'd like to know your source for this. Hm. And a long chat about other bits of your life.

"I talked to Xuyalix about the Caan Cerex. He was somewhat reluctant to chat on the topic. Turns out Cerex is some sort of relative who had a patch of bad luck. Got caught with smuggled goods on a world with a low opinion of smugglers. Pulled a term in contract labor and was sold offworld. His kin put together a fund and tried to redeem him, but the Labor Service wouldn't cooperate. I'd say the ananiles are meant to buy his contract with enough left over to get him home to Acaanal.

"Woensdag is on the way to Acaanal to check with Cerex about how close you got to the way the theft was worked, but I don't see any reason to make more trouble for the poor schlup. He's not important enough to bother with. I'll send a drone your way with a report on the interview. It should reach you before you make Ambela.

"The little one is the convincer. She's got impressive reasons for needing that disruptor."

In the screen a planet swam against a star ground while Digby's image sank to Thumbelina size. The turning world was mostly water with polar icecaps, two largish continents, one with a tapering tail of islands that came close to joining it with the third continent which was about half the size of the other two. A single moon drifted past in the stately gravity dance of satellites.

Icon Digby set fingertip to fingertip, tilted his head so the fez tassel brushed along his jaw. "What the original state of Ambela was no one knows, but sometime after it developed rudimentary flora and maybe fauna, the folk generically called Impix arrived—even they don't know where they came from. They settled in and mauled the world in the usual way, had some wars, lost hold on the tech that brought them there, began slowly building it back. They'd reached steam power and rudimentary elec-

trical services, rediscovered radio, when the Ptak arrived
as part of the outpouring when the Ptakkan Empire broke
up. Ptaks are not a bloody lot, but they have their peculiar
ways. They don't like being overlooked by strangers or
having outsiders controlling any of their space. As an
aside, that's one of the reasons their neat little empire
broke up—too many non-Ptakkan species kept resolutely
away from any touch of power.

With that in mind, they uprooted every Impix they
could catch, hauled them to the continent they called
Impixol, and set up a satellite-controlled force field
around the continent to make sure none of the Impix got
loose to bother them." The Digby icon tapped finger
against finger. "Unlike the Impix, they kept contact with
the outside, and with a low birthrate and the resources of
a basically untapped world behind them, particularly the
drajjul opals, they were a comfortable if not a wealthy society for their first millennium on-planet. When the
drajjul mines began to play out and the shipping companies started dropping away, they opened casinos and used
the third continent as a hunting preserve, pulling in hunt-
ers and gamblers. Fads and fashions being what they are,
revenue from this started big, but tapered off considerably
until two factions of Impix began fighting each other and
the Ptaks found they had a new tourist attraction.

They set up flights of cameras to track the battles and
keep the action crackling for their War Viewing tours."

The image on the screen changed, and Shadith found
herself watching hand-to-hand fighting on the banks of a
river with a burning boat in the background. The fighters
were a good match with her favorite in the ghost stakes,
though somewhat larger and more muscular. Males, perhaps.

The scene changed—a city being bombarded—changed
again, fighters overrunning a nomad camp—changed a

third time—a group of seven males roasting bits from a smaller, darker version of themselves over an open fire.

"By arming and supplying both sides, some judicious prodding, and sending assassins after those arguing for peace, the Ptaks have kept the war going for more than a decade and have prospered from it enormously." The Icon wagged a finger. "I put this in just for you, Shadow. If the Ptaks suspect you want to interfere with that war, they'll slide you down a black hole, so mind yourself. And when you get to Impixol, do your best not to get yourself photted by one of those cameras, hm?"

The image on the screen shifted again, swept down to water level and hovered around wavetop, focusing on a series of flickers moving horizontally along an invisible surface.

"The Fence." Digby's voice was prim and disapproving. "An essentially simple force field that kills whatever comes near it. Near being approximately two meters. Easy maintenance, almost no moving parts. By using the disruptor, your little ghost-candidate could punch a hole in the Fence without starting up all kinds of alarms, a hole big enough to let a boat through, if that happens to be what she wants. Not that it will do her much good, the power differential between Ptak and Impix is just too great. What she should do is go after the ground controls of those satellites. When you locate her, Shadow, you might mention that little notion—as long as you're sure no one else is listening.

"Rose, tact not being one of our Shadow's gifts, I strongly suggest you provide cover and maintain the link to the ship. Their orbital facilities are crude at best and definitely not secure, so you had better groundside the ship and secure it against ordinary probes. You'll have to let Ptak security probes find their way through, but give them a tale to play with, hm?

"I've encoded into a zipfile all we know of Ambela,

the Ptak and the Impix war, so this lecture is essentially unnecessary, but it pleased me to make it." The world image vanished and Digby was floating before them again, a mischievous grin on his simulacrum's face, a sparkle in his bright green eyes. "Happy hunting, my dears. And be ready to tell me all when you get back."

2. Ambela

Autum Rose took the hand of the driver and stepped with stately elegance into the hotel shuttle. She wore a lace-edged privacy mask; her hair was dyed black and swept into a braided knot atop her head, her earlobes were stretched into long flesh loops with a black pearl set in silver at the apex of each loop, her face paint was a stark white, widow's mark for the Suvvojan femme she was supposed to be.

Shadith stood scowling on the metacrete, using the toe of a worn boot to herd luggage that kept trying to ramble off until the driver could lose sight of his tip long enough to open the back doors of the shuttle.

The driver was a Ptak male in premating molt, the soft curly feathers on his head detaching themselves at intervals to go floating off on the acrid, eye-biting breeze that swept across the landing field. Once Rose was seated, he came rushing back, his toe claws scratching irritably at the 'crete. He slapped his hand against the palmlock and stood twitching with impatience as Shadith chased the bags up the ramp and crowded into the servant's bay after them.

Digby's notes said the Ptak are roaring snobs, she thought, stroking her fingers over the faux skin that covered the hawk etched into her cheek. *I'd say he underestimated it. Useful. Now that the sorting's begun and they've got my place in the hierarchy settled, they'll ignore me nicely.*

* * *

Disdain in the lift of her chin and the set of her shoulders, Autumn Rose inspected the suite. "Adequate, but not what I'm accustomed to. Ah-ay-mi, Mar Tana, what a widow must endure." She patted a yawn. "I am tired. I'll sleep a while. Set the shield so I'm not overlooked, then see what there is in this tedious place that might possibly prove amusing."

Inconspicuous in her dull gray-brown tunic and trousers, her hair hidden in an intricately folded kerchief, Shadith stepped from the service tube, ambled through the busy traffic of flesh servitors and 'bots and emerged onto The Strip.

Lala Gemali was the largest city on Ambela and the only place where off-worlders moved about with any freedom. It was a mix of Ptakkan towers and generic star-street architecture, of brilliant primary colors and muted browns and grays. Holoas swarmed like confetti, brushing through the visitors riding the chain chairs and the mover mats, turning the air into a kaleidoscope of color and ghostly shapes, whispering the glories of the viewing palaces, joy houses and casinos.

Songbirds flew everywhere, alone and in flocks of hundreds, blipping unconcerned through the holoas, flitting from tower to tower, tiny patches of jewel-bright color.

The Ptakkan towers were airy open structures, more glass than wall because of Ptak claustrophobia, with great play of arches and flying buttresses as if the Ptaks sought to recreate the tree forms of their natal world. And every surface was painted a different color or a different shade of one of the colors already used. There was no place for the eye to land and linger; the din of the colors as noisy and persistent as the twitter of Ptak voices that overrode all other sounds.

The dull, squat outworld buildings scattered among

these elaborate towers were like basso roars, jerking the eye to a halt on broad planes of gray or buff or muted green. The rambling streets went suddenly straight each time they passed one of those structures. The contrasts were disturbing and reinforced the effects of the floating holoas. After a while the visitor had to get inside to rest his eyes and ears.

Out in the middle of The Strip, chain chairs clanked and shook in continuous circuits. Mover mats ambled along at a slow walk beside them, rubbery ovals about three meters wide and four long, with polychrome rails and leaning posts for the drunk or merely shaky. The area closest to the buildings was an ordinary walkway where the visitor could maneuver on his own feet without the pavement shifting under him.

Though it was still early afternoon, The Strip was filled with visitors. Shadith began to understand Digby's warnings as she listened to the talk that swirled around her.

Phrase fragments from the Viewers—a mix of fascination and disgust, avidity, indignation, blasé boredom.

Talking about cannibalism, blood, exploding flesh and bone.

About stalking. Men stalking men like beasts.

A sense that the Viewers go back and back to this place and that, like a tongue worrying a sore tooth.

Pleasure and pain. Pleasure in pain.

Savoring horrors that made the speaker's comfort more precious.

The Ptaks talked money.

Rolled the count of obols on the tongue.

Tallied the aliens like sheep in their fields, sheep to be sheared to the last curly hair.

Shadith wandered unnoticed among them, growing more depressed by the moment; it was a huge city not only in numbers but in area, difficult to hold in the mind because she didn't yet understand Ptakkan patterning despite the weight of data Digby had provided.

Play the game, she thought.

Walk the edge.

Tsah! I'm on a job.

She sighed as she contemplated her sense of responsibility.

Bourgeois to the bone.

Edge. You're as bad as this lot, wearing a safety tether, hunting carefully tamed thrills.

Ah-weh. Don't be silly, woman. You do what you do. Playing head games with yourself wastes time and energy. Spla! You better get back in gear.

A group of offworlders came like a dark wave from one of the joy houses; chattering in Cobben-speak, moving with complete disregard for the others on the street, they took over a mover mat, continued their comments as they slumped against the supports.

Shadith swallowed hard and stepped onto another mat, careful to keep a somber Bawang between her and the group two mats ahead of her.

Nightcrawler Cobben? Digby didn't mention there were Cobben involved. Assassins and mercenaries, yes. Maybe his sources didn't know. Or they *could* be here on holiday. Do retail killers find wholesale slaughter a relaxing hobby?

She smoothed her fingers across the faux skin covering the hawk, checking to be sure it was firmly in place. The Cobben of Helvetia had more than one reason to be annoyed at her. She leaned against a post, found a birdmind, and eased into it enough to keep it circling above the Cobben while she watched through its eyes.

They reached the end of the mat's route, stepped off, and strolled along a side street, too busy talking to notice a small fretting bird that flew in sweeping circles above them, uttering agitated twitters.

Eyes on the ground, only enough mind on what she was doing to keep from bumping into things and people, Shadith slouched along two streets over, a rambling narrow way that ran roughly parallel to the one the Cobben was taking.

They passed through an area of blocky warehouses whose utilitarian forms were concealed behind hedges and thick ropy vines, emerged into what looked like the bedroom community for the imported laborers who did the unglamorous jobs of cleaning and repair, servants, waiters, translators, guides, all those who kept Lala Gemali running smoothly. There were small houses, duplexes, ottotels, transient lodging for all purses from scab joints to militantly respectable boardhouses.

The Cobben went into one of the ottotels, a gray-faced anonymous structure that sat among thick shrubbery and small trees almost as if it pulled a cloak around itself.

She turned her mindmount loose and ambled about the neighborhood, getting it set in her mind and looking for another ottotel where she could settle and keep an eye on the Cobben. If they were Ptak-hires, they knew things she needed to know—and sooner or later they'd be heading over to Impixol. She meant to hitch a ride on their transport.

There were no Ptak visible on these streets, only a mix of drab offworlders she decided were leaving for shifts on The Strip; here and there grifters of various sorts worked cons on the off-duty souls, a scatter of streetwalkers smiled with painted tenderness, while other furtive types scratched a living selling assorted and usually adulterated drugs.

The flocks thickened overhead, the cries became more raucous as waterbirds took over from the singers. She watched them a moment, smiled. Odd how on every world that had seas, birds that lived by the sea produced almost the same sound, as if there were a sort of optimum noise that carried across water.

It was mid-afternoon by the time she reached the lake-shore and there wasn't much going on. The fishboats moored there were empty, waiting, their owners and crews gone home till it was time to leave for the next day's catch, the tourist docks were mostly deserted, the brightly painted boats rocking empty and idle. Some distance along the shore she could see a few container ships still unloading grain and other supplies from the farms on the far side of the water and there were more such transports in view out on Lake Incunala.

She walked to the end of a deserted wharf and settled on a bitt, swinging her booted feet and lifting her head to the damp cool wind coming off the water.

"Haven't seen you around before."

She turned her head. The speaker was a bald old man with a face like polished teak and a body still hard but perhaps more brittle than it had been a few years back. He set his bait bucket down and eased himself to the planks beside it. She watched as he dipped a chunk of bait from the bucket, gave a dexterous twist to a hook, and sent it smoothly through the dark meat. With an equally dexterous flick of his wrists he sent the line swinging out, the weighted end dropping into the water with a quiet splash.

"Haven't been around," she said. "We just got here."

"We?"

"My employer and me. Widow. She decided she wanted to spend her official mourning time watching folk slaughter each other and her kin provided the coin real fast."

"Like that, hm?"

"I'm a woman of strong moral convictions, or I would have strangled the bitch two days into the flight. With a little luck she'll fire me, that way she'll have to cede me a severance."

"You don't want to get stranded here, young and juicy as you are. You'd be thinking that time with the widow was paradise."

"Maybe." She went silent as his line jerked, watched him reel in the fish, unhook it, and drop it into the bait bucket. When the line was out again, she pointed at the wooded island and the spray of rocky islets that trailed from its base. "What's that called?"

"Graska Wysp. Government run for government business. The Ptaks can get real nasty if they think folk are sticking their noses where they don't belong."

"Hm." She glanced at the buttonchron clipped to the breast pocket of her tunic. "Ti-ta, I need to be there when the Widow wakes. Good fishing, man." She slid off the bitt and strolled away, stopping at the mouth of the alley to wave to him.

Autumn Rose was stretched out before the suite's wall screen, watching bands of fighters stalking each other. She clicked it off, turned her head as Shadith came in. "Anything interesting?" She flicked a hand toward the shield generator sitting on the table, a small green light glowing against the dark plastic cover.

"Yes. I had a bit of luck, ran across a Nightcrawler Cobben and tracked them to where they live. Remember what Digby said about hired assassins?"

"Mm. Planning to hitch?"

"I think so. We should probably have our quarrel in the morning. I need to listen in on what they're talking about and the closer I am, the better."

Rose sighed. "Just as well. I'm going to have to find a game, I've never been so bored."

Shadith watched the door slide closed behind Autumn Rose, shook herself, and sighed with relief. The careful politeness between them could get more wearing than hard labor. She moved about the suite, picking up Rose's discarded clothing, cleaning the bathroom, turning down the bed, playing the servant's role for the watchers who'd be looking in on her at intervals now that the shield was turned off. Digby's assessment. The Ptaks are paranoid about visitors interfering with the cash flow. Unless shielded by a caster whose capacity you're sure of, assume you're watched.

She moved to one of the long mirrors beside the door, ran her fingers through her short curly hair, checked the faux skin to see if it was still sealed in place, and went out to do her own kind of playing. She wasn't looking forward to the quarrel; they'd choreographed it on the way here, but there was too much negative energy between them to make that fight an easy thing.

The light came on suddenly enough to blind Shaddith as she came back from her night ramble.

Autumn Rose caught her by the shoulders, shaking her, screaming insults in a guttural Suvvojan, finishing, "Where were you? I don't pay you to go whoring round the town, you miserable piece of nothing. You're to be here when I need you, you hear me? Get that look off your face. I won't tolerate insolence." She swept her right arm back and slapped Shadith hard enough across the face to send her staggering backward into the hallway.

Shadith straightened, stared at Rose; she touched her face, looked at the smear of blood on her fingertips from the cut one of Rose's rings had made, then she returned the slap with as much force as she could put in it (wondering even as she swung if Rose had found as much relief in this exchange as she was enjoying right now).

Autumn Rose recoiled. "That's it. That's all. Get your things, I want you out of here now. Now," she screamed. "Five minutes, then I call the authorities."

* * *

The cut scabbed over, a bruise forming around it, her gear beside her feet, Shadith stood in the middle of the lobby and looked around. Behind a long counter a female Lommertoerken clerk sat at a keyboard, eyes on the screen, her long, deeply lined face intent.

When Shadith rapped on the countertop, she looked up. "Yes?"

"Is there somewhere close I can rent a lockup?"

The Lommertoerken smiled, wrinkles spreading like stage curtains, her large brown eyes shining conspiratorially as they swept across the bruise. "I can let you have a locker here for a few days." She lifted a bony shoulder. "Have to charge you for the keycard, company policy. You need a place to stay?"

Shadith sighed. "That I do. Somewhere cheap, she has to pay me severance, but. . . ." She shrugged. "You know anything down near lakeshore? My fa was a fisherman, I can catch my dinner if I have to."

The clerk ran her fingers over the keyboard, tongue clicking rhythmically as she worked; after a moment, she tapped a key, waited for the printing to finish, then tore off a sheet with half a dozen addresses on it, short paragraphs beside them listing requirements and costs. "You want to be careful," she said. "Some of the boardhouses out there funnel women to bordellos and worse; they advertise cheap prices and give you more than you pay for, but nothing you'd like. These are all right, though." She pushed the list across the counter. "If you'll get your things, I'll show you where to put them."

3. Spy on the job

Shadith had her choice of ears. The ottotel was clean enough outside the walls, but inside was a busy haven for vermin of various sorts, much of it off the ships that landed here—mice and other small rodents along with as-

sorted spiders and insects. Exterminators cost money and
random sprays of toxics were likely to make some of the
clients sicker than the vermin. 'Bots and servitors didn't
care and the Ptakkan owners of the 'tel had no intention
of coming near the place. The rooms were sealed and
small seeker 'bots took care of complaints, if any.

Shadith stationed a mouse in the air duct, put it to
sleep, and used its ears to pick up what was being said in
the main room of the suite the Cobben infested.

She rather missed Autumn Rose, though she certainly
hadn't expected to. There was no one to talk to. And she
couldn't even go play. With all this passive mindriding,
the concentration it needed, all this lying in dark rooms,
not moving, trying to keep awake, she was too exhausted
most nights to do anything but watch the vids. Everything
in Lala Gemali, even around here in this bedroom community for low status workers, was geared for plucking
the offworlders of their last coin. Coin viewers in every
room. Watch the war and feed the Ptakkan greed.

She scolded herself, reminded herself she was here on
a job, not chasing one of her own shadows or running
down a personal threat. *I have to get used to this,* she
thought. *I'm on someone else's time. Again. Well, I managed to get used to the diadem, this shouldn't be too hard.*

Listening to the Cobben was depressing. Despite what
they did for a living—or maybe even because of it—there
was a closeness between them that made her want to
break off and go cuddle with Swardheld for a while. It
reminded her too forcefully of the lack in her life. Reminded her that she had to yearn after Autumn Rose just
to have someone about who shared a common purpose.
Several times she bailed out quickly as sex play started
developing. Made her envious and queasy at the same
time. And curious, wondering what it'd be like to be part
of a multiple arrangement that had been going on for a
number of years.

Odd. She could spy on them to find out what they were going to do, to learn their skills and interactions in case she had to fight or even kill them, but spying on their sex lives to satisfy curiosity was something she simply could not do.

"The Blivvy was looking at you, Feyd, you know she was." A rolling giggle. "Don't know what she'd do with a little playtoy like you, you'd get lost in those rolls of fat."

"Oh, he likes them lush." A rumbling growl of a voice.

"Someone turn on the shield?" A light dry voice, ambiguous as to gender.

"Why bother." The first speaker, a mid-range female voice with harsh edges. "Government issue. You know it has to have holes in it."

"Hoy, Sarpe, you said it." Slow, rather dragging male voice, the words interrupted by a loud yawn. "I'm beat. Rest of you want to min the chik you'll have to yob without me."

"Yo, Orm, you right." A quick ripple of a voice and a long sigh. "It's sleep for me."

Dragging sounds, giggles from the fresher, slap of flesh against flesh, coughing, smells of kava brewing, of soap and damp and dust stirred up. More coughing, sighs, creaking from the pallets, soft rubbing sounds from quilts moving over flesh. Silence for a while, punctuated by a few snores before one of the Cobben made an exasperated sound like a mix between a snort and the clicking of tongue against teeth and shifted the snorer onto his side, or perhaps her side.

More silence for a while, then sounds of movement converging on a corner of the room away from the sleepers. Quiet voices.

"Sarpe, we getting good money for this, but I've about had it here. How long's it been, six years? Feels like six centuries. We're getting to be like contract labor, if you ask me."

"Yeh, Meya's right. Stuck in a yobbing rut worse'n any bourgie snek." A soft groan, stretching sounds. "I'm getting sloppy. If I had a real hit, chances are I'd blow the Cob. Don't like it. Don't like losing my edge. Don't like feeling maybe it isn't just me."

A short silence, then the harsh clipped voice of the Coryfe. "You challenging me, Kayr?"

Sound of snort, then the quick light voice with a hint of laughter in it. "Don't point your fangs at me, Sarpe Coryfe. I'm just telling you."

A longer silence.

Sarpe's voice, quieter now, the edges smoothed over. "I'll be meeting with the Clo-Kajhat two days on, he said he's got something special for us. We'll talk again when I know what it is."

Shadith took the mouse through the ducts until it was far enough away so its reaction wouldn't reach the Cobben, then she turned it loose and let it go squealing off, tiny claws scrabbling on the plas of the duct floor as it ran for familiar territory.

She pressed the heels of her hands against her temples, then rubbed them across her eyes. She was exhausted but too nervous to sleep. With a whispered curse, she hunted out a handful of coins and settled back to watch the war unfold. Once again the war. It had an awful fascination. After a week of watching she almost understood what brought the tourists here.

She drowsed as war scenes flowed across the screen, minor engagements and assorted overvoiced scenes meant to harrow the soul or something like that, with adverts for the bloodier action inserted at intervals.

Battles on pay per view. See Pixa phelas ambush an Impix farmer and his workers. See Impix overwhelm a Pixa ixis on its way to the Meeting Ground.

Total sensory immersion in the Sensarams. Be a Pixa warrior fighting for the purity of his faith. Feel what it's like to live in a city shelled day and night. Rape. Slaughter. Cannibalism. Feel it all, relive the primitive thrills your culture has left behind.

Music swelled, the camera's point of view swam among clouds, then swooped down to drift above a road paved with ancient yellow bricks worn hollow by centuries of feet passing along them.

"They can only walk," the voiceover said, a resonant baritone oozing with sentiment. "On this roadway their faith permits only feet. They come from everywhere, from the mountains, from the plains, Pixa and Impix alike. They come in groups like this family, the tribond of fem-mal-anya and children, all they own in those packs on their backs, see the starved, weary faces of children too exhausted to be afraid any longer. Sanctuary lies ahead, just a few more hours of walking and they can rest, protected by the sanctity of the Holy City Linojin.

"Many come alone, the last survivors of slaughtered families or outcasts who have rejected faith and friendship, refusing to fight for the soul of their people." The POV dipped lower, floating in front of a small solitary figure. "You can't see cowardice on their faces, only dust and that bone deep weariness."

The little Pixa trudged along, unaware she was being watched, her eyes shifting constantly, moving from the farmworkers in the fields to the other pilgrims behind and ahead of her, dark green eyes, wide and enigmatic, set aslant in a narrow face with smooth shiny skin like gray-green bark.

Shadith sat up, slapped her hand on the bed beside her. "Gotcha. Nice timing, O Fate. Hello, Yseyl."

She crossed to the small kitchen alcove, set water to heat for cha, and hurried back. She folded the thin pillows and tucked them behind her, stretched out on the bed, ankles crossed, fingers laced behind her head, ignoring the treacly narration, her eyes fixed on the figure until the POV shifted to hover over the city.

Luck. It usually balances. I wonder what's waiting to hit me in the face. Mp. Souvenir shops. Wonder if they've got anything useful on Linojin?

The POV swooped over the largest independent standing structure in the city, a white marble confection, every surface carved with interlocking, stylized forms of plants, birds and beasts, and with intricately interlaced knots, spirals, and other symbols. There were towers with pointed domes, grass growing green on the roofs, courts with ponds and streams and leaping fountains.

And a high swaying tower of angular openwork steel with wide flung steel cables bracing it against the wind from the sea.

Radio. Digby said you'd worked your way back that far.

The POV followed WhiteRobes pacing along the paths by twos and threes, hands invisible in wide sleeves, eyes on the ground. Male with male, female with female, anya with anya.

"This is the most sacred place on Impixol. The Grand Yeson. This is the center of worship for the Impix God. And these you see are the holy ones who govern in this city. The Anyas of Mercy, the Sisters of the Godbond, the Brothers of God. These are the ones who will question the Pilgrims, the exiles, these are they who decide who will remain in the city and who must be sent away to dwell in the poverty and hard labor of the nearby fishing villages." The image of the exiled family trudging along the street briefly shared the screen with the Yeson. "Will they be allowed to huddle in the barracks of the Holy City or forced to fend for themselves?" The little ghost's image replaced the family. "Is she hohekil, a refugee, or simply one too tired to fight any longer, seeking rest with her God? Will she be allowed to stay or will the Brothers find her unworthy?"

The screen blanked and the adverts reappeared:

Battles on pay per view. See Pixa phelas ambush an Impix farmer and his workers. See Impix overwhelm a Pixa ixis on its way to the Meeting Ground.

Total sensory immersion in the Sensarams. Be a Pixa warrior fighting for the purity of his faith. Feel what it's like to live in a city shelled day and night. Rape. Slaughter. Cannibalism. Feel it all, relive the primitive thrills. . . .

The cha pot beeped. She went to the alcove, made her cha, brought the mug, and settled down to watch the rest of the show about the Holy City Linojin.

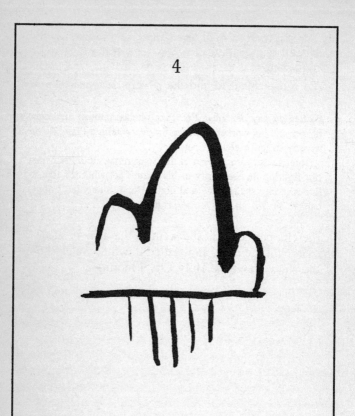

Clouds cover the sun, curtains
of rain hide what is ahead.
Danger or nurture?

Chapter 5

1. Thann's trek

Mikil fidgeted near the door as Thann checked the straps on Isaho's pack, made sure her bootlaces were tied and her coat was properly buttoned and belted tight to her slight body. In the anya's room the radio blared suddenly, and a mal's voice spoke through static; a moment later a fem began singing. Isaho didn't say anything, but her mouth tightened into a thin line and her eyes started looking at something only she could see.

Thann got to xe's feet, pulled xe's daughter against xe and held her until the small stiff body softened.

Xe wanted someone to do the same for xe. Xe was scared rigid. Xe didn't want to do this, didn't want to go away from the place where xe'd lived all xe's life. For the past week as Isaho was healing, as xe was preparing for the trek, assembling food, tools, balls of cord, matches, a fire-striker, a folding knife, whatever xe thought of that was small enough to carry, as xe was trying to ignore Ankalan's scowls and his angry mutters about parasites, every hour of every day xe's mind scrambled endlessly for a way to escape this trek. Xe spent hours flattened against the earth in the rubble-filled caricature of a garden behind the battered, half-ruined apartment house, praying for guidance. The earth was silent. If God listened, there was no sign to show it.

Xe hefted xe's own pack, let Isaho help xe into it, then tied into quick-release knots the laces that kept the strap in place across xe's chest. Xe sucked in a breath, exploded it out, turned to Mikil. +Give us the Journey Blessing, Cousin. Please.+

Isaho made an impatient sound, but Thann pulled the child into place beside her and bowed xe's head.

Mikil's hand shook when she touched Thann's shoulder with the ritual double tap. "May your feet go lightly on God's earth and may your journey be safe and your days pleasing." She tapped Isaho's shoulder, repeating the blessing.

Thann felt Isaho stiffen, but again the child minded her manners and made no protest. This hardening in xe's daughter troubled xe deeply; xe felt that Isaho was slipping away from the Company of the Blessed, that her soul would blow endlessly across the earth and never again know peace. *Maybe in Linojin,* xe thought, *maybe they'll know what to do, how to call her back.*

Mikil opened the door, then stepped aside. "I'm sorry," she said. "I wish ... if things were different. . . ."

+I know, Cousin. I leave only blessing behind me. May you and yours fare well.+

Mikil laughed then, a harsh unhappy sound that broke off as a wavery whistle came from the other room. As soon as Thann and Isaho were through the door, she pulled it shut. Thann could hear the bar dropping, then the quick heavy steps of the fem as she went to tend her anya.

Isaho tugged at Thann's sleeve.

Thann slapped sharply at the femlit's forearm, got her attention. +If you get yourself hurt again, you'll never make it to Linojin. Let me listen for trouble and behave yourself.+

Isaho blinked, her eyes gleaming liquidly in the moonlight coming through the broken windows of the hallway. Then she nodded. "But we have to get started," she whispered. "Now."

+Yes, but stay beside me and keep your eyes and ears sharp.+

The cratered, rubble-filled street was a pattern of gray and black, the light from nearly full Phosis making strange angles out of shadow so that everything looked different. There was a strong warm wind blowing along the street, dead leaves and debris rattling before it, but the guns were silent. Now and then Thann could hear snatches of music from radios close to shattered windows, now and then the sounds of people talking or laughing or screaming at each other or sobbing.

Getting around in the city would be easier in daylight, but the snipers in the hills shot at anything that moved and the big guns hammered and hammered at the dying city. Night meant slow going and the scavenger gangs that roamed the streets breaking into places, destroying what they couldn't use, but thinta would warn xe when they were about, so they were easy to avoid. Xe didn't understand how they could do that, but it was of a piece with everything else; xe couldn't understand why Pixa and Impix killed each other over a different reading of God's Law.

Xe's hand on Isaho's shoulder, Thann crept along the street, thinta roving in an arc ahead of them. Xe wanted to know when anyone was coming at them, so they could hide till the danger passed. The chances were small indeed that such a person might be Sisters of the Godbond or Brothers on the way to the bedside of someone sick or dying.

Street crossing. That meant moving into the open, away from the sheltering walls. Thann stood a moment, turning slowly, straining to feel danger.

Nothing.

They ran across the street and into shadow again, comforting, blanketing shadow.

The moon slid through shreds of cloud, its light waxing and waning unpredictably, hiding and baring them in that random dance, giving them no warning of potholes and the concrete chunks that caught at the toes of their boots with what seemed to Thann like malice as if the inanimates of Impixol were striking blindly back at those who'd maimed them. Xe shivered and pushed the thought away, but each time xe staggered or caught the toe of xe's boot, the fancy came sidling back into her mind.

One street crossed ... three ... nine ... fifteen. ...

Xe's legs trembled with weariness and a cold sweat dripped down xe's face, burned into xe's eyes. Xe wanted to stop, but there was no safe place xe could see, and besides, Isaho wouldn't stop until she fell, and arguing with her would make too much noise.

Xe grabbed Isaho's arm, used all xe's weight to shove the femlit over a crumbled wall, then tumbled over after her. Before Isaho could speak, xe clamped a hand over her mouth, frantic because xe's lack of speech might bring death on them all since xe couldn't use xe's hands to explain until xe was sure Isaho would stay quiet.

Xe felt stiffness, then a relaxing. Isaho nodded, her head moving against Thann's hand.

Xe took the hand away, signed, +Someone coming at us.+

Isaho nodded again, signed: +How many?+

+One band seven.+ Thann flicked a finger straight down the street. +One band six.+ This time xe pointed to the north and brought xe's hand quickly toward them. +Side street.+

+Will they meet?+

+If our luck has left us. All we can do is stay quiet and wait, Shashi. And pray.+

Isaho's body went stiff, and she turned her head away. Thann sighed, set xe's hand on earth coming to life again after its years of sterility beneath pavement. *So much anger. Forgive her, she hasn't reconciled herself to pain and loss. So young.* Xe broke off that thought before it led to the areas xe didn't want in xe's head and sent thinta roaming again, feeling the life fires come closer and closer.

Fear sat in xe's stomach like an expanding stone, cold, hard, heavy; fear was a below-the-skin shaking in xe's legs and arms. Xe wanted to be back inside somewhere. Anywhere but here. Xe'd been frightened before, many times, but xe'd never been alone with it, there'd always been xe's clan or xe's bondmates to comfort xe. Now there was only Isaho, and Isaho was a child; it was up to xe to keep her safe, to stand between her and danger, and xe knew in xe's bones xe was no more a barrier than wet paper.

The stone in xe's belly grew and grew as they waited, until xe felt glued to the ground by the heft of it.

Sudden chatter of shots.

Screams, shouts, curses, clattering noises.

Silence.

The air around Thann felt as if it were stretching, pulled out and out and out into an unbearable tension.

A shot. Another. A whine as pellet ricocheted over their heads and thunked into the broken wall behind them.

The noises grew louder, came faster, surged toward them then away.. . .

The encounter went on for another hour, then both sides broke off for reasons as invisible to Thann as those that brought on the attack.

Thann waited as long as xe could keep Isaho quiet, sweeping xe's thinta across and across the area around them just to be sure the streets were clear. When xe could feel the child's restlessness about to explode, xe got stiffly to xe's feet and signed to Isaho to walk beside xe.

The wait had been no rest; xe's body screamed with fatigue, but xe crept on as xe had before, shuddering as xe nearly stepped on a body sprawled on the street. There were half a dozen dead scavengers scattered about, the bodies moving in and out of visibility as if they were actors on a spotlit stage. Isaho was silent beside xe, not looking at the dead, content for the moment with simply moving west.

Gradually the ruins grew wider apart and the rubble heaps smaller. Mill owners and merchants had lived here once, building large compounds with walled gardens. They were among the first to fall to the Mountain Guns, easy targets and tempting since the Pixa hated everything about Impix commerce. Thann could remember the first days of xe's tribond when xe and Bazekiyl and Mandall used to ride the jittrain out here and walk along the streets enjoying the damp earth smells, the sounds of water from the hidden gardens, exclaiming over the mosaic murals that decorated the outsides of the walls. Once the bombardment started, though, the jittrains stopped running. The story of the destruction came through the news reports on the radio, but no matter how deft the reporter, it hadn't been real until now, until xe felt it with xe's fingertips, saw the ruin of xe's memories in the dim light from the setting moon.

Xe caught hold of Isaho's arm, pulled her to a stop beside a wall more intact than most while xe's thinta scanned the area for life.

Nothing larger than small rodents scurrying about in their hunt for food.

+Shashi.+

Isaho wouldn't look at xe, just kept tugging at the hold on her arm as if she meant to walk forever without stopping until she reached Linojin.

Thann moved in front of xe's daughter. +Shashi.+ She made the movements large, a silent shout.

Isaho blinked, then seemed to crumble as her concentration broke and the automaton that had been wearing her body disengaged. "Thanny?" The word was dragged out and blurry.

+We need a place to rest a while and sleep. Seems to me, this is as good as we'll find inside the city.+

Isaho leaned heavily against xe. " 'M sooo tired, Thanny."

+Listen, Shashi. This wall is still pretty high. I'll lift you, but you've got to pull yourself over. Soon as you're down inside there, stay very still and wait for me. Do you understand, Shashi?+

"Mm. Unnerstaahhhh. . . ." The word was swallowed by a huge yawn.

Thann dragged xeself wearily onto the broken stones, eased around, and let xeself fall into the weeds at the base of the wall—and, for a moment, fell into a panic when xe couldn't see Isaho anywhere. Xe pressed xe's back against the wall and thinta swept the garden until xe touched the child's small bright life.

Lost in the hot flush of fear/anger, mouth gaping in a soundless scream, xe ran toward the life fire, pushing xe's body through the thick overgrowth of hedges and gone-to-wild plants until xe reached an old garden shed, shaky and smothered in plant debris but still standing. Isaho was stretched out beside the small stream trickling from beneath it, scooping up water and drinking avidly from her cupped hand.

Thann caught her by the shoulders, yanked her onto her feet, and stood shaking her and sobbing, mouth opening and closing with the words xe wanted to scream at her but could not.

"Thanny?"

The weak wobbly cry broke through the spasm of rage

and Thann caught xe's daughter hard against her, hugging her and shuddering.

After a moment xe stepped back, brushing a hand across xe's burning eyes, then signed, +I told you to wait for me.+

"Thanny, I was sooo thirsty. So I came here to get a drink."

+How did you know there was water here?+

Isaho blinked. "I dunno. It was kinda like I smelled it. Anyway, I knew it was here and there wasn't anybody to bother us, just some mayomayos and a nest of wejeys and some little brown birds hopping around."

Thann closed xe's eyes, drew a long breath, let it trickle out. +Shashi, I almost died when I saw you weren't there. Don't do that to me again. Please, daughter meami.+

Isaho stiffened, then flung herself at Thann, her hands clutching frantically, her body shuddering. "No no no no, Thanny don't die, don't die eee."

Appalled at what xe's thoughtless words had done, Thann held her and whistled softly until her shaking stopped, then xe unhooked Isaho's fingers and patted the small hands. +So let's get camp made. Do you think you could pull some of that dry wood off the shed? A little fire under the eaves back there would be safe enough, and we can have a hot meal before we sleep.+

Thann sat by the small fire gently massaging the egg in xe's pouch and watching xe's daughter sleep. For the first time in weeks Isaho wasn't writhing in the grip of nightmares; her face was smeared with dust and a crust of dried moss, but it was calm and sweet, and the sight of it was balm to Thann's weary spirit.

The red faded in the dying coals as the sky lightened. Finally xe emptied a mug of water onto the last patches of fire and curled in xe's blanket next to Isaho, listening to the femlit breathe and wondering if xe was going to be able to sleep. Almost in the middle of the thought xe was gone.

Thann woke not remembering where xe was, lay staring at the crooked lacery of twigs and leaves over xe's head until last night's events came back to xe. Xe sat up and smiled despite the aches and stiffness of xe's body. Isaho was kneeling close by, a little pile of broken wood beside her. +Did you sleep well, Shashi?+

"Ground's hard." She rubbed at her side. "And there was a stick poking me. But I didn't dream." She wrinkled her nose. "Thanny, I saw some plants, they looked like pictures in my farm book, you know, tatas, I was thinking maybe we could dig them and cook them? And there was some qanteh, I pulled one and it was fat and yellow, see." She reached behind her and brought round a dirt-crusted root with the three leaves like feathers growing from its crown. "I remembered Mam . . . I remember you washing them and cutting the tops off and slicing them for me to eat. I liked them."

+Must have been a kitchen garden, Shashi. Let me get my teeth cleaned, then you can show me where you found those things.+ Xe pushed the blanket back and got stiffly to xe's feet, then turned to frown at Isaho. +Did you clean your teeth and wash yourself?+

"Ahhh, Thanny. . . ."

+No matter. We can have our wash together.+

The wild garden was quiet and peaceful in the waning hours of the day; the pop pop from the snipers and the scream/boom of the shells from the Mountain Guns seemed distant and somehow muted. As the sun slipped lower in the west, Thann found xeself increasingly reluctant to leave. Xe and Isaho could live here well enough, at least until the egg hatched and the anya inside began to suckle, venturing out only when they needed things the garden couldn't give them. They could clean out the shed and use debris from the house to weatherproof the walls, and the war could go on around them, but they'd be safe.

Each time xe's mind traveled that road, xe would catch sight of Isaho watching the sun, measuring how soon they could leave. Then the dream would slip away from xe. And even without Isaho's urgency it would still be only a dream, xe knew that. Peace anywhere was ephemeral, to be treasured and dismissed.

They left the garden as the red was fading from the western sky and crept on through the fringes of city, an area deserted, ruined, gone wild. Several times they ducked behind a wall or under a hedge to hide from peddlers or farmers packing in produce on the backs of munymys, but that was only because Thann didn't want anyone to see or question them, not because there was any danger in these folk. The scavenger gangs never came this far, setting their ambushes deeper in the city.

By midnight even the ruins were behind them. The road was a collections of shell holes and erosion, but it was at least an open space in the tangle of weeds and plants gone wild, berry bushes whose long tough canes had brittle thorns that caught at anything that brushed against them and broke off at the slightest pressure. The small farms that had once lined this road and provided fresh vegetables for the city had been deserted for years, the families who worked them driven from the land by the Pixa phelas who killed as many as they could and burned out the rest.

Thann was back to being scared again. Xe didn't like having no straight lines xe could depend on to orient xeself, didn't like knowing nothing about what lay on the far side of any bend in that awful road. Letting Isaho guide xe's steps, xe sent the thinta sweeping round and round again, tearing that Pixa phelas or the murdering robber bands xe'd heard about on the radio would some-how slip past xe's senses and come down on them.

The anya-in-egg was restless, kicking and scratching at the leathery shell; Thann's fear was like nettles rubbing at it. Xe knew that, but xe couldn't control xeself. All anyas had trouble dealing with uncertainty; they liked order and calm, with their cousins and bondkin close about them.

The road grew slightly better as Thann and Isaho left the city behind; there were no more shell craters, only ruts and potholes decorated with the dried manure from packer munymys and teams of draft skazz, wheel tracks from the farm wagons and the footprints of the small lives that ran in the briars and birds hunting out grass seeds.

Thann kept to the road because there didn't seem to be anything else to do, but it worried xe. Their only hope of actually reaching Linojin was to stay elusive and apart like mayomayos living near a mahay's lair. The road made them targets.

Near moonset they came on tilled land.

The field was enclosed by a double fence of barbed wire, the strands only a span apart, the outer fence at least two meters high. In the narrow lane between the two lines of barbed wire a pack of hunting chals came running to-ward them, throwing low threatening growls at the walk-ers in the road. With a small squeak Isaho crowded against Thann, clutching at xe.

Thann patted her, led her to the far side of the road, one eye on the chals. The extra distance stopped the growls, but the beasts paced along with them until they reached the end of the field and moved into a stretch of wasteland.

It was another indication of how dangerous the road might be, and it was all Thann needed to convince xe that they had to get off it right now. Besides, dawn was less than an hour off and they had to find a place to camp. Xe tapped Isaho's arm to signal that xe meant to sign.

+Your eyes are better than mine, Shashi. Can you find

a way off the road and into the thorns? We need to make camp.+

"Thanny, the river's that way." Isaho pointed. "I can smell it. It's not far. If you want, I think I can find a way there."

Thann felt the child grow steadier as she spoke. Having something important to do pushed away the fear and fretting. Xe nodded. +Yes. We've got to get away from the road, and the river will keep us going the right direction.+

As Isaho moved ahead and began working her way into the mess of thorns and weeds, Thann followed, wondering what Isaho's newly discovered gift meant. This was the second time she'd had spoken of smelling water. A gift she hadn't needed in the city, so no one ever knew it was there? *Hahkeh! if it's true, it's God's benison for sure. Crossing the Plain without following roads ... shay ya!*

No matter how carefully Isaho led and Thann stepped, the wind blew thorn canes against them, canes that acted like saw blades cutting into their boots and trousers and sometimes even flew up to slap them in the face, drawing blood wherever the thorns touched skin.

The eastern sky paled to gray, then flushed pink.

Isaho kept going. She glanced back now and then to be sure that Thann was still following, but mostly she moved quickly and surely through the fields, heading for a goal that seemed clear to her, though Thann rapidly lost any sense of direction. Even the dawn colors didn't help to orient xe. *An eight-year-old child,* xe thought. *It should be me taking care of her.*

Despite xe's disturbance at this tumbling of roles, Thann felt relaxed for the first time since they'd left Mikil's apartment. *The thread of order,* xe thought. *That's what it is. God's presence in Shashi, caring for us both.* Xe nodded as that thought finished, feeling cradled in caring hands.

The thorns gave way to trees.

From the darkness of the soil and the dead stumps, fire had swept through here a few years ago, clearing out the weeds and brush and thorns, giving a new crop of saplings room to spring up, delicate maka trees and the sturdier, slower growing vevezz.

Isaho led xe in a complicated twisting path through the thicket; though the going was less painful without the thorns, pushing through the dense growth of young trees was hard, slow work. The sun was well up by the time they reached the riverbank and stood looking at the water flowing eighty meters below. Isaho had brought them there as straight and true as if she'd been following a blazed trail.

Broad, deep and muddy with a small island poking around the bend just ahead of them, the Khobon River rolled along with the illusion of serenity a shallow mask on the surface, broken by the occasional snag or sudden sucking eddy. Watching the hypnotic shift of current lines, Thann felt fatigue settle over xe, weighing down xe's limbs more and more heavily with every breath xe took. Xe touched Isaho's arm. +That glade a short way in, let's make camp there. We can eat some of Mikil's way cakes, then catch up on our sleep.+

Isaho shook her head. "Here, Thanny. Let's camp here. I don't like all those trees. And look, if anyone comes at us, we can just jump in the water and get away."

Thann shuddered at the thought, then nodded. +But we should move back a little. Into the edge of shadow so travelers on the river won't see us.+

Isaho yawned and smiled sleepily at xe. "All right, but I don' want any cakes, Thanny. I just wan' go to sleep."

Thann woke and started up. Isaho's blankets were empty. Xe swept thinta round, relaxed as xe felt xe's daughter close by. Xe got groggily to xe's feet and moved from under the trees, following the pull of the thinta, found the child curled up on the edge of the cliff, deeply asleep.

Thann looked from Isaho to the river below. It was as if the water had pulled her as close as she could get, reaching her with a call so strong that it overrode mind and will. Xe listened a moment to Isaho's steady breathing and wondered if xe should carry her back. Finally xe shook xe's head and returned to xe's blankets to get what sleep xe could before it was time to move on.

They left camp while it was still light, following the bends of the river as closely as they could.

It wasn't easy walking. Nothing was easy anymore.

When they made camp the second night by the river, Thann brought out the balls of cord xe'd put at the bottom of xe's pack. Half asleep, Isaho watched as xe carved a crude shuttle from a bit of deadwood, wound a length of cord about it.

"What's that, Thanny?"

Xe set the shuttle down so xe could sign. +A long time ago, when I was an anyalit about your age, in the days before the war when Khokuhl was a happy place, my father took me fishing along the edge of the estuary marshes. In the summer we went almost every day. I learned the netting knots because he said I couldn't fish with any other net but one I made for myself. It wasn't proper, he said. When I finished a net he liked, he taught me the way of casting it. In the morning I'll try out this net, and with a little luck we'll have fish for breakfast. We'll need to find our own food, Shashi. There won't be places to buy it, and we haven't the coin anyway.+

"Oh. Is there enough cord to give me some?"

+I put some in your pack, too, down at the bottom. Why?+

"I thought I could make snares. You remember how

Mam taught me to catch rats? Maybe I can trap some mayomayos and wejeys."

+Ah! Yes, that's a good thought. Dig out the cord and see what you can do.+ Xe took up the shuttle and went back to making the net.

As the twist and slide of the shuttle grew more automatic, xe found time to watch Isaho gather sticks and play with the bits of cord until she had the nooses arranged to her satisfaction. The Need for Linojin hummed down deep in her, but it was overlaid now by a purring contentment. *Ah, Shashi, why didn't I see this before? You need something to do, to take your mind off Linojin. Diversion. I could have done it in Khokuhl and maybe . . . I don't know . . . God give you game in your snares.*

In the morning, while Thann was tossing the net for fish, a river peddler sailed round the bend behind xe and brought his boat to shore before xe knew he was there.

2. Walking with the Ixis to Linojin

Wintshikan woke into the warm gray light of a summer dawn with her shoulders burning and cramps in her legs that made her want to scream when she moved. She floundered in the blankets and tried to sit up.

She couldn't. Her legs had no strength in them, and the muscles of her arms and shoulders seemed turned to jelly. She lay back, staring at the leaves arching overhead and wondering how she was going to manage this day and the next and the next if she couldn't even stand.

Zell heard her moving and came trotting over to her.

Wintshikan glowered at her anyabond and for a moment hated xe's wiry agility.

After looking her over, Zell nodded and went away. When xe came back, xe had a stout staff with xe, a sturdy bit of limb xe'd trimmed and polished before Wintshikan woke. Xe laid it beside her. +I thought you were going to regret pushing so hard yesterday.+

Wintshikan tried to use the staff to pull herself up, but she couldn't get the proper grip or brace it effectively. She let the staff fall and lay back in the tangle of blankets, her eyes blurring with angry tears.

Zell bathed her face with a bit of rag dipped into the mug of warm soapy water, drew the rag along her arms, and washed her feet, then xe took the bladder of maphik balm xe'd rescued from Oldmal Yancik's body and began kneading the greasy cream into Wintshikan's arms and shoulders, then her legs. As xe worked, xe stopped now and then to sign comforting words to xe's fembond.

Anger at herself and the body that wouldn't obey her fading as the heat from the balm sank into her muscles, Wintshikan managed a twisty smile. "Worn-out old mapha fit for the stewpot and not much else."

Zell's lefthand fingers fluttered in an anya-giggle. +Oh, we need our Mama-mapha for more than eating. Now, see if you can bend those knees. And I'll go behind and shove.+

On their second day in hohekil, the Remnant of the Shishim Ixis walked north along their Round Path, foraging as they moved. The pickings were small, though it was high summer; it was as if the land itself had grown weary from the war and was turning hohekil.

Adding to that, they'd already passed this way, and there'd not been enough time for the land to renew itself.

It was a quiet day, wind whispering through the treetops though the air down on the trail was still and hot. Somewhere in the distance she heard a boyal's coughing bark. Songbirds twittered and shrieked at intruders, a celekesh sent an exquisite trail of notes to the sun, a hudahuda's harsh cry following it like a clown after a bride dancer. Around her, mayomayos and sasemayos rustled through the underbrush. The red dust puffed up round her feet, its hot acrid bite filling her nostrils.

Wintshikan hadn't walked so much in years, not since she'd gotten stiff and unwieldy and her knees started going on her. She'd ridden the ixis wagon, sitting beside Oldmal Yancik who took care of the team of maphiks that pulled it. She wasn't a young fem; Her malbond Ahhuhl was only two years older and he was fifty when he took the spear and a little later laid down his life in one of the early battles against the Impix. And there were the ten years she'd gotten through since. It was hard, so hard to move this old body. The first day of this trek she'd had fear and anger driving her. And stubbornness. Today the only thing left was stubbornness.

Luca and Wann scouted the country ahead of them, watching for Pixa as well as Impix phelas. With the ixis bonded in hohekil all fighters were their enemies and dangerous.

As the hard, weary miles slipped behind them, Luca was suddenly strong and happy, shouldering her new responsibilities with a zest and joy that set Wintshikan to flaying herself with the knowledge that she'd been remiss for a long time, coasting on the comfortable pillow of custom, not searching for and healing the sores within the ixis. The war had made everything so difficult that custom was the one place where she could relax, the one support that was always there.

I am not clean in God's Sight, she thought. *I've let my ixa-daughters stray from the Path. It's good that we're going to Linojin. A Holy Place will turn thoughts back to the Right Way.*

She thought about Luca's continued absence from all Praise, the shutters that dropped before her eyes when any of the others spoke of God or the Prophet. It was as if the femlit were trying to be polite enough not to rail against

God in the hearing of the others, though she no longer walked the Path. *I don't know what to do. If I say anything, it will just drive her farther away. I wish we were in Linojin now, the Speakers of the Prophet will know what do, they have to know. How can I bear it if her soul is lost to the Pixa, never reborn among us? It'll just drift about until it fades to nothing. And it will be my sloth that did it.*

Zell worked balm into Wintshikan's limbs again when they made camp that night, wrinkled her nose at the smell, and took her blankets upwind.

Lying along for the first time in years, breathing in the vapors rising from her shoulders and arms, Wintshikan stared up at the moon riding in the arms of a tree killed by lightning sometime last year; she thought about the children of her bond. They were long gone from her, one way or another. Her son Hanar joined a Pixa phela and was killed in a raid two years ago. Her daughter Kulenka married out-ixis into a clan from the far north, her new Round centered on the Meeting Ground Isilo. It was an ache to see her go, but she was Heka's daughter and couldn't stay with the ixis she was born to. Her two anyas, little brown Mali and golden Mishi, they had bonded into equally distant clans, and she and Zell hadn't seen them for over five years. She didn't even know if Kulenka, Mali, and Mishi were still alive.

On the other side of the banked fire Xaca made whimpering sounds in her sleep. She was dreaming again. Wintshikan grimaced. To help Xaca purge the night evils, she listened to those dreams as they walked. Evil indeed. Torments. Hidan didn't dream, but xe stayed close enough to Nycn to touch her again and again, as if xe saw Impix in every shadow, ready to jump out and eat xe.

Hidan and Nyen. A bond, maybe? It would be something good from this terror, she thought. *Xaca . . . her anyabond is bones now. I have to think up something she can do to take her mind off her fears . . . she's worrying the children . . . nightmares . . . food, not enough for anyone, hm . . . wonder if it would help if I put Xaca in charge of the foraging. She'd have to mind something besides her own fears. . . .*

In the middle of worrying over that problem, she finally fell asleep.

On the ninth day of the walk, near sundown when the shadows were long on the trail, Luca burst round a bend and stopped in the middle of the Path. "Hussssshhh." She waved her hands to stop the questions and went on in a low, intense voice. "Don't want them hearing you. Impix, downslope, some fifteen minutes away."

Hidan started trembling. Wintshikan gripped xe's arm, glanced rapidly around.

"Xaca, take Hidan and the children, and find cover. Kanilli, you and your cousins go with them. Uphill. Impix're less likely to climb if they feel like looking around. Nyen, get a handful of bracken and brush away our tracks, but don't spend more than a minute or two at it. Good work, Luca. Get back to Wann, and the two of you go to ground."

Zell trembled as xe listened to the Impix strolling along the Round below them as much at ease as if they were in their own home streets.

Wintshikan tapped xe's arm, signed, +Not much woodcraft to this lot, they made more noise than a rogue skazz in must.+

Zell wobbled xe's hand in silent laughter.

Words drifted up to them, phrases, casual laughter, broken bits that like the inlay of different colored woods on the ixis wagon's sides told a story. An ugly story. Another chapter of that tale the two phelas before them had begun.

Disregard and death. The currents of war shaping phela to phela, Pixa to Impix until they were mirror images staring at each other.

Open-eyed and silent, Wintshikan wept for her own folly and that of her people.

3. Yseyl's homecoming

Yseyl flew the disruptor out to the Fence—out beyond the Prophet's Finger, that stony barren headland where no one bothered to come, not even smugglers.

In the end, Cerex had been more generous than he contracted, giving her a stunner and the skip along with a medkit and several packs of emergency rations when he dropped her off in her home mountains.

"The Lady watch over you, and if you survive this, give me a call." He handed her a small gray square. "My drop box on Helvetia. Get to a Splitcom and shove the flake in the code slot. Leave a message, and I'll come fetch you."

He touched her cheek, his fingertips silky and delicate, then turned away and busied himself with the sensor board, doing things she suspected were essentially unnecessary. They'd gotten to know each other rather well on those long insplit journeys when there was nothing else to do. Different species, oddly alike despite that.

We're sports born to be pinched off and thrown away, she thought. *Nobody loves us. We should go eat worms.*

She smiled as she opened the case and took out the disruptor. *Worms and wormholes. Maybe I'm even making sense.* She pointed the business end of the thing at the Fence, a round patch that was blacker than any night she'd ever known, touched the trigger sensor.

For the longest time nothing seemed to be happening. Maybe Cerex had lied after all. She stared at the Fence and tried to ignore the coldness in her stomachs.

The flickers developed paired waves, one dipping and the other rising. The waves turned into a swirl about a circle of emptiness, a circle that grew and grew until the bottom edge dipped below the water and the emptiness was big enough to run a steamer through. The growing stopped, but the hole stayed.

She camped on the Finger and watched it, waiting for the Ptaks to notice, wondering how long it would last.

At the end of the third night it flowed together until there was no sign anything had happened. No visitors either. The disruptor was all Cerex had claimed.

Yseyl's mouth tightened into a grim line as she checked the alignment of the peaks. When she was sure she'd reached the Wendlu Round, she eased the miniskip below the treeline, maneuvered it into a thicket of young mutha saplings, and let it settle to the ground near the decayed giant whose fall had made room for them.

With a groan of relief, she left the saddle, stood rubbing her mistreated buttocks, and muttered to the birds and the air, "Why do offworlders who know so much about everything, make something so miserably uncomfortable?"

Air and birds having no answers for her, she removed the packs strapped to the skip's carry grid and set them on the crumbling trunk. She settled beside them and pulled off her boots, then sat wiggling her toes and enjoying the feel of the earth against her feet. It was good to be back where all the tugs on her body were familiar, where the smells and colors and textures felt right.

The Wendlu Round.

The next peak over marked the camp where she was hatched. "By Minyama Stream I first saw light/Dancing waters blue and bright," she sang as she kicked her heels against the trunk, her voice a breath on the breeze that rustled through the pale green mutha leaves. "By

Minyama Stream I first knew pain/My love is gone, won't come again. . . ."

The memories were hard ones. She forgot them when she was away from here, but when she set her feet on the Round, they were back again. Always back again.

Her Mam and Baba were killed in a rockslide while she was still in egg. Her anya went into howling grief and was kept tied to the ixis wagon after xe tried to fling xeself over a cliff. A week after Yseyl hatched, a vein burst in the pouch and nearly drowned her as the anya's body emptied itself of blood. The Heka saved her life and ordered the anya Delelan to pouch her. Crazy Delelan whom nobody would bond with. The ixis fed xe and looked after xe, but otherwise stayed as far from xe as they could. And as far from Yseyl as they could when she emerged from the pouch.

Delelan didn't care. Xe had xe's voices and the ghosts that xe saw with such conviction that sometimes Yseyl thought she could see them, too. As she grew older, there were moments when she hated Crazy Delelan, blaming xe for the weirdness in her that made the other children afraid of her; they tormented her because they were afraid. They called her Crazy Yseyl. They yelled at her that she'd killed her anya. They pinched her and bit her and fought with her and stole her food and broke her things. Delelan protected her as much as xe could and loved her in xe's odd way, comforted her when the dark closed round her, when she wondered if the taunters were right, if she were a death-dealer from the egg.

It didn't help when her God-Gifts began manifesting themselves. When she discovered she could make people see whatever she wanted them to see, even if there was nothing there. That she could pull the shadow of shape around her and be anyone. That she could make radios play even when the batteries were dead. She didn't say much about these Gifts, but people saw her using them and that was enough to make her seem odder, more frightening to the others. And so more isolated.

In the eighth year after her hatching, she found the caves that twisted through this mountain, hugged the secret of them to her heart, and spent hours exploring them, crawling recklessly through convoluted, cramped spaces barely larger than she was, a handlamp she'd stolen from a peddler at the Yubikha Meeting Ground shoved out ahead of her, batteries long dead but still glowing at her touch.

When the shadows from the saplings crawled across her toes, she clicked her tongue and got to her feet. "You can loll around watching grass grow when this is over, Crazy Yseyl." She stretched, yawned, set to work organizing the packs she was going to carry up the mountain, getting them balanced properly on her back so she'd have the mobility she needed to reach where she meant to go.

Sketchily concealed by the leaves on the crooked red branches of a silha bush growing from the weathered stone, Yseyl dropped to a squat beside the boulder she used as a marker and contemplated the triangular aperture in the side of the mountain that she knew better than the lines in her own palms.

She sat very still, waiting for the web of small lives to quiet and scanning the gravel and coarse sand in front of her for sign of intruders. When she was satisfied that no one had been interfering in her business, she dropped onto her belly and wriggled into the mouth of the cave.

For a moment she thought she was going to get stuck in the right angle bend that came just before the tube widened suddenly into a large chamber, but a twist of her body and a shove of bare feet against a fold of stone pushed her around and she burst free of the tube with scraping sounds from the packs and a loud rip. She wrinkled her nose. "What I get for being lazy."

She slipped out of the straps, eased the packs onto the floor, and got to her feet.

Sunrays dancing with dust motes poured through the cracks in the stone, painted fluttering leaf shapes on the thick gray dust that covered the floor, playing shadow games with the tracks in the dust, the three-clawed mayo-mayo prints, the larger sasemayo spoor, and the scuffs of her bare feet from the last time she'd been here.

On the inner side of the chamber were half a dozen holes, some hardly large enough to admit a sasemayo, the rest of varying heights. One of them was low and broad, rather like a partly open mouth.

Yseyl stretched, yawned. "Hoy-ha, ol' fem, get your body moving. Have to get away from here by sundown."

Her way lit by a handglow she'd bought at Marrat's Market, she inched into the mouth hole, pushing the disruptor case ahead of her this time. The case kept getting hung up on bulges and cracks in the floor, and several of the turns required a lot of wriggling and shoving, but she managed and some ten minutes later emerged into a second chamber.

Lumpy and echoing, a stream hardly wider than the span of a mal's hand meandering along the back wall, it was considerably larger than the first and filled with a velvet darkness that seemed reluctant to yield to the light from the handglow. The flattest surface was that next to the entrance hole and there Yseyl had built a knee-high platform from mutha branches, binding and knotting them together with grass rope saturated in nivula sap. On this platform she'd built herself a small hutch with a three-sided storage shed. The front of the shed was closed off by a piece of heavy canvas.

Setting the disruptor case on the platform, she climbed

up beside it. She untied the canvas, fetched out a box of
candles from the half-a-hundred she had stored in the
shed, a candelabra that had taken her fancy once in Icisel,
and a blanket which she shook out and dropped beside the
box. She twisted the candles into the holes and lit them,
smiling as the gentle wavering light woke the shadows
she called Delelan's Ghosts.

She watched a moment, then went back for the rest of
her gear.

For a while she played with her treasures, all sense of
time lost in counting and caressing them, the hand-
hammered gold and silver coins of the Pixa, the machine-
struck coins of the Impix, a long necklace of polished
turquoise and jasper beads, a bronze statue of a running
boyal, a soaring celekesh carved from jet, a Heka's ring
broach, a mosaic prayer icon that had belonged to a group
of Bond Sisters, all the bits and pieces that had stuck to
her fingers from the years when she'd been only a thief,
before her calling came to her and she began hunting
arms dealers.

Finally she sighed, put most of her treasures away, and
slid the disruptor case into the slot she'd left for it. She
kept back one sack of coins and a few pieces of jewelry
for living costs in Linojin, then tied the canvas into place
and left.

Yseyl came to the Outlook where the Pilgrim Road began mid-morning of the next day, a hot, still summer day,
so quiet and filled with peace that the War could have
been a nightmare she was waking from.

Beyond the patchwork fields of the farms and the nub-
bly green of the fruit orchards, there was the city—white
marble lace on an emerald green ground, the streets like
darker threads winding through it, the ponds and fountains jewels on those threads. And the radio tower rising

above them. And the fishing village to the south, a dull, ugly blot that only emphasized the beauty of the rest.

And out where the sky met the sea, was the Fence. Yseyl stared at it. *You aren't so great. Not any more. I put a hole in your gut, and you didn't even know it.*

The first time she'd seen the Fence, there was an agony in her head as if someone pounded a nail from temple to temple. That was gone. *I put a hole in your gut. I watched it ooze shut, but I can do it again, any time I want.*

She turned away because she couldn't think while she was looking at that THING, sat down on the half-moon of polished stone, and pulled off her boots. She added the boots to her pack and pressed the heels of her hands against her eyes. *Slow,* she thought. *Be careful. You don't know who you can trust. Be the proper little Pilgrim. Be like all the rest. Have your story ready. Who am I? Yes. I'll take my mother's name. Lankya of Wendlu ixis. Visit the Prophet's Grave. Gahh, just the thought makes me sick ... I have to do it. I have to find someone who can lead people. I can escape, but I can't lead. I knew that. I didn't think it through. Someone HAS to know how to use that thing. Drive holes through the Fence, let the people out who want to go, let the killers keep on killing. God! I wish I could still believe ... I wish ...*

She shook off the sudden malaise and rose; feet dragging at first, she stepped onto the Pilgrim Road and started for Linojin.

The Road was paved with yellow brick, hollows worn in it by thousands of bare pilgrim feet over centuries of use. The bricks were warm from the sun and gritty from the dust the summer breeze blew across them. How strange to walk here. Yseyl felt old ghosts rising in and around her—warm and slightly stale ghosts like three-day-old bread in greasy sandwiches, shoved into a back pocket for lunch that never got to happen.

She began to pass the outlying farms.

Short-legged, with curly horns and flickering tails that continually showed their white undersides, herds of lowland maphiks grazed in fenced pastures.

Farmers plowed fields behind teams of skazz, the iron plowshares turning over rich black earth. The smell of that earth was pleasant in her nostrils, though as Pixa, she should be appalled by such slashing at the body of God.

The iron plowshares roused a memory that chased the other ghosts away.

When she was six, already on her way to being the target of all the malice in the ixis, a Prophet Mal came to Wendlu Ixis and spent tedious time at Night Praise inveighing against Impix sins, particularly their mines and mills.

In the morning he gathered the ixis children and quizzed them about their learning, asking them to recite the Sayings of the Prophet and giving out wrapped candies to those who had the answers he wanted. After a while he noticed Yseyl squatting at the back, scowling and silent. She knew she wasn't going to get any candy, and even if she did, Shung and Huddla would jump her and take it away. They were the oldest and the strongest and they knew from long experience that anything they did to her would not be punished. If she complained, it was she who'd get the whack.

He beckoned to her.

She tried to pretend she didn't see him.

"You, femlit," he said. "Yes, I mean you. Come here."

She trudged through pinches and hisses of "don't disgrace us," "crazy Yseyl," "you mess up, we gonna get you." When she reached the Prophet Mal, she stopped and stood staring at the ground, not daring to look at him.

"You have not tried to answer." He caught hold of her chin and lifted her head so she was forced to gaze at his stern, lined face. "Have you no answers?"

He smelled sweaty and something else she didn't know but didn't like, and his hands felt wrong, like polished leather, not skin. She wanted to pull away, but his hold was too strong; all she could do was drop her eyes again and stare at his chest rather than his face. The loose thing he wore that wasn't quite a shirt—it was made from Impix cloth. Silk. She knew that because just a month ago at the Yubikha Gather Thombe and Busa and Anya Bilin had a yelling, slapping argument over Busa taking her lace money and spending it on a piece of silk. And he had an Impix knife on the leather strap that belted it to his body.

"What is the Path of the Child? Tell me the first Saying."

Despite her fear and her nervousness, the Whys had got hold of her. Crazy Delelan said Why was the first word she spoke when she crawled from the pouch. Without thinking, Yseyl lifted her hand and pointed at the shirt. "If Impix are so bad," she said with regrettable clarity, "if the things they make are hated by God and the Prophet, why are you wearing Impix silk and how come you use an Impix knife?"

Yseyl shook her head at the memory. *Bad timing,* she thought, *but the truth, for all the whipping I got.* It was a question no one had ever answered for her. The Pixa couldn't live without the things they fulminated against. No mines, no iron, no mills, no steel. And no fine cloth or thread. No ax heads or axle bolts, no needles or knives or chains. Not the first time nor the last she'd experienced the twisty logic of adults.

Except for a few soaring spires and the openwork steel radio tower, now that she was down on the plain, the city was hidden from view by the ancient thile groves, huge trees with curving triple trunks that arced over and out

with smaller limbs growing straight up from the arches,
limbs thick with hand-shaped leaves of dark green.

A number of walkers were ahead of her, a few Impix
pilgrims in their bright yellow robes, two or three Pixa in
dark green; the rest were refugees from both branches of
the Impixol family, dressed in whatever they wore when
they turned hohekil and ran from their kin and their
homes.

*Much more of this and half the people left alive will be
coming here. God, I hope there is someone behind those
walls who can whip up enough heat and light to organize
this escape. Funny, or maybe not, now that I have the disruptor, there's nothing I can do with it. Not alone. I
should be steamed at Cerex because he must have known
it was just a stupid gadget and no use at all to what I
want.* She wasn't angry, not really. After all, she'd started
out by trying to kill him. Which he'd accepted with remarkable equanimity. And she liked him. *I just have to
figure it out,* she thought. *Find some way to make it useful.*

Up close, the walls of the city were more like lace than
she'd expected, the white marble facing carved and
pierced in an intricate flow of images and words, Sayings
of the Prophet, Songs from the Book of God. And all of
it was exquisitely clean. As she waited in the line of those
seeking entrance to the city, she saw a group of fems and
anyas in coarse unbleached robes carry buckets and
brushes to a section of wall. They chanted a Song as they
scrubbed delicately at the stone.

The line of folk ahead of her curved round a screen and
vanished inside the gate. Step by step she moved forward,
weary and bored but putting on a face of patience. She
wanted no one looking at her and remembering her.

When she rounded the screen, the stench of Pilgrim
sweat and dirt hit her in the face, no breeze to dilute that

consequence of days of walking and privation. She took shallow breaths, let her eyelids droop while she examined what lay ahead of her and listened intently to the questions so she'd be prepared to answer them when her time came.

Long table. Four Brothers of God seated with pen, ink, bound registers, writing down the responses.

Two doors in the far wall. Those with money for their keep went through the righthand door, those who cast themselves on the Mercy of God passed through the left.

"Pixa or Impix?"

"Pixa."

"Name."

"Lankya of Ixis Wendlu Clan Enzak."

"Reason for visit."

"Sanctuary. I am hohekil."

"Have you coin to keep yourself, or will you be a Guest of God?"

"I have coin to keep me for a while."

"You understand, it is not likely that there will be paid labor you can do."

"I understand."

"This is a place of peace. Weapons are not allowed within the walls. If you have any such, they will be sealed and returned to you when you leave."

"I have this." She took her belt knife from the sheath and laid it on the table. "No more."

It was a lie, of course, but she wasn't about to let herself be wholly disarmed. Besides, even if they searched her and found Cerex's stunrod taped to her back, they wouldn't know what it was.

He took the knife, wrote on a strip of paper, and sealed the paper to the knife with a bit of heated wax. He set the knife in a box by his feet. When he straightened, he said, "If you are found with a weapon inside the walls, you will be cast out and not allowed to return. Do you understand?"

"Yes."

"You will be required to do Service to God for five hours each week. You will be given a token for each hour completed and should display those tokens to any Brother, Bond Sister, Anya of Mercy, or Prophet Speaker who requests to see them. Do you understand?"

"Yes."

He opened the much carved wooden chest that sat at his elbow and took out a small bronze square with a hole in one corner. "This is a luth. It is your key to the Freedom of Linojin. You will see that today's date is stamped into the metal. Six months from today you will go to the Grand Yeson and put forth your reasons for remaining in Linojin. If these are accepted, you will be given another luth at that time. If they are not, then you must leave. Do you understand?"

"Yes."

"Carry the luth with you always. If you are found without it, you will do penance and then must leave. Do you understand?"

"Yes."

"Then welcome to Linojin, O Pilgrim. God's blessing be yours."

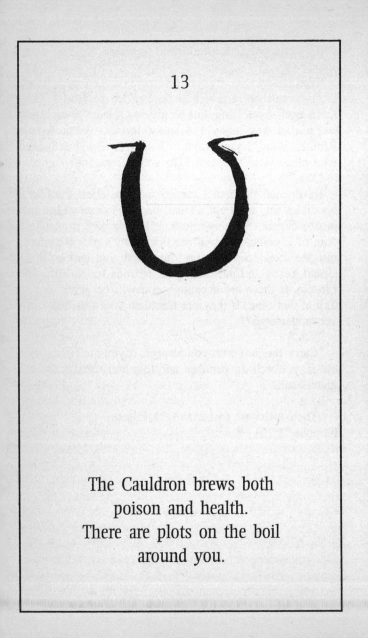

The Cauldron brews both
poison and health.
There are plots on the boil
around you.

Chapter 6

1. Figuring a way from here to there

> *In the distance*
> *the smell of hibiscus*
> *crying out risk us*
> *eyeing with askance*
> *I sing the mythos*
> *of cosmos in prim pose*
> *preening for glances....*

Shadith dropped the stylo onto the clipboard's magnet, leaned against the bitt, and let her legs swing, her bare feet almost touching the water the high tide had brought in. The scribbles on the sheets of paper were there as camouflage, an excuse for sitting where she was sitting and staring out across the water (though she'd surprised herself by rather liking some of those lines).

Graska Wysp. The island chain was a sprinkle of dots just beyond the mouth of Lala Bay. She had a good view of the largest island, the one called k'Wys; the wharf where she sat was at the edge of the bay, old and deserted, rotting back to the earth it was built on.

Though the north end of k'Wys was a rocky tor with scraggly windblown shrubs growing from every crevice, the southern third was flatter, a tangle of brush, vines and heaps of pumice except for the areas cleared off for the flier pad and a large hangar. The fliers in that hangar were the only ones allowed in the air over the sea between Ptak-K'nerol and Impixol.

The water was deep under her feet, but the currents were strong and there was a lot of crosschop—probably why the wharf was no longer in use. An ancient eel lived in a hole below her, a huge creature long as a python and three times as thick, with the temperament of a rabid wolverine. She knew him well by now, having mindridden him a dozen times, using his predator's eyes to explore the area around k'Wys. Old Tiger had given her some wild rides.

During high tide she swam him into the blowholes that riddled the base of the island, forced him to follow one after the other and stick his nose out the surface openings until she'd found the one she needed, the one that led to the surface north of the hangar, in a waste area filled with twisted stone and stunted thornbush. His temper got worse the longer she rode him, but after a few slashing fights with the smaller eels that laired in those holes, he settled down and was tractable enough when she took him out again.

The eels were part of the islands' defense—no swimmers in those waters. As she leaned back and swung her legs, the picture of an idle dreamer, she saw another part of that defense.

Jet boats were zipping back and forth on the lake beyond the islands, pairs of them racing, others playing elaborate games of tag and bluff. One of them turned through too broad an arc and passed on the far side of a bright red buoy. The man at the wheel went limp and fell in a heap, the boat's motor died. A few moments later a patrol shell left k'Wys and came alongside the intruder.

There was a swift flicker along the water as the field shut down. The men in the shell tossed a howler into the jet boat, then shoved it past the buoy into unwarded water. They sat a moment listening to the howler whoop and watching to make sure the current carried the boat away from k'Wys, then a lifted arm brought a second flicker as the field went on again. The shell hummed back to the landing.

Why does everything on this world have to be double the work? Shadith reached for the clipboard, tapped the stylo against her chin. After a moment she started writing again.

Howl said the honeybear	*Shaking in a shrieking fit*
Growl said the hoaryboar	*Dropping in a digger pit*
Foul said the holyman	*Cursing at a biting nit*

She wrinkled her nose, scratched the lines out, started as a voice sounded behind her.

"Why'd you do that? I kinda like it."

She looked round. It was the old man she'd spoken to the first day. He was leaning on the bitt, looking over her shoulder. He'd come up so silently she hadn't heard a thing—though that might also be due to the howler which was still going off at short intervals as the jet boat rocked and turned in the waves.

"Mp. You spooked me. Why? Too forced. Whimsy that feels forced is worse than week-old cake."

"Got y'self fired, huh?"

"She started using her hands on me. I'll take a lot but not that." Shadith dropped the stylo onto the magnet, patted a yawn. "Thought I'd have a little vacation before I started looking for work." She grinned up at him. "Nice out here and cheap entertainment. Been pondering on getting a pole and fishing for dinner. My da had a fishboat and I went out with him sometimes when I was a kid."

"You want to be a bit careful along here. Seen the eels?"

"Yeh. One thing sure, swimming's not on my program."

He chuckled, straightened, shading his eyes with a

gnarled hand as he watched a pair of polizer 'bots fly over to the jet boat and start towing it back to shore.

Shadith nodded at the boat. "He dead?"

"Nah, just stunned. In an hour or so he'll come out of it with a bodyache that'll make him sorry it didn't kill him. Told you. Don't mess with the Graska Wysp."

"Not much chance of that; with my finances I'd have to walk on the water to get there." She felt around, found her sandals, and began strapping them on.

"You thought of selling your poems?"

She got to her feet. The clipboard tucked under her arm, she smoothed her dress down, ran her fingers through her hair. "I've sold a few, but I know better'n to think I can live off them, Grandda. Well, see you round. Good fishing."

She strolled away, didn't bother looking back. Twisty old man, but a bit more obvious than he thought he was. One small knot in the Ptakkan security web. Ah, well, it was nice to have such a credible witness to her innocence. Irritating, though, if he showed up at the wrong time.

2. Music and mouse ears

That night Shadith drifted along The Strip, absorbing color and noise through her skin as much as through eyes and ears; it was a garish gaudy tasteless mess and she loved it, a sensory overload energizing her, filling her with zazz. She'd painted her face, neck, and shoulders with swirls of black and white, pinned a crimson crest and horsetail to her brown-gold fuzz and wrapped her body into bright blue glittergauze. Her feet were bare, her toenails painted gold to match the fauxclaws she'd glued on. She moved in the beats of the clashing music, riding the whipped-up excitement of the crowd around her, mind shut down, eyes searching for something, she didn't know what, just that she'd know it when she saw it.

She slashed her nails against a groping hand, laughed over her shoulder at the angry man, slipped away from him around a band of small brown Pa'ao Teelys, past a Menaviddan matron with a dozen miniatures of herself clinging to her stiff black hair, lost herself in a motley aggregation of Cousin types on a guided tour.

Holoas swooped at her, whispered in her ears: Watch the rape and murder of a nomad tribe. Harnke's Picture Palace has it all. See the secret orgies of the White Brothers. Harnke's Picture Palace has sensearound, you'll have every sensation as if it were you in the white robe. Learn what the Bond Sisters do in the heart of their Enclosure. Things so secret and perverse you won't believe your senses. Harnke's Picture Palace has group rooms or private viewing, whichever you prefer. Watch the torture and eating of an Impix anya. Bring a friend or meet a stranger with your tastes. Who knows what might come of it. Harnke's. . . .

When she moved from the set area of one holoa, another began its pitch, whispering, insinuating, enticing.

Her distaste for their wares started to gray down her pleasure, so she ducked into a dingier side street where there were more dangers for the unwary, but at least she'd be free of the whispers. The facades of the playhouses on this street were almost as garish as those on The Strip, with the delights inside flashed across the fronts iike the painted flats in an ancient carnival. She tossed her crimson horsetail, danced to the music blaring from the houses, reveling in the slide of muscle on muscle, the vibration that shook her to the bone, wanting no praise or blame from outsiders, no intrusion on her enjoyment of herself.

For a while she was left alone, but the sensual energy in her body began to attract interest in ways she didn't want, so with a touch of anger and some reluctance she stopped the dance and slipped through a holo-facade that proclaimed the virtues of the Utka-Myot Fight-o-Drome. Two srebs bought her a night's membership and a battered flake reader that was set to lead her through the delights the playhouse offered.

She moved to the main public arena and dropped onto a bench beside the door to watch a firstcut knife fight. A man and a woman circled each other on the sand. They were quick and well trained, with a number of crowd-pleasing moves that were mostly spectacle. She smiled. Rohant would have wiped the sand with them in about thirty seconds, but she wouldn't want to face either of them in a real right.

A hand settled on her leg, moved up her thigh, squeezing as it moved. She slapped the hand away and slid down the bench. The man's face looked familiar, maybe one of those who'd started crowding her on the street.

He slid after her. "You shakin' it real good out there, minka. Give y' a good time?"

"Not interested, 'spois. Leave me 'lone and go find other meat." She slid further from him along the nearly empty bench.

He followed, put his hand on her leg again. "Don' be like that, whore. You sellin', I buyin'."

"Haul ass, chyr." She raked the fauxnails across the back of his hand. "Shove y' chya at me, y' pull back a stump."

He cursed her, started an openhanded swing at her face. A metal claw clamped on his wrist, the arm of the peacer 'bot under the bench, and its minimalist voice grated, "Stri king a cli ent is not per mit ted."

She used the respite to leave the arena, annoyed with herself for dropping her wariness and allowing this stupidity to happen. Spla spla, it fit well enough into the persona she was throwing into the face of Ptak-sec, so no harm done. She shook the horsetail and laughed at herself. No one watching that bit of folly would possibly see her as a professional investigator on the job.

She looked into two more of the public arenas, found nothing that interested her, and left the fight-o-drome.

"You worry me, little Voyka."

She scowled over her shoulder at the old man. "You following me round?"

"You aren't hard to see, got up like that."

"Not in the mood for sex, if that's what you're after. Just want to have some fun." She moved her shoulders impatiently, put a touch of whine in her voice.

He clicked his tongue, shook his head. "Nothing like that, Voyka, just sayin'. You got any your poems in memory?"

"Some I set as songs. Why?"

"There's this place down a bit closer to the lake. Man I know runs it. Lots of Ptaks go there, mind that?"

She shrugged. "Their world. So. . . ." She saw the crewman emerging from the fight-o-drome looking ready to chew nails. "Um . . . let's move on, hm? That's a cross street where the shadows are, isn't it?"

"What's wrong?"

"Just a creep I had some trouble with." She sighed, yanked the crest and horsetail from her head, and moved hastily around a clutch of Cousins coming from a playhouse. "Mood he's in, I don't want him anywhere round me."

Shadith glanced at the holo, frowned. "The Hungry Harp?"

"Saul, he's the owner, he says if you have to have everything explained, you don't belong there."

"Mm."

The old man chuckled. "Come along, Voyka. You can

buy kaf or wine at the bar; if you want something else, it's likely hanging in the shadows."

Inside was dark and smelled of the herbs in the smoke drifting from the torches in gilded cages scattered about the long L-shaped room, hanging on chains from ceiling beams, swaying in the breeze from the coolers, torches that cast confusing, multiple shadows over the faces of the people seated at the tables. There was a small stage with a guitar, a flute, and a keyboard sitting on chairs as if they watched the watchers.

Saul was a round little man with eyes so pale they seemed bleached in a face the color of charcoal; he was bald on top but wore his fringe of long gray hair in double plaits tied off with leather thongs. He had a wide, thin-lipped mouth that was never still, squeezing together as he listened to the old man, a corner twisting up, then down, lower lip sucked in, then both lips pursed, then moving from side to side.

When the old man finished, Saul turned his head, called, "Zaddo."

A man came through a beaded curtain, tall and thin with straight blond hair hanging loose. "Huh?"

"Talk to her." Saul jerked a thumb at Shadith. He touched her arm, pointed at the stage. "You got fifteen minutes. Zaddo here plays keyboard. Get up there and tell him what you want."

Shadith fixed the red crest in her hair again, moved with the elaborations of the tune she'd whistled for Zaddo; when she was ready, she sang, playing with the words, turning them to fit the music:

> *"I am fathoms deep*
> *In love with dark*
> *I fill my mouth with night*
> *And drink the absence*

Of the light
Dense and stark
I think
I will not endure
The pure white silence
Of the day
I will sleep the bright away
And rise
With the moon
To reprise
The melodies of night."

Five songs later, hoarse and weary, humming with the praises of her audience, quite pleased with herself and starting to wonder if the old man was really a spy or just a whacked piece of beach wrack, Shadith ambled back to her boardhouse.

After a long hot shower and a pot of caloury tea to soothe her throat, she stretched out on her bed and went hunting for ears so that she could listen to the Cobben.

Sound of a door closing. Feet, sighs, grunts, a thud as one of the Cobben knocked something onto the floor.

"Meya, you're drunk!"

"Am not. 'F you'd turn the light up."

"Heb, you stink like a whorehouse. Where were you anyway?"

"Whorehouse." *Sound of honking snigger.*

"Ta-tse, how's the talent?"

"Talented. Sarpe, you back?" *Hebi's growl loudened to a shout, then he answered himself.* "Hunh. Guess she is, looka that, shield's on."

Sound of door sliding open. A confusion of footsteps, sound of yawns. Sarpe's voice had a post-orgasmic muting of its usual harsh edges. "So you lot are back."

"You getting shy, Coryfe?"

"Don't be more of an idiot than you have to, Feyd."

"Any news?"

"Clo-Kajhat finally came through with what's on his alleged mind. More than just strangling some hapless git. He wants Linojin brought into the war. The tourists are getting bored with the sniping, he needs something big to get their juices going."

"Huh? Don't get it, Sarpe. How'n Tarto's Hell we supposed to do that?"

"He's targeted three mals. The Holy Piz who plonks that Temple thing . . . ahh, Brother Hafambua, Humble Haf the preaching mal, the jinners go round licking up the sweat where he walks, they think he's so righteous, then there's a Prophet Speaker called Kuxagan, got a mouth on him could talk you into a spate of celibacy, Heb, need I say more? The third's the hohek leader, the one they call the Arbiter, name of Noxabo. He keeps the peace between Pixa and Impix, which is something I wouldn't like to try. Clo-Kajhat figures we do 'em and fix it like one of the other factions killed 'em. That should stir the pot real nice."

"So when we getting started on it?"

"Day after tomorrow; be ready to catch the boat for k'Wys straight up noon."

After she let the mouse run free, Shadith lay on the bed staring at the ceiling. The horns of this dilemma had very sharp points. It wasn't her job, it wasn't her war. Why should she feel pushed to get to those people to warn them? And who said they'd believe her anyway? And yet. . . .

Finally, tired of the ruts she was running in, she shoved that problem aside and began to consider how she was going to explain disappearing after that performance. *Ah Spla! I STILL haven't gotten into work mode. Or stayed in character. Doing what comes naturally will have to wait till the job's done, or I'm going to mess up worse than this some time soon.* She sighed. *If the old man isn't a spy, just a nice old guy who's convinced himself I could be a daughter or something like that, he's going to make one big fuss when I stop showing up. If he is a spy, I'm in the soup for sure.*

She laced her hands behind her head and lay scowling at the ceiling. *Say I write him a bit of thank-verse, say I've met this neat guy and we're going to do some snuggling, so he shouldn't fuss if he doesn't see me for a couple weeks. Give the thing to Saul, tell him to pass it on. Just stupid enough an excuse he might even believe it; the way I've been acting, it'll be right in character.* She sighed and turned to working out the final details of stowing away on the Cobben's flier.

3. Night swimming with eels

Shadith slipped out of the long dress she'd worn to cover her swimming tack and stuffed it into her gearsac, pushing it down behind the break-in kit Digby had provided along with other bits and pieces he thought would prove useful. She knelt in the deep black shadow at the end of the wharf where the weathered stone rose a dozen meters above the surface of the water. Old Tiger was moving in his hole. She could feel the hunger developing in him; if she left him alone, in another half hour he'd come gliding out to chase down some dinner. *Sorry, old son,* she thought. *But this won't take long.*

She pulled on the breather hood, clamped down on his brain, slid over the side, and lowered herself into the water.

Old Tiger was a horror mask snarling in her face as she kicked herself down to meet him. She caught hold of the ragged crest that ran down his backbone, positioned herself beside him and sent him swimming at top speed toward k'Wys.

When his body brushed against her as they plunged through the darkness, she could feel the slide of those long live muscles fighting the resistance of the water. It was a wild intoxicating ride and made her want to howl at the moon for the glory of it all.

She scolded herself to order as the slopes of k'Wys loomed before them, set the eel to searching for the configurations around the blowhole she wanted.

The crescent moon was low on the horizon when she pulled herself cautiously from the hole and wriggled through the thornbush until she could stretch out on a mix of gravel and dead grass and use her nightglasses to sweep the area around the hangar.

Quiet. No one around. As usual.

She eased up, squatted, and pulled the gearsac round where she could get at it. Screened by the brush and the folds of rock, mindtouch reaching out to warn her if anyone came round, she stripped off the wetsuit, rolled it into a tight cylinder, and tucked it into a crack in the stone. No point in dripping on the hangar floor. The breather hood she contemplated for a moment, then slid it into a press pouch on the outside of the sac. There might come a time when she needed it.

By the time she was ready to move, the moon was gone and clouds were blowing across the stars, thickening the darkness. The wind had risen and was whipping dead leaves and grit across the ground. She let it whip her along with them, turned the corner of the hangar, and stopped before the small personnel door. She clicked on the reader Digby had given her, confirmed what her own senses told her. The only barrier was mechanical. She flipped the reader over, extruded the quickpic, and inserted it into the slot.

A moment later she eased the door open and slipped inside. As she started to turn so she could relock the door, there was a swift scrabbling and a sudden weight slammed into her, knocking her flat.

Carrion breath.

Feet on her back, nails ripping into her shirt and the skin beneath it.

Teeth closing on the nape of her neck.

The instant she felt the weight, her mindride stabbed out, froze the beast.

She lay with her face in the dust, holding desperately to the grip she had on him.

Focus. Slow. No hurry. You know how to do this. Follow the pathways, take control, bleed off the rage. . . .

In another few breaths she had him.

She opened his mouth, walked him off her back, then rolled up and scowled at him and through his eyes at herself. It was a weird feeling. She eased off on the hold, played a moment in his pleasure centers, then brought him closer so she could rub her hands over him and get him used to her scent.

The faint light coming through clerestory windows high overhead showed her a black canine with a flash of white on his neck. She dug her fingers into his droopy jowls, scratched behind his ears, worked down his spine, evoking slobbery whimpers and an ecstatic wriggle of his hindquarters. Gradually she removed the controls, starting to breathe again as he stayed friendly. He was an intelligent beast and not mad at the world, no meanness in him, just doing his job.

"Yes, you're a good dog, aren't you. With a good trainer, you like him, don't you. He's my friend, you're my friend. Feels good when I scratch you like that, doesn't it. Ah, spla, your breath's enough to knock over an ox. So I'll get up. Down, boy, feet on the floor. That's right. Head at my knee. Now let's go explore."

Panting and dripping slobber, he trotted beside her as she moved about the hangar, using a minute pinlight to see what the Ptaks kept in that vast gloomy building.

There were four fliers parked in the center of the stained metacrete floor. A fifth was racked with one of the lifters stripped, waiting for repairs which a certain thickness of dust suggested no one was rushing to complete.

None of the locks were engaged.

They were standard haulers with the cargo hold below the passenger module. The hold was a rectangular box with a grating floor, straps for tying bales and bundles, and a series of wall bins. Stowing away wouldn't be difficult if she could figure out which flier the Cobben planned to use.

She moved away from them and stood, hands on hips, scowling at four large shadows. "Well, dog, it's really too bad you can't talk. Or would you even know? Maybe they haven't decided themselves which beast they're going to ride. Shays! I really don't want the noise it'd make if I had to steal one of those things. It's a nest in the rafters for me, dog. Sleep out the night and watch which one they load up with supplies and hope they do it ahead of time."

The dog pushed his muzzle against her hip and wagged his stumpy tail as she dug her fingers into the ruff round his neck.

"You're a love, aren't you?" She chuckled. "Deadly little love. I'd be cold meat without the mindride. Ah, spla, my fault, not yours. Should have read the building before I went in. Hmp. Time for you to get back to work and me to find myself a perch."

Early morning sunlight was streaming through the narrow clerestory windows when the large doors slid open. The dog trotted to the door, stood a moment, ruff bristling, a ridge of hair rising along his spine. There was a sound that Shadith felt rather than heard. The dog relaxed and trotted out of sight. A moment later a cargo carrier hummed in.

It settled beside the nearest flier, then a small wiry man followed the handler out. Lying on a rafter high above them, Shadith smiled tightly as he spoke. Cobben on the job. The voice told her which. Orm.

With the loader 'bots working steadily and in spite of Orm's fussy interference, the transfer of the goods was quickly finished. As the handler loaded the 'bots onto the carrier, Orm climbed into the passenger section of the flier. Shadith tensed, listening to the clinks and clunks he made, wondering if he were going to settle in and wait for the others. The Coryfe said noon and that was several hours off, but maybe they'd changed the time.

The handler walked round the carrier, making sure the 'bots and the stakes were properly in place, then he slammed down the locking lever and climbed into the cab. The hum of the lifters filled the hangar. Orm dropped from the flier's cabin and ran to the carrier.

A moment later the hangar's door hummed shut.

Shadith circled the flier, Digby's readout telling her that Orm had activated some sort of alarm. The readout wasn't sensitive enough to do more, so she clicked it off and crouched in the shadow next to the cargo hatch, eyes shut, trying to trace the energy flows. Since most of the system was potential rather than actual, it was a bitch to read. She was sweating and her head was throbbing by the time she managed to trip the switch and shut the thing off.

She used the quickpic to unlock the hatch and crawled inside; there was just room to wriggle along on top of the padded crates. At the back of the hold there was a small pile of unused padding and a space large enough for her to sit with some comfort. She slipped her arms from the straps of her gearsac, pushed it to one side, lowered herself onto the padding, then sat scowling at the crate in front of her, trying to decide if she should reset the alarm.

If it was internal as well as external . . . if she needed

a passpartout to convince it she was part of the cargo . . .
dogs were easier. . . .

The Cobben might have gotten sloppy through easy living, but she couldn't count on them missing an obvious
thing like a switched-off alarm. She closed her eyes,
found the configuration after a few moments of fumbling
about, sucked in a breath, and flipped the switch.

Nothing happened.

*Right. Now all I've got to worry about is boredom.
Hours of boredom. Do I dare sleep? Better question is
how do I stay awake?* She yawned, arranged one of the
pads behind her, curled up as comfortably as she could,
and went to sleep.

When the Twig is broken, Peril.
Body, mind, and soul
on the brink of the Abyss.

Chapter 7

1. All that effort undone

Thann adjusted the net with a flex and bend of xe's wrists and sent it skimming out, the wet cord resisting the mischief of the wind that boomed in xe's ears and teased the water into jadeite shards. Xe's father had a saying—a talking wind makes bad fishing—which had proved itself over and over this day. Xe tugged at the steering lines and began pulling the net in, alert to a certain liveliness in the feel that told xe that xe'd finally caught more than weed and driftwood.

A scream. Isaho! Thann dropped the guides and started to turn.

Hands caught xe's arms, a loop of rope was round xe's wrists and dragged tight. A moment later, xe was facedown on the river bank, another loop about xe's ankles pulled tight and tied off. Xe writhed around, spat dirt from xe's mouth, and began struggling against the ties.

The mal who'd trapped xe wore a peddler's red shirt, faded and stained, a peddler's humpy hat with the wide brim to keep the sun from his eyes, a peddler's iron rings in his ears. The bits of his crest hair poking from under the hat were streaked with gray. He watched xe struggle, his leathery face impassive, then cupped his hands round his mouth, yelled, "Got the kid, Yal?"

"Ehyah, Baba, but she fighting like crazy, you wanna stake that 'un down and come gimme a hand?"

* * *

Thann whistled xe's distress as Yal and the peddler came from the vevezz brake, Isaho's limp body slung over the mal's shoulder. Yal was a mallit perhaps two or three years older than Isaho, swaggering along beside his father, a red rag braided into his crest and wooden plugs where the rings would go when he finished his apprenticeship.

The peddler dumped Isaho on the bank beside Thann, turned to his son. "Keep y' eyes open." He flicked a bony forefinger against barrel of the pellet rifle the mallit carried. "But don't go wasting ammo on shadows, or I take it outta your hide. You hear?"

"Ya, Baba."

"And keep y' hands off the femlit. She worth good coin if she fresh meat."

"Ya, Baba."

The boat was a flat-bottomed scow with a single mast and a shack built of weathered planks for a sleeping cabin, the deck cluttered with barrels and bales, an old sail that was more patches than original cloth tied over these. It was nosed against the bank, the sail dropped in a crumbled mass on the boom, an anchor cable taut and straining over the side, holding it against the push of the current.

The peddler splashed into the water on the downstream side and swung himself on board. As he began turning the crank to lift the sail, he called to his son, "Yal, haul 'em over. Hop it, mallit, you want that Imp phela to come over hill and see what's happenin'? Nah! Not the femlit, the anya. That's the one that's real walkin' money. What I keep tellin' you, make sure of the money first."

"Ya, Baba. Uh ... anya, xe's made a mess of xe's wrists."

"Ne,' mind that, Patchin' comes later. Move it."

Yal hefted Thann and rolled xe over the side. The ped-

dler caught xe before xe hit the planks and dumped xe
down by a bale of old clothes that smelled of sweat and
rot, then went back to working the crank as the mallit
struggled along with a writhing, screaming, biting Isaho.

When he reached the boat, Yal dropped Isaho over the
rail and swung himself up after her, hauled her across to
Thann, and went to help his father.

Thann nuzzled at Isaho, trying to comfort her, driven
half insane because xe's hands were tied and xe couldn't
speak. In the middle of xe's anguish, xe remembered the
peddler's words and felt a flare of hope. *Impix phela, he
said. If only they would come, anything would be better. . . .* Xe's hope died as quickly as it was born. He
wasn't really worried, he was lessoning his son. If he
thought the Impix were close enough to be trouble, he'd
have done the carrying himself instead of leaving it to the
mallit, and we'd be going down river already. *Isa, ah, Isa,
we'll get out of this. Somehow. I promise . . . hush, Shashi
. . . hush, baby . . . oh, God, help us, give me strength. . . .*
Xe moistened xe's lips, tried a soft whistle; it was more
air than sound, but xe turned it to a lullaby that seemed to
comfort xe's daughter.

As soon as the boat was out in the middle of the river,
the peddler lifted Isaho and carried her to the stern, then
dropped her at the feet of his son who was tending the til-
ler. "The anya gives trouble, strangle the little bitch."

He went into the shack and came out with black iron
chains draped over one arm, a bundle of rags and a battered tin box in his other hand. He dropped the chains beside Thann, squatted beside xe. "You heard?"

Xe nodded.

"Good." He set the box on his knee, pried the lid up
and took out a half-used tube of salve. "So you don't
move when I cut the ropes off." He went to work and had

xe's feet free, squeezed out a dollop of salve and spread
it where xe'd cut into skin and muscle trying to kick free.
When he had it well worked in, he tore a strip from one
of the rags and wound it round xe's ankle, his fingers sur-
prisingly deft, almost gentle. As soon as he was finished
with the second ankle, he clamped iron cuffs over the
bandages, locked them in place. They were joined by a
chain about the length of xe's arm.

He dealt with the wrist wounds in the same way, locked
cuffs around xe's wrists. These fit so tightly he could
barely close them over the bandages. The chain that
joined them was shorter, but xe felt an inexpressible relief
when xe saw that xe would be able to sign.

He wiped his hands on a rag, sat on his heels, his eyes
moving over xe. "Anya in egg," he said after a while. "So
you won't be trying to go overboard. Femlit's your
daughter?"

Thann hesitated, signed, +Yes.+ Xe's hands shook with
the weight of chains.

"Up to you to see she behaves. She gives too much
trouble, we knock her on the head and drop her overside.
Understand?"

+Yes.+ As he started to get up, xe signed rapidly,
+Why? Why are you doing this?+

He laughed as he stood up. "You ask a peddler why?
Coin, anya, coin. There's a hungry market 'long the coast
for anyas in good health. Femlits still bring in something,
too, but there's getting to be a glut in them, so not near
so much as an anya. What that means is what I said. Too
much trouble, we get rid of her."

Thann sat with xe's back against the bale of rags, Isaho
crouched beside xe with her head in xe's lap. Xe stroked
xe's daughter's shining black hair with small careful gestures that didn't make the chains clank and watched with
despair as the wind and current carried them swiftly back

along the ground that had cost them so much time and strength.

Xe made Isaho eat the biscuit and stew the peddler fed them. +If you don't eat, you'll get sick, and we'll never get to Linojin. As long as we have our strength, Shashi, there's always a chance. If you get sick and die, there's none.+ Over and over, the same things, over and over till the glaze faded from Isaho's eyes and she forced the food down.

As the sun rose on the second day, Thann heard again the boom of the mountain guns.

On the third day they were gliding past the ruined towers of Khokuhl; they spent the night tied up at a half-drowned wharf at the far end of a waterfront that used to be the busiest on the east coast of Impixol. The only things there now were rats and rot.

On the fourth day the boat crept along the south shore of the Bay of Khokuhl, standing out only far enough to escape the jagged stone teeth at the foot of the cliffs. Around noon it reached a high-walled inlet like a bite out of the stone.

The peddler dropped sail and hove to at the mouth of the inlet, lifted Thann off xe's feet and carried xe into the cabin, leaving xe in the stinking darkness. Xe heard the hasp clank shut, the scrabbling as he pushed the padlock through the staple and clicked it shut. *Protecting his assets,* xe thought. *Please, oh, God, watch over Isaho, don't let them hurt her. Please. . . .*

As xe kept up xe's desperate prayer, xe felt the boat shift, then settle to a steady dip and surge. Xe licked xe's lips and put all the force xe could manage into the whistle code xe and Isaho had worked out as they walked. Xe broke off, kneeling taut with fear, waiting for an answer.

Isaho's voice came to xe, sweet and true, stronger than it had been, almost a fem's voice though she was still too young for the Change. "Thanny," she sang, "Anya meami, they have taken the chains off, I am well." Then she whistled the code that meant she was truly all right.

A lie, but a brave one. God watch over you, my baby. Thann sighed and settled to wait for whatever came next.

The boat shifted direction. Xe could tell by the sound of the wind and the tilt. The next few minutes as it negotiated the crosschop at the mouth of the inlet, xe was thrown off xe's feet, rolled about, slammed against one wall then another. By the time the worst of the motion stopped, xe was bruised and dizzy and xe's throat burned from the bile xe's first stomach cast up.

After another fifteen or so minutes, there was a thump, a shudder, and the movement gentled further to a slow rocking. Mixed in with the raucous cries of shorebirds, xe heard scratching and rasping as the fenders rubbed against something, probably one of the wharves. The peddler's voice came muffled through the weathered wood of the door. "Yal, you listen now. Anyone tries to come on deck, take out their knees. Don't kill 'um, I don't want that kinda trouble. And you don't listen to no yammer, y' just keep deck clear till I get back."

"Ya, Baba."

"Hoy! Anya! Got a choke lead on your femlit here. You whistle her she should be a good chal, you hear?"

For a moment Thann's lips trembled so badly, xe couldn't make a sound, then xe whistled the warning note and hoped Isaho would mind it.

Xe felt the dip and the outward thrust that told xe that the peddler was stepping off the boat.

It hadn't been real somehow before this. *We're going to be sold,* xe thought. *Maybe to different buyers. . . .* That pierced xe like a knife. Xe hugged xe's arms across xe's chest and rocked forward and back in a storm of grief/fear/rage *God, oh, God, where are you, how can you let this happen? Isa Isa Shashi my baby. . . .*

Xe rocked and wept, prayed and lashed at xeself for not thinking. If xe'd put xe's mind to it, surely there must have been at least a moment or two when xe could have tried to get xe and Isaho away. No, xe'd let fear make xe helpless, and now it was too late. . . .

The spasm passed and xe crouched exhausted for a time, then xe began to move about the shack, hands splayed out, fingers groping, eyes straining in the faint light that crept through cracks between the planks, cracks around the shutter blocking the single window in the wall across from the door.

It was a filthy place, a pallet by the shuttered window that xe avoided touching as long as xe could, the blankets greasy, smelling of stale sweat and other bodily fluids, probably crawling with vermin. There was a chest at one end of the pallet, battered and heavy with iron bands around it, iron hasp and padlock. At the other end of the pallet, there was a sawed down box that served as a bed table, two inches of each side left and partitions set into it to keep a water crock and some unwashed dishes from sliding about too much. Among the crockery xe saw a glint of metal; xe lifted a plate and found a spoon and a three-tined fork. Xe took up the spoon and tried to bend it; the metal gave only a little and sprang back when xe loosed it. Good steel. Stifling xe's distaste, xe took the edge of a quilt and wiped as much of the food away as xe could, then put the spoon and fork in xc's trouser pocket.

Xe moved about the hut, testing the walls, pushing at them, trying to find a board rotten enough to let xe break through.

Nothing, nothing, nothing.

The word beat in xe's throat like blood. *Nothing, nothing, nothing*. The wood was weathered and cracked but too sound for xe's strength.

Xe started at a thump against the door, stood with xe's

hand pressed against xe's mouth until xe's heart steadied and the mix of sounds told xe what was happening.

The mallit was tired of standing; he'd dumped himself down and had got himself arranged with his back against the door. A moment later, he started whistling, flatting notes and garbling the beat so xe almost didn't recognize the tune, though it was a song xe'd heard on the radio dozens of times in the weeks before xe left Khokuhl, one they said was popular in the cities along the southern coast. The noise plucked at xe's nerves, but xe tried to ignore it as xe looked around and considered what to do next.

Trying without much success to ignore the images in xe's head of a hoard of body izin crawling up xe's legs, xe stepped onto the noxious bedding and began pushing gently at the shutter. It was thinner than the walls or the door, and xe could smell the dryrot.

Xe's heart leaped into xe's throat as xe's fingers passed along the latchhook. *If it was secured from the inside....*

The hook was stiff, with a hump in the end meant to hold it firmly in the staple. Xe didn't dare use much pressure. Too much noise and the mallit would notice. Pull in, push up. Pull harder. Tight, the fit was tight, easy, thumb under the end, up, push up, ahhh!

Xe caught the hook before it could swing loose. For a moment xe couldn't catch xe's breath, just leaned xe's head against the wall and gasped in the stinking lifeless air.

Then xe pushed against the shutter and it moved.

Xe jerked xe's hand back when the hinges started to squeal, waited to see if the mallit had noticed.

He was singing now, beating time with the flat of his hand against the deck; there was a chorus of sorts that he shouted out every few slaps of his hand, the words so mangled and slurred that she couldn't make out what they were. That didn't matter. The only thing important to se was that they were loud and if xe fitted xe's actions properly to them, xe could get that creaking shutter open.

Inch by inch, hands trembling with that strain, shuddering as the hinges squealed and groaned, xe edged the shutter back. After an eternity, xe pushed it against the wall and stood with xe's hand bent, gulping in the acrid, briny air off the bay.

Yal broke off the song.

Thann straightened, stood tense, hand pressed across xe's mouth.

He started whistling "Bashar's Lament," the last song Mandall had announced on the day that he was killed.

Thann forced back the wave of grief. Xe had no time for memories now. Mandall was dead, Isaho was alive and needed xe.

Xe turned xe's back to the wall, hitched a hip onto the sill, and got xeself up into the window. Xe caught hold of the roof's overhang, used that to pull xeself out as slowly as xe could force xeself to move, struggling with desperate attentiveness to keep the chains from clanking.

When xe was out, xe crouched and shuffled across the deck, crept under the sail tarp and wriggled through the bales until xe could see the wharves and massive warehouses that edged the end of the inlet.

Xe counted the masts and funnels of half a dozen steam coasters tied up at the wharves and smaller, sleeker ships that had to be smugglers' craft. Behind the slate roofs of the warehouses a massive stone wall rose so high she could barely see the crenellation along the top. *Fort Yedawa. We built it to keep pirates away from our cargoes and our shores. Now the pirates have moved behind the walls and turned into slavers and whoremasters and arms dealers.*

The peddler's boat was tied at the last of those wharves, moored to a pair of crusted bitts. The nearest of the steamers was two wharves over; it was long and broad in the beam, with auxiliary masts, short, stubby things that looked as if sails run up them would be absurdly useless at shifting the rusty bulk of the ship. She could see several crewmals working without much enthusiasm on repairs that seemed to involve a lot of hammering and scraping.

Birds glided overhead or sat the chop between the boats like miniature boats themselves, white and black with long greenish-ocher beaks. Cats lay sleeping in the sun or prowled among the bales and barrels piled on the wharves, killing rats, dodging the feet of the few ladesmals and sailors in view. Two of the steamers farther along the line were being readied for departure; the other ships were deserted except for watchmals dozing at their posts and a crewmal or two working with a lazy lack of enthusiasm.

Xe couldn't get onto the wharves. Deserted as they were by all but a few, there were still were too many eyes about; listening to the peddler speculate with his son about the price xe'd bring convinced xe that the first person here to see xe running loose would put the grab on xe faster than the peddler had. But xe couldn't stay here among the bales; it'd take about five minutes to find xe. Xe was a strong swimmer, but the iron chains would drag xe down if xe tried that.

Hiding places . . . anywhere I think of, the peddler would see too . . . he's a horror, but he's not stupid . . . if he got a search started . . . no, he wouldn't do that, he doesn't trust folk here enough for that . . . so, that's a small plus on my side . . . if I can't figure out something . . . might as well crawl back in the window . . . he's sold Isaho by now . . . I can't . . . God, why did you let this happen . . . why?

Thann lay with xe's face pressed against xe's arms until xe's breathing steadied, then xe listened a moment to Yal's whistling. When the mallit began a series of elaborate trills, xe slipped over the side of the boat, used the rotting fenders to haul xeself along until xe was under the wharf, then began making xe's way south in the cold and filthy water beneath the wharves, fighting the down-pull of the chains and fatigue, moving hand over hand along the cross bars between the piles, blessing God's beneficence at giving xe a receding tide.

Near the far end of the line of wharves the water began to stink even more than it had and it was filled with bits and pieces of things xe didn't want to think about, things being swept outward by a powerful current that would have caught Thann and taken xe with them if the smell hadn't stopped xe.

Xe clung to a cross bar and scowled at the water boiling up a few feet in front of xe; below the murky surface, xe could see a rounded dark blotch. Sewer outfall. And in a short while the tide would be out enough to uncover it. The thought made all xe's stomachs heave, but it did offer the only hideaway xe'd found in all xe's cogitations.

Xe pulled xeself from the water and perched wearily on the bar. As soon as xe was settled, xe checked the egg. The sealing sphincter of the pouch had held, God be blessed; xe didn't want to think of the infection that swam in that filthy water. Xe sighed and leaned against the weedy stone to wait for the uncovering. With a little luck the peddler wouldn't get back to the boat before the tide started coming in again and xe'd be tucked away up in the sewers where even he wouldn't think to look. *Oh, blesséd God, keep Isaho safe and grant me grace and patience to do what is necessary.*

2. Crossing the mountains

Wintshikan watched Luca and Wann come loping along the Round, got to her feet, and made her way down the mountainside to wait for the rest of the Remnant to come from hiding.

Under the thick foliage of the trees the night was dark and quiet; the moon wasn't up yet and a drift of thin clouds muted the starlight. Wintshikan found that darkness oppressive and walked ahead a short distance to a place where a windstorm two years ago had blown down a huge old tree and opened out the forest. She sat down on the crumbling trunk, pulled her Shawl more tightly about her; the cold that gripped her had little to do with the night and a lot to do with the decision she'd taken up there on the mountainside.

Xaca came silently into the open patch, the children holding her hands, pressed close against her, their eyes huge, their faces old with the strain from being afraid. Arms hugged tight across her chest, Nyen followed them with Hidan close behind.

Wintshikan felt in her belt pouch and took out the box with the Tale Cards. She sat with the box on her thigh, her two hands clasped loosely about it. "We have thinking to do," she said. "Questions to ask. We will bespeak the cards and consult our hearts. It is a hard way that lies ahead, and we must get ourselves ready to bear it."

As she opened the box and took out the cards wrapped in their silk scarf, she murmured the words of the Prophet. "Bless the unfolding, O God. Guide the mix and the draw, O God. Speak to our hearts, O God. Guide our days, O God."

She lifted the cards clear of the silk, held them out, the pile resting on her two hands. One by one, the Remnant passed by, touching the pile with fingers of the left hand, the heart hand. Luca was the last of them. Her eyes were laughing as she set her fingertips on the top card and before she walked on, she murmured, "In this I do believe."

Wintshikan gave the silk to Zell who spread it on the log, then she shuffled the cards and began to lay them

out, two in the top row, three in the middle and one last
below them.

"Come round and see," she said, and when the Remnant was kneeling by the downed tree, she touched the
base card. "Death it is. Death is the gate to the change
from which there is no returning. This defines us. We are
dead to the Round and born anew as hohekil."

She touched the cards in the middle row, one after the
other. "These are the determinants that mark the days to
come. The Gate that looks forward and back. The Broken
Twig, peril to the body or the mind. The Spring from
which comes wisdom. There is more danger ahead of us
and a choice, perhaps many choices. It is necessary to
make them wisely."

She touched the cards in the top row. "These are the
guides to direct us to the Right Path. The Spiral which
embraces all. It is God Himself who speaks to us, who
will be our Light through the darkness of our unknowing.
If we walk the Right Path, we will pass through the dark
and the dangers unharmed. Think, Oh, Remnant of
Shishim, on the double meaning of Path. And the last
card, the Fire upon the Altar. What we do, though it may
not seem so, we do in the service of God."

With slow deliberation she took up the cards, set them
back in the pack, and squared it. She gave the silk and the
pack to Zell, straightened, pulled the Shawl closer about
her body, and spoke as Heka. "The Tale of the Cards has
echoed the thoughts that came to my heart when I lay in
terror and listened to the obscenities of the Impix phela
walking that Round that was once ours to keep and bless.
As the Twig is broken, so must we break our lives. We
must leave the Round. Now. So much sooner than I'd
hoped. We must leave behind all we know, cross the
mountains and walk the lowlands if we wish to live long
enough to see Linojin. The Peddler's Trace is half a day's
walk to the north of us. Can anything be more of an omen

than that?" Slowly, deliberately, she removed the Shawl from her shoulders, folded it and placed it on her lap, rested her clasped hands on it. "Oh, Remnant of Shishim, if there are those with another course to offer, or anything to add to what the Heka has said, this is the time to speak."

She moved her eyes from face to face.

Luca and Wann held hands and smiled at her. Nyen was grim faced, though she nodded as Wintshikan looked at her. Xaca bit her lip but nodded her agreement. Kanilli and Zaro leaned against Xaca's knees, eyes wide with fear and excitement. Hidan nodded. As anya, xe had more to fear than any fem or mal.

"No one has spoken. Thus let it be." She got to her feet. "Omylya Creek lies ahead another hour. It'll be late when we reach it, but we'll camp there for the night. We'll speak the Praises as we walk and pray God's blessing on our choice."

In the morning the Remnant—even Luca, this time—gathered on the Round and sang the Blessing of the Absent, blessing themselves by it, for they would absent from the Pixa Rounds perhaps for the rest of their lives. Then they moved quickly, warily, along the Path, going hungry because they were afraid to slow for foraging.

As day slipped into night, night into day again, they wound through the mountains, clinging together the more closely because now all they had were themselves. Everything they'd known had vanished from under their feet. Even the land was different now, harder and even more ungiving.

Luca and Wann moved more deeply into their bond and farther from God's Path.

Xaca no longer dreamed horrors. It was as if her fears had been purged from her with the other losses. She sang as she walked and foraged for food, the tunes were old ones, the words new.

Hidan was quiet, anxious, never far from Nyen, as if xe couldn't forget that xe was food to any phela that came across the Remnant. That was truth. They were hohekil and cursed of God in the eyes of those who still pressed for war. Whatever was done to them was just, for they were traitors to the Cause.

By nightfall on their fifth day on the Peddler's Trace they'd reached the end of the winding vale that was Kakotin Pass and had moved a short distance down the western slopes, the silver grass of the savannah intermittently visible as the Trace twisted about.

"Po po po, didna expect to see Pixies on t' Trace." The mal who stepped from the shadows under the trees lifted his free hand as Luca came to her feet, her knife out. "No no, young fem, no trouble am I." He bowed. "Just old Bukha the Needle Mal with his pack and his faithful yuzz."

Peddler Bukha was a short wizened mal with a face more wrinkled than a shirt slept in for weeks. The bits of his crest visible under the hard peddler's hat were patchy with gray, his small shrewd eyes were the yellow of old cream. His voice was a comfortable growl, oddly pleasant despite its lack of harmony. He gave a tug on the lead rope and a small shaggy yuzz almost obscured by a covered pack came ti-tupping into the firelight. It shook its head at Kanilli, drawing a giggle from her as its long ears flopped about.

Wintshikan got to her feet. "We are Pilgrims," she said. "On the road to Linojin to pray at the Grave of the Prophet for the souls of our dead. We have nothing to tempt a peddler to bargain."

"You discount the pleasures of your company, Heka. The Peddler's Trace is a lonely road." He canted his head, looked sideways at her, a yellow-eyed bird spreading his plumage to please. "I see you're about to make supper. I could add a pinch of shlah tea to the pot and some rounds of waybread."

Though Zell pinched her and Luca looked sour, Wintshikan smiled at him. "Be welcome, Bukha. Though if you stay, you should understand that we are sworn to keep ourselves apart and will not offer dalliance."

"Most gracious Heka, I'll abide by your rules while I'm in your company."

In the shadow beyond the reach of the campfire, Wintshikan stood with Zell and Luca, watching the peddler doing his finger magic for the children. "Say your say," she murmured.

"Heka, why did you ask him to stay? I don't like anything about him."

"Nor do I, Luca meami. But isn't it better to have him by the fire where you can see him than to leave him prowling about us in the dark?"

Zell touched her arm. +Peddlers don't give things away, not for the pleasure of anyone's company.+

"Yes. He's not as clever as he thinks or as charming. Luca, you and Wann are the best we have at woodcraft, you've scouted for us all day, could you do more?"

"Yes. What are you thinking?"

"There's not much moon, but the road is open here, the soil is pale, could you track that yuzz, see where he and the peddler came into the Trace?"

"Easy enough. You think. . . ."

"I believe nothing about him, not even the direction he came from. Don't leave until we say Praise and tuck the children into their blankets. I'll show you where Zell and I will be sleeping." Her laugh had edges on it. "Pretending to sleep, that is. Come to us and tell us what you found."

* * *

Luca slid into the thicket where Wintshikan waited, sitting cross-legged on her blankets, her back against the trunk of a small tree, Zell crouching beside her. "Where is he?"

"Back by the stream with his yuzz. Hidan is watching him. Xe'll let Zell know if he moves."

"He's a spy. Didn't even bother trying to cover his trail. He circled round to come from the east, but he started west. There's a camp about half an hour downroad. Five mals, armed. Not a phela, sneak thieves and bandits, making more of themselves than is there. Sitting round the fire drinking stilled phuz and boasting what they're going to do to us." Luca closed her eyes and shuddered. "Fems 'll be dead when they're finished, but they'll keep the femlits and the anyas to sell. There's a roaring market for healthy anyas. And the Freetowns are always looking for new, clean whores." Her voice shook. "Seems like the ones they have don't live very long."

"Good work, Luca. Did they say when they're coming for us?"

"Tomorrow night. The spy's going to stay with us, make sure that all the arms we have are a few knives."

"Yes. How drunk are that lot?"

"They're celebrating pretty hard. In another hour or so, you could kick them in the face and they wouldn't know it."

"Do you think it would be worthwhile to rob the thieves?"

"Ahhhh." Luca pressed her hand across her mouth to keep in the laughter. Eyes dancing, she nodded.

Wintshikan rose to her feet, took the Shawl Zell handed her, flung it round her shoulders, and spoke in formal mode as Heka of the Shishim ixis. "For the crimes of planned murder and enslavement, I declare Bukha the Needle Mal neither Pixa or Impix but beast, and I require of that beast its life." Sighing, she dropped the Shawl on the blankets. "All very well, these grand pronouncements. Now I have to decide how to do it."

"Leave it to Wann and me. We can cut the bhasit's throat while he sleeps."

"No, Luca. This must be execution, not murder. And he must have his chance to make peace with God."

"Why? Would he give us a chance?"

"This isn't about him, it's about us. Do you really want to use that lot as your standard?"

Luca scowled, then stalked off.

Zell touched Wintshikan's arm. +She's hurting and filled with rage, Wintashi, I can feel it. She'll leave us if we push her too hard.+

+I know. Seems everything I try is wrong. Has Wann . . . ?+

+Wann will not speak to us. Xe has given pledge to Luca.+

+Why didn't they tell us, let us bless them?+

+They will not accept a blessing. What Wann has said to us in anyabond is that it would be a blasphemy, and that they will not do.+

+It is the war, Zizi. Why was I so slow to see? I find myself standing too close to Luca's ground, too often tempted to hurl curses at God for letting such horrors happen.+ Wintshikan rubbed the sudden rush of tears from her eyes. "So let us go, my sister, my love, and do a horror of our own."

Bukha came awake fast and fighting, but Wintshikan cast herself across his middle, pinning him to the ground, Luca and Wann got ropes on his wrists, Nyen and Hidan caught his ankles, first one, then the other, and tied them together.

Wintshikan levered herself up and stepped away from him. "We tracked you to your friends and listened to them boast, Bukha the Needle Mal. Out of their mouths you are condemned."

"What is this? What right . . . ?"

"God's right. And by God's Law as spoken by the Prophet, you may have a thousand heartbeats to be mindful of your transgressions against that law. Make yourself right with it before you die. Gag him, Luca. Nyen, make the rope ready. Cleanse your soul, oh, Bukha, for on this night you face your judgment."

He did not die easily; he fought his bindings as Nyen tied the end of the rope to the yuzz's packsaddle, made hideous sounds past the lump of waybread Luca bound in his mouth to gag him. When the beast took its first step under Nyen's urging, his muted howl was an ugly thing.

Wintshikan walked to Kanilli and Zaro who stood with Zell, watching with wide eyes and frightened faces. "You have shared in the judgment of the Remnant. Have you questions?"

Kanilli looked down, but Zaro lifted her head with a touch of defiance and said, "I thought he was a nice little mal. I know he meant bad things for us, but why? Why would he do such a thing?"

"For gold, Zaro meami. Perhaps for the pleasure of it. Use this as a warning when we reach the lowlands. You can't trust anyone there. They have all kinds of excuses for what they do, but mostly it's just to pleasure themselves or for the gold they worship."

Kanilli raised her head and shied as the hanged mal groaned and twitched; she fixed her eyes on Wintshikan's face. "Then why are we going there? Why can't we stay in the mountains?"

Wintshikan sighed. "Death is a part of the compact with God, but it must come in its own time. To stay would be to go seeking for death and that is forbidden."

"But. . . ."

"We'll talk more tomorrow, I promise you, little sister. Now you go with Zell and get things packed up so we can leave. We have to be past the bandits before the sun comes up."

She watched them follow the anyas into the gloom under the trees, sighed heavily as they vanished. *Words WORDS! Oh, God, help me. My faith is slipping from me. I don't understand anything now. If You leave me, what have I got left?*

"Heka."

Wintshikan turned. "What is it, Luca?"

"We tied the rope to that other tree. We want to leave him hanging there as a warning."

He was still jerking a little, not quite dead. Wintshikan twisted her mouth and turned away. "Yes. Off the Trace like this, anyone who sees him will be his own kind." She made the avert fork with fore and middle fingers of her heart hand. "May his ghost be turned from us."

"Xaca's going through the pack to see what we can use; she'll toss the rest, but we figure the yuzz will be handy for carrying some of our own load. Nyen and Hidan want to come with Wann and me to see what we can lift off the bandits."

"Luca, nothing they have is worth your lives. Remember that."

The young fem grinned. "I'll remember," she said and went gliding off with that easy soundless stride she'd learned somehow since the Remnant had gone hohekil.

Wintshikan forced herself to look up at the hanged mal, sickened by the puffy blackened face and protruding tongue. "Your soul will peel away and vanish like fog on a spring morning. May it find peace."

Zaro squealed at the crack of a shot that went echoing around the mountainsides, following by others so close together they were like the sputter of frying maphik. The yuzz jerked on the lead line and tried to run, almost pulling Kanilli off her feet, but Xaca caught hold of the rope behind her and their combined weight was enough to hold him while Zell used xe's thinta to soothe him.

When Wintshikan spoke, her voice was high and shaky. "Zell, are they . . . ?"

+By thinta they are alive and well, all four. I thin death, but it isn't ours.+

"I told her. . . ."

+Hush, Wintashi, Luca's no fool. Don't judge her till you hear her reasons. It's better if we keep moving.+

Wintshikan straightened her shoulders. She was Heka, and it was time to remember that. "Kanilli, you and Zaro go ahead now; take the yuzz and don't look back. Xaca, go with them. Zell and I will follow. The others will come when they come."

And come they did, Luca and Wann, Nyen and Hidan on riding jomayls, rifles strapped to their backs. Nyen and Hidan were leading three more laden with canvas-covered packs.

Wintshikan felt a coldness at the bottom of her belly. *Not yet,* she thought, *but soon, it'll be time to pass the Shawl to Luca. God guide her, I cannot.*

3. Settling into Linojin

Clutching the luth in her left hand, Yseyl turned from the table, shied as a novice in brown opened the righthand door for her. As she stepped through, she heard the Brother's voice droning through the same set of questions for the next in line.

The door hushed shut and she found herself between high white marble walls that jagged through acute angles like the SkyFire sign on the Tale Cards. *No time to stand gawking,* she told herself and moved briskly along the slate pavement. From the corner of her eyes she could see damp streaks on the marble and remembered the fems and anyas washing the walls. *People here must wash this place every few hours to keep it so clean. God's hot breath. Service. Me and a squeegee. Well, we do what we have to, I remember the time. . . .*

The thought broke in half as she stepped from beneath the walls into a place of blinding whiteness, open to the sky, the sun pouring in as if to cleanse her of all the ills that life had brought her.

All it did was make her angry. She felt small and dark, like a poison burr, and she wanted to spit that poison over everything. The powers here were trying to manipulate her as they had when she was a child. It hadn't worked then, thanks to Crazy Delelan, and she wasn't going to let it work now.

She charged across the enclosure, slapped her hands against the double doors with the Egg carved on them, split the Egg wide, and marched into Linojin.

And into a swarm of children circling about her, shouting at her, offering themselves as guides.

A small compact femlit came wriggling through the mob with the use of elbows and knees; she had a scrape on her nose, bruises on her arms, and eyes fiercer than a hunting boyal. Unlike the others, she wasn't shouting, she just stood in front of Yseyl, head up, a challenge in every line of her body.

Yseyl smiled. She couldn't help it. "Your name," she said.

"Zothile. Call me Zot if you want me to answer."

Yseyl heard the doors swing open behind her. The crowd of children rushed away to importune the new arrival. "Done, Zot. What's your fee?"

"Copper a day, I take you wherever you want to go and get you whatever you want."

"Hm. I could bargain that down, I think, but I'm not

going to bother." She took a copper from her belt purse, tossed it to the femlit who plucked it from the air with a dart of a small scuffed hand. "Your first day's pay. Take me to the Grave of the Prophet."

Zot shrugged. "You call it. You want the Holy Way or the fast way?"

"Make it the fast way, hm?"

"Right." Zot started off at a quick pace, leading Yseyl into a maze of narrow streets, dark and cluttered with mals sitting slumped against the walls or huddling in niches, many of them maimed by the war, a leg gone or an arm off at the elbow, a patched eye, a face so scarred it was painful to look at—or the wounds might be on the inside, the only evidence a constant shivering, a mouth moving in soundless endless speech, a dullness on the face. A few fems passed by, ignoring the mals as Yseyl ignored them, moving along the center of the pavement with a quick pattering gait that carried them rapidly from turn to turn.

The smell wasn't as bad as it had been in some of the coast cities Yseyl had visited in her first career as thief and her second as assassin, but there was a sour hopelessness that hung in the air which made a nonsense of the bright whiteness only a few streets away. Yseyl savored the sense this gave her of the rightness of things. It was, in its way, a recapitulation of her whole life.

She looked thoughtfully at the back of Zot's head, then took a few quick steps to catch up to the femlit. "Changed my mind," she said.

Zot's eyes laughed at her, then went blank. "Thought you might. What you really wanting?"

"At the moment, some talk. Where?"

"Maybe I take you somewhere and me and my friends rob you?"

"Been tried another place. Didn't work. Besides, you'll get more if you keep your friends out of it."

"You're no Pilgrim."

"Not since I was younger'n you."

"I hear y'. Teashop round a couple corners."

"Teashop?"

"What they call it. Backrooms 're something they don't talk about with the Godmen. And what comes in y' cup's not tea if you know the right words."

"Just so you know, I'm no spy either."

"Hunh. I know that."

"How?"

"I just know. Come on."

Compared to some of the rat holes Yseyl had passed through in Icisel, Yaqshowal and Gajul, the Spiral Knot was painfully clean and well lit. "They polish the surfaces well, don't they."

Zot grinned. "Us maggots we know how to duck the broom." She led Yseyl to a booth at the back of the room where the light wasn't so intense and customers were thin on the ground.

Yseyl slid in and sat with her hands resting lightly on the table, her head on the incurve of the high wall separating this booth from the next one. She smiled at Zot. "I was hohekil before it had a name. Lot of them in here?"

Zot knocked on the table. "You want to know who runs them?"

"That, too."

"Humble Haf—um, that's the Brother of God who runs us all, Hafumbua's his long name—Humble Haf digs up excuses to shove most of the hohekil out of Linojin. Doesn't like 'em. Thinks they mean trouble. He's Imp born, but he don't even like Imp hohekil. Anyway both sorts end up in coast villages trying to feed themselves off the sea. If you lookin' for someone, you likely find 'em there." She stopped talking as an old mal shuffled over. She ordered tea and sandwiches and waved a hand at Yseyl. "She payin'."

Yseyl nodded, counted out the coppers. When the mal shuffled off again, she raised her brows. "Pushing your luck, young Zot. So sing a bit more for your supper. Tell me about the big one, the one who keeps Impix and Pixa hohekil from killing each other."

"Him? It's a mal named Noxabo. The knot of hohekil who stay, they live near the Sea Gate round the Broken Twig, that's the inn old Fashile owns, xe was anya to a coast trader from Sithekil just south of here. Storm shoved him into the Fence which ashed him and fed the ashes to the fish." Zot shrugged. "Happens all the time. If kishin' Ptak let us have weather reports, well. . . . Anyway, Fashile and xe's fem Jawele had kin here, so they brought their coin and set up a place for hohekil. Jawele, she died a couple years ago. You want someone who don't like Ptak a lot or Humble Haf or much else, Fashile fits fine. And like I said, Noxabo lives there."

She kept talking as the old mal shuffled toward them carrying a loaded tray, but switched to describing the city in more neutral terms. "To find your way around, all you have to remember is that the Grand Yeson and the Radio Tower mark the exact center of Linojin and the Progress Way cuts the city in half. North of the Way, in the west quarter you have the Chapter Houses of the Brothers of God, the Anyas of Mercy, the Sisters in Godbond. In the east quarter you have the Grave of the Prophet, the Speakers' House, the Seminary and the Speakers' Park." She took the plate of sandwiches from the mal and set it between the two of them, pulled her drinking bowl in front of her, nodded as Yseyl did the same.

"South of the way, in the west quarter you have the Orphan Halls, that's where I live, and boarding houses for workers and lots of small family houses and some bigger ones for merchant families who made their stash and got away from the coast while they still had it." Zot inspected the sandwiches, took one. "You want to pour the tea? I take two spoons sugar, but that's all. In the east quarter you have the hostels for the Pilgrims and a few places for the folk who take care of them. And on the boundary between, out near the wall where Humble Haf won't be offended by the stench of commerce, there's the Market. And you want to be sorta careful who you tell your business to, hm?"

"I noticed. Your hint was strong enough to flatten a skazz. How do you go about getting to be a guide?"

"You have to be older'n seven and younger'n thirteen and you or your folks have to get one of the Godfolk to speak for you." Zot scowled at her. "You askin' about me, this Bond Sister at the Hall, she got me the place. Nothin' special, she does it for all the kids, she gets money to run the Hall that way."

"And expects you to be grateful, hm? Don't need to say. I know the feeling." Yseyl nodded at the rest of the sandwiches. "I'm not hungry. You want those?"

The sandwiches vanished inside Zot's shirt. "So what's this leading up to?"

"You're twelve pushing thirteen, aren't you? What happens after that?"

"Look, I'm a guide. You get off on sob stories, find yourself a whore. You want, I'll show you where and that's it."

Yseyl grinned at the femlit. "Vumah vumay, no one ever said I had any manners. What this is leading up to, I've got some things to sell and I need to know a buyer who's reasonably honest and no gossip."

Zot stared at her a moment. "You come to Linojin the Holy City looking for a fence?" She refilled her drinking bowl, added the sugar and bent over the bowl, stirring the lukewarm tea with a vigor that sent the spoon clinking loudly against the porcelain.

Yseyl looked at the straggly black hair falling past the closed face and wondered if she was going to get any answer at all, then Zot lifted her head, her mouth stretched into a broad white grin. "Today?"

Mehll looked like one of those round dolls Pixa mals carved for their children from sija wood, the base sphere filled with lead shot so that when you tapped it, the doll rocked back and forth but didn't tip over. Xe's face was round with a cascade of chins and a web of smiley-wrinkles digging into the soft pale flesh. Eyes like plum bits in a hana bun flicked from Yseyl's face to her hands as Yesyl laid out on a black display cloth some of the pieces from her stash.

"This and this. . . ." Yseyl's forefinger nudged a brooch, then a necklace. "I acquired in Icisel. The rings come from Gajul. I've had them for several years now."

+You get around some.+ Mehll pulled an embroidered length of cloth hanging from the ceiling. A beam of yellow sunlight touched the display cloth, making the gems shimmer and glitter like the sea on a summer day. Xe fixed a glass in xe's eye, lifted the necklace, and began inspecting it.

"So I do."

Zot sat on a stool in a corner, reading one of the books Mehll kept on a shelf there; she was very much at home in this place—which Yseyl found interesting.

It was a comfortable room, shadowy except for that one bright ray, filled with armies of small carvings and decorated boxes and other intricate ornaments of a size to fit in the palm of the hands. As the shadows shifted in the room, they leaped to the eye and sank back into obscurity a moment later.

Mehll set down the last of the rings. +Nice pieces,+ xe signed.

Yseyl raised her brows.

+I don't haggle, dear. I know what I can sell these things for, and I subtract my profit. What's left I pay you, if you choose to take it. Which is four hundred grams silver. What do you say?+

"I'll say it's fair, and I'll take it." She reached for her backpack and lifted it into her lap as Mehll opened a cashbox and began counting coins into a balance scale. She leaned back in the chair, turning her head so she could see Zot who was bent over the book, her body shouting her immersion in what she was reading. That was as good an endorsement as any words would have been. "I've a feeling you know people better than most, Anya Mehll."

+So?+

"I've got a problem. No. Better to call it a puzzle. I think I want to talk to you about it."

For several minutes Mehll signed no response, just kept adding coins to the pan. When the weights balanced, she tipped the coins into a leather pouch, pulled the drawstrings tight and pushed it across the table toward Yseyl. +My question is do I want to listen? I don't think so. There's a darkness in you that worries me. I feel myself being sucked into it and I won't allow that. Do what you have to do, but let me be. Let Zot be.+

Yseyl didn't touch the pouch. She folded her arms on top of the backpack and gazed coldly at the old anya. "I earned that darkness the hard way, Anya. I've stalked and killed nine men in the past three years. Offworld arms dealers. Vumah vumay, more than that, but I don't count the others."

+You'd better go. Now.+

"The tenth dealer I stalked convinced me to let him live by giving me something. I can open a hole in the Fence, Mehll. Anywhere, anytime, with no alarm. A hole big enough to let a ship sail through. I want to lead people away from this stinking war. But I'm a thief and a killer. My ixis counts me dead and anyway, they always thought I was crazy. Probably right, too. You see my puzzle? I've got this wonderthing, but how do I use it?"

+Why me?+

"Anya. And what you do. You can read I'm speaking my truth, and you might be able to look beyond that to what's really there. And that." She nodded toward Zot. "How many children read those books?"

+They say Humble Haf loves his cat.+

Yseyl nodded wearily. "If you won't hear, then you won't. Think about it. Think about sailing to Sigoxol, walking free on land where there's no war." She lifted the money pouch and stowed it in her pack. "Eh, Zot, let's go find me a place to stay."

By the Spindle
Plots are spun for good or ill.

Chapter 8

1. Operating on Impixol

Shadith woke to the sound of voices, laughter, and the hum of lifters. Her head throbbed from the stale air and her muscles were cramped; she started to stretch, froze as she remembered where she was.

She listened a moment. She couldn't make out words, but she relaxed anyway because the voices were easy and unworried, a good match for the emotional tone she was picking up from the passenger cabin above her. Her ringchron told her she'd been asleep for more than three hours which probably meant the flier was over the Wandel Sea at the moment.

She rearranged herself cautiously, did a few tense-relax exercises, closed her eyes, and sent the mindride searching. She brushed against a bird mind, slid into it, and found herself looking at the long blue heave of the sea and a distant glitter that she knew had to be the Fence.

She let the bird slide away and tried to work out what she'd do once the flier touched down, but the steady droning, the stuffy air, the futility of planning without data was a soporific mix, and she was soon mindsurfing through nightmare.

She woke again with the sudden glare of light, cursed herself for sleeping too long and sent stiff fingers after the stunner in her sleeve.

"What?" Orm's voice, sounding irritated.

"What I said. Let that wait unless you feel like hoisting those bales about yourself. The 'bot developed some kind of epilepsy and either won't lift at all or hurls stuff over its shoulder. Bijjer's working on it, but he won't have it back together before tomorrow."

Spitting out a curse, Orm slammed the hatch shut and went stomping off.

Shadith started breathing again.

When the outside sounds had faded, she got her supplies together, crawled over the padded bales, and eased the hatch open a few inches.

She listened for several minutes, but the only sounds she heard were the distant twitters of several birds, the whisper of the wind, and an abrasive hiss that she didn't recognize until she looked down and saw the grit wind-driven across the stone floor of the place where the Cobben had parked the flier. A brief mindsweep confirmed what her eyes and ears had told her. She finished opening the hatch and jumped down.

The flier was sitting near the edge of an immense hollow wind-carved into the stone of the cliff face. A few meters to her left there were boxes and bundles piled in ragged dusty heaps on a floor of loading pallets. Some of them were covered by tarps, but most were abandoned to the wind, their padding tattered by the abrading grit. At the back of the hollow, protected by a sheet of transparent plas, a row of two-seater miniskips hung from clamps set into the stone, looking like a dozen witch's brooms waiting for a Sabat.

She brushed away dust-clogged webs and chased off the minute arachnids that had spun them, then went after an assortment of fur-covered slugs with dozens of tiny legs, sending them scurrying into cracks and beneath the pallets.

After she'd got herself and her supplies cached in a

nook behind the dustiest of the bales, she forced down some hipro paste and washed the aftertaste from her mouth with gulps of water. *You'd think they'd have fixed this stuff by now so that eating it was a little better than starving. Gahhh.* She pulled padding around her head and shoulders, leaned against the cavern wall, and began feeling about for eyes she could use to explore the area.

The light outside was fading, the day almost over in this part of the world. The bird was sleepy, wanting to find a perch for the night, but not fratcheted enough to fight Shadith's hold. It wound upward in a rising spiral and rode the wind in circles over the Ptakkan camp.

This was the caldera of a large and long-dead volcano; dark green conifers grew on the slopes around the periphery, rising to an uneven rim that bit like black teeth into the darkening sky.

There was a round lake in the center, a clump of small wooden houses built in the Ptakkan style with much bright paint, dozens of lacy balconies, huge windows, and cascades of arches, all of them connected by glass arcades. Beyond the houses there was a flat field paved with a dull red rubbery substance. *Playing field? Drill field? Makes one wonder about Ptak military.* Shadith grinned at the thought of polychromatic spectacle of a collection of marching Ptaks. The word *uniform* didn't exist in Ptakkip.

Two buildings were more utilitarian. The one nearest the playing field was a pitched roof chalet profusely balconied with shutters on the windows. Not a place where Ptaks would be comfortable. *Cobben,* she thought. *Assassins' Hall.* The second was built close to the lake, almost touching the thick line of slim lacy trees that grew at the edge of the sand. It was a long wooden building shaped like a brick, painted white and set inside a tall hedge of thornbush. Part of it was storerooms. That was the section with the small square windows. Where the Ptaks worked, the windows were fifteen meters by five, acid etched over the bottom third so outsiders couldn't see in, but the light could come through. The roof above the storerooms was flat and held a bouquet of assorted antennas—and what looked like a Rummal shield generator. *Last time I saw one of those was in the tech museum on University.* She brought the bird spiraling lower until she could hear the warning hum and feel the faint tightness in the skin that she got when she or her surrogate passed close to heavy power. *Control center,* she thought. *Where they manage the Fence and keep contact with their spies. I've got to get in there. . . .* The bird started fighting her, and she let it climb again.

There were a few Ptak children playing at the edge of the lake, an old male past his last molt sitting in the shade of the trees and watching over them. More Ptaks wandered through the arches and rockeries, the rapid patter of their high voices carried in broken bits by the wind currents to the bird gliding above them.

The contrast between the tranquillity of that scene and the images of the war reheated her anger at the Ptaks. They managed to ignore just what it was that gave them their comfortable life.

Distracted, she let the bird slip away, and the view vanished abruptly. She swore and began feeling about for land-bound eyes and ears, something that would get her into the Center.

The building was old, maybe even as old as the Fence, and it had a colony of furslugs that might have been in there since it was built. Shadith slipped into a juvenile slug who was scuttling along through the thick gray dust, the humping wriggling gait considerably faster than it looked; he pounced on a bug like a plate with legs, crunched it down with a degree of smug satisfaction that nearly started her giggling. He darted into a hole in the wall, curled his legs under him and slid headfirst, chittering to display his enjoyment, into a maze of tunnels in the dirt. Round pink ears swiveling, nose twitching, he wriggled and humped along the tunnels until he emerged through the tangled roots of a thornbush. He found a patch of sun, flattened himself on the warm dirt, and went to sleep.

Shadith chuckled, shook her head, and went hunting for another mount.

". . . katakreen anomaly. Avo! Where'd you put the list, it's ignoring the new string." The tech was a female Ptak, a sleek brown hen with corrective lenses in gold frames perched on an arrogant nose. Shadith was so startled by those, she nearly lost control of her mount.

A small and very young male came from a glassed-in cubicle at one end of the workroom. "O Great Vourts, O Four-eyes of Immeasurable Power, if it was a fidd, it'd bite you. By your elbow." He leaned against the doorjamb. "Anybody hear if the assessment passed?"

Another tech looked around from her station. "Don't hold your breath. The Kasif snuffed the last seven tries, this'll go the same way. Upgrades cost some, satellites more. This stuff still works, so why bother throwing away good coin for things you don't need."

Vourts sniffed. "No point in sarcasm, Tippi." She scowled at her station, snorted, and pulled a thin black book from a crack between two monitors. "At my elbow, huh?"

Shadith took the furslug across the ceiling studs until she found a crack above Vourts' head, close enough so she could see the screen and read what appeared there.

Vourts leafed through the book, found the page she wanted, and slid the book into a holder. She entered the first key, scowled as access was denied, tried a second, then a third. "Ah! Got it. Kreecher prog decided to forget the last two centuries. If it takes this much k'thar to make a simple course correction. . . ."

Interesting. Maybe useful. Hm. That's enough here. Let's see if the Cobben's where I think they are.

". . . this all you've got?" The harsh, clipped syllables of the Sarpe. A rattle of stiff paper, something being passed from hand to hand.

"It is a finely detailed map, Coryfe." The Ptak's voice was near a squawk from suppressed irritation. "Drafted from satellite phots, with data entered from extensive interrogations. There's a copy for each of you on the table by the door. If you'll look at these?"

"What are they?"

"Floor plans of the Houses where your targets sleep. You don't have to worry about security, these are holy types. Your only problem will be ·getting them alone; they're almost always surrounded by hordes of other religious. The envelope holds flat phots of the targets, plus flakes with as many images of them as we have acquired over the past year, some are stills, others show them moving about. The page clipped to the envelope is a schedule of rites and other observances, where the targets will be on each night of the week and who will be with them. Unfortunately, because of the way we were forced to acquire this information, it is some months old. However, your targets do lead rather regimented lives, so that shouldn't be too great a problem for you. To optimize the chance that the schedule won't be interrupted by events— and to get a maximum reaction, there's a Holy Day coming up. Four days from now. We suggest you do the job then."

"We were told to leave certain evidence. . ."

"Ah. Yes. That has been assembled. I'll bring it round

tomorrow after you've had a chance to look over this material."

Sound of chairs scraping across the floor. Sounds of movement, one set of feet marching across the plasta matting. Sound of a door closing.

Sound of a case opening. A click.

Pain flashed across Shadith's brain, transmitted by the furslug trembling in her mindgrip. She let it move away inside the wall until it was comfortable again, within the block instead of pinned at the border.

A snort. "Like to shove that medo's crest up his arse, teach him manners."

"Shut up, Yoha. He's no worse than the others."

"Not saying much, that. Sarpe, do they really expect us to . . . ?"

"Don't they always? Send us in blind, expect us to make like ghosts. Orm, get that map pinned down, and let's get a look at what we've got to work with."

More sounds of shifting, chairs drawn across the floor, paper rattling.

"Hm. The Brother of God, he's in this huge pile right in the middle. Meya, that packet of plans, which one's the big sucker?"

Rustle of paper as the Cobben looked through the material handed them.

"Third down. And calling it a plan is . . . tsah!"

"I see what you mean. We'll have to do our own scouting and that's going to be tricky." Sound of tearing paper. "Ugly zurl, isn't he. Old frogface. Hm. We'll need some of those white robes. About the only plus in this mess, those robes, they'll cover a lot. Meya, Keyr, you're the closest in size to these Imps. Best be you two doing the scout."

"All right by me. Lethe dust?"

"Good idea, if you get spotted, we don't want them remembering you. And since we'll probably be dropping in next night, we also don't want a lot of corpses stirring them up."

"We get a chance at him, do we take it?"

"Good question. They want us to take out all three the same night. Given this slop . . ." slap of hand, faint rustle of paper "what do you think?"

"I say we do it our way." Feyd's rumbling growl. "Do the Brother first, since he's the hardest to get to. Wait a couple days, hit the Speaker. Wait another couple, maybe three days, hit the Arbiter."

"I like that." Keyr's quick whinnying voice. "Confusion makes things easier."

"Sometimes." Orm's slow drawl. "Sometimes not. Clo-Kajhat give you any reason, Sarpe? I never heard any, just here it is, go do it like we said."

"All he said was he wants to blow the city apart, get the different factions shooting at each other."

"This isn't our kind of thing, Sarpe. You know it isn't." Meya's voice, light, rapid, unhappy. "I think we should put it to the vote, we finish this, then we tell Clo-Kajhat to go min his own chik and get back to Helvetia where we belong."

As a general argument arose, Shadith soothed the slug to sleep and withdrew enough of her attention to think over what she'd heard.

Up till now she'd concentrated so hard on getting here, she hadn't thought much about the difficulties of finding Yseyl, one small Pixa in a city full of Pixa and Impix. *I have to get one of those maps. After they've left, maybe. Do I need to hear any more of this? No. I don't think so.*

She woke the furslug and let it go humping off, then took another swallow of water and tried settling to sleep.

Sleep wouldn't come.

Three people were targeted for death. She knew about it. It wasn't her business. Digby would be furious. He'd warned her; if she went on working for him, she'd be

bound to come across things that appalled her about their
clients and she'd better make up her mind to ignore them.

But. . . .

It wasn't her business. . . .

"All right," she whispered into the dusty darkness. "I
don't like Cobben, I never have. They aren't clients. Ptak
aren't clients. I'm going to kick their little plans into
moondust." She thought about that a moment, shook her
head. "Ah Spla, I'll do something. Don't know what right
now . . . ."

She pulled the padding closer about her and this time
dropped into a dreamless sleep.

2. Linojin

Shadith lay on a grassy flat high in the mountains above
Linojin, a tarp pulled over her as camouflage against
Ptakkan cameras. She had her binocs strapped on and was
turning her head slowly to scan the city, cursing her stupidity. Even listening to the Cobben grouse about their
problems hadn't prepared her for this.

Linojin was big. There was that pile at the center. The
Grand Yeson which translated roughly as cathedral, with
its surrounding maze of small courts and arcaded walks,
its spires like twisted horns and its extraordinary roof.
Looked as if the tiles or whatever were squares of grass
sod, the grass a brilliant emerald, rippling almost seduc-
tively in the brisk wind off the ocean. The steel lace of a
broadcast tower in one of the back courts rose twice the
height of the highest spire.

Then there were the Religious Houses. Warrens filled
with mals, fems, and anyas, the members of each group
dressed in identical garments which made their resem-
blance to ant swarms all the greater. And the common
streets teemed with people, Pilgrims, tradespeople, workers, refugees. All looking alike, from this distance any-

way. Same species. Pixa and Impix, different cultures, same shape. Stupid, stupid, not thinking what it meant when Yseyl went to ground in a Holy City where everyone was closely monitored by locals as well as the Ptaks through their spy satellites—where any kind of alien would stand out as if she were painted red.

Disappearing in a polymorphic stew like Lala Gemali was simple, but this?

The anyas were tiny, hardly more than a meter tall, their heads about at the shoulders of the fems, heart-high to the mals. Even in one of those white robes there was no way she could pass herself off as a Brother. She was at least a head taller than the biggest of the mals.

"Can't go down there. Can't ask questions. Shadow girl, you didn't think this through very well. Shays! There must be a hundred thousand of them. Maybe more. How am I going to do put my finger on one particular Pixa?"

She turned the binocs on the Pilgrim Road, sighed as she saw the thin but continuous line of newcomers. More people to add to the mix. "Yseyl, ah my Yseyl, if I had your gift. . . ." She smiled at the thought of putting on a face and shape to fool that lot, then shook her head. Wishes only wasted air and energy. "Digby's right. If I can hook you for him, he can put that talent of yours to good use."

She shoved the binocs up off her eyes and examined the map unfolded before her, its edges pinned down with bits of stone. "So. I ask myself, why did you come here? The answer's obvious, isn't it. Those three the Cobben are targeting are the only ones who can use the disruptor to get more than a few people past the Fence. People will follow them. Believe them. Trust them. Not you, little thief. Hmm. Nothing interesting on the radio. No sudden interest in gathering people together. No excitement down there. You haven't figured it out yet, have you? No one listening to you. No one believing you. Do you even believe you? Fairy gold, that disruptor. Pretty thought, but gone with the sunrise.

"And where are you? Not with the religious. And not with the Pilgrims. I don't think you could stand that piety, little assassin. Not from what Cerex said. Among the hohekil. Most likely. That means the southwest quarter. All right, let's take a look and see what's there. Maybe I'll get lucky again. After all, it did happen once."

Shifting from map to city, city to map, she spent the rest of the afternoon identifying buildings and streets, locating the market, checking out gates, associating the data written on the map in minuscule glyphs of interlingue with the objects named. Always a chance that Yseyl would go walking down one of those streets the moment Shadith swept the binocs along it. Lightning could strike twice if the Lady decided to smile on her.

By nightfall the only thing she'd gotten from that continual scanning were eyes that burned as if someone had taken steel wool to them. She folded the map, rolled up the tarp, got the miniskip from under the bushes where she'd stowed it and flew cautiously back to the hollow where she'd made her camp. Still two clear days before the Cobben struck. She fixed a meal, then settled back to brood over what she'd seen and plot strategies for thwarting the assassinations.

She spent the second day scanning faces, because she couldn't think of anything else to do, but saw nothing of Yseyl.

Toward the end of the day a powerful wind began blowing inland, driving black clouds before it. She could smell the sea and hear a faint humming that she couldn't pin down until she looked at the broadcast tower and saw how it was quivering despite the cable stays that helped hold it upright. Those cables. She shouldn't have been

able to hear them hum this far away; it must be some kind
of atmospheric freak.

Was Yseyl was still in Linojin? It was three weeks
since she'd seen the little ghost walking along the Pilgrim
Road, and who knew how long ago that scene was
flaked?

"This is not working. I could sit here till this body rots
and still not pick her out of that mess. Hm. If this was one
of Autumn Rose's games, she'd finesse. Force a move.

The broadcast tower.

She stared at it.

A song. Maybe a song cycle. Cover all bets. Shop it
round the coastal cities, get them to play it, send the call
out as far as it'll go. Wear one of those Brother robes
with the cowls. Antiwar songs. One of them talking to
Yseyl. She must be getting frustrated about now, trying to
find a way to use the disruptor. Hm. She was stalking and
killing arms dealers before she went off with Cerex.
Bloody little creature, more than a bit crazy, killing to
stop killing.

She must have cached the disruptor before she came
into Linojin. She certainly didn't have it with her in that
scene where she was walking barefoot on the Pilgrim
Road. Well, it's what I'd do. And it means I have to get
my hands on her if I want that thing back. Hm. She can
be talked into things. Cerex did it, I have to figure out
how I . . . hm . . . maybe . . . nice if I can combine the two
things . . . warn the Cobben's targets and set my trap. . . .

She gathered herself and went back to her camouflaged
camp as the first raindrops began pounding down.

3. Radio show

"Who are you?"

"You don't need to know that. Which one of you's the
technician?"

It was a small room, filled with unlikely looking gadgetry, clumsy stuff she could just barely recognize from experiences in her first life. The lighting was harsh, provided by two bare bulbs in ceiling sockets. One of the turntables had a reddish-brown disk on it with an arm moving across it. She could hear a faint hiss but no other sound. One mal sat before the turntable, an earphone harness on his head, the other stood with his back against the wall, clutching a cup of congealing tea. Both of them kept glancing at the pellet rifle in her hand, then looking away.

"Why?" It was the seated mal who spoke. He shoved a phone off his ear and swiveled his chair about till he was facing her, using his body to cover the subtle move of his hand toward the standard of a microphone.

"Don't opt for dead hero, mal. Put both hands flat on your thighs." She waited until he complied. "Why? I want you to record some songs for me."

"Huh?"

She could feel the surge of curiosity that almost overcame his fear. "That's a studio on the far side of that window, right?"

"Right. What kind of songs?"

"Laments, my friend. Hohekil songs." She glanced at the disk revolving slowly on the turntable. The business end of the pickup had progressed very little since she'd walked in. "You've got about an hour there, haven't you."

She felt his annoyance. He wanted to lie, but he didn't quite dare. Not yet. "Just about," he said.

"Should be plenty of time. Besides, it's way past midnight. I doubt you'll get many complaints about a bit of dead air. What's your name?"

"Kushay."

"And yours?"

"Habbel." His voice was sullen. He was considerably younger than the other mal, an apprentice perhaps.

"All right, Kushay and Habbel, I want you to listen

carefully. I don't intend harm, but I do mean to sing my songs for people to listen to, even if only the few who are out of bed tonight."

"You're not Impix or Pixa. Why are you doing this?"

"Say that I'm moon mad, hm?"

"What makes you think we won't shave the master once you've gone?"

She laughed. "I trust my gift, Kushay. You won't want to throw them away. I'll give you a sample." She repeated a few of the vocalizations she'd gone through before coming here and when she felt easy, she said, "The first song is called 'Phela Mal.'

> *"We dance at the jerk of puppet strings*
> *worked by feathered Ptakkan fingers,*
>> (her voice sobbed over fingers, putting anguish
>> and anger in the syllables, then dropped to
>> a hush for the next line)
> *playing out our games of war*
> *for the watchers' ghastly pleasure.*
>> (pleasure was soft and drawn out, controlled fury)
> *Oh, the joy that killing brings!*
> *The joy the joy that killing brings . . .*
>> (the sibilant at the end of brings hissed then
>> softened, melting into the next line)
> *But the thrill so briefly lingers*
> *Our burning blood cries out for more.*
> *Let us be lavish with our gore*
> *Fill the Ptakkan purse with treasure*
> *Inflame the watchers' endless leisure*
> *Kill until Pix and Imp are gone*
> *And this song's forever done."*

As he understood the nature of the song and her voice crept under his skin, Kushay shivered. When Shadith was finished and Habbel started to speak, he raised a hand to stop him. "You said songs." His voice was hoarse. "Like that?"

"Yes. Like that. And the profit's all yours. Moon mad, remember? All I want is for those songs to be heard as widely as possible."

"Habbel, take her into the studio. Help her get set up. I'll run the board."

"Kush, Brother Umbula won't like. . . ."

"Listen to me, Hab. You have any idea how much Icisel or Gajul and the rest will pay for a voice like that? And we don't say word one she isn't Impix or Pixa, you hear me?"

". . . and this song is called 'Children of War.'

> *"Child of the hill,*
> *Child of the city,*
> *why do you kill*
> *with absence of pity?*
> *Blood taints the land*
> *till only weeds grow*
> *and the only one pleased*
> *is the carrion crow.*
> *Your children demand*
> *food you can't find.*
> *The farmer who tills*
> *is smoke on the wind.*
> *Friend murders friend*
> *and families decay.*
> *Child of the city,*
> *Child of the hill,*
> *with half of us fled*
> *and the other half dead,*
> *who will repay*
> *the blood that you spill?"*

When she'd finished the other two songs, she turned to face the window. "That's done. Put on another master, please. I have an announcement I think you'll need to record and pass on."

"What's this?" His voice came through the grill with an eerie mechanical aura to it.

"I promise you it's important."

"All right."

When she got the signal, she drew in a long breath, let it trickle out.

"I am one who will not countenance what is being done here. What I say is truth, the proof will come on the night. Assassins have been sent to Linojin. These are their targets:

The Holy Brother Hafambua.

The Blesséd Kuxagan the Prophet Speaker.

Noxabo, Arbiter of the Hohekil.

On the Night of the Unshelling, twelve strangers come to kill. And not just to kill but to lay blame among the factions of Linojin. Those who Fenced you here wish it said that the Prophet Speaker ordered one death and the Arbiter another two and so on till each is blamed for the other's dying. Those who Fenced you here have sent them to destroy the peace of Linojin.

Guard yourselves. Be not alone.

Believe me or not, it does no harm to be sure.

Blessed be Linojin.

May its peace endure.

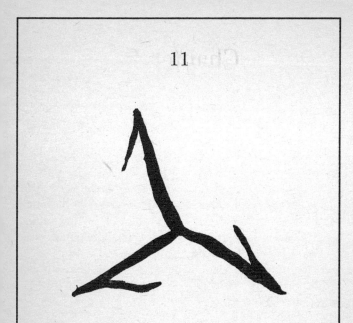

The Trivadda is the sign
of decisions.
The parting of ways,
The sundering of
past and present.

Chapter 9

1. Transit

With filthy water lapping at xe's heels, Thann scrambled up the ladder in the maintenance shaft. It was corroded and shaky and, from the layers of crud on the rungs, hadn't been visited since the war began. The darkness in the shaft was thick, impenetrable.

A rung sagged suddenly as xe put xe's weight on it and xe slipped. For a moment xe hung from one hand while xe's feet felt for lower rungs. Xe's free hand waved about, went past the outside of the ladder into an opening beside it, fingers plunging into light-weight, granular rubble. Xe jerked xe's hand back, knocked it into a rung, and grabbed onto it.

When xe'd caught xe's breath, xe wrapped an arm about a rung and began exploring that hollow place. It was a shallow niche half filled with litter, big enough to hold xe. Trying not to think about what xe was touching, Thann scraped away much of the dry, crumbling rubbish, swung off the ladder and made xeself comfortable in the niche.

Xe leaned back, closed xe's eyes and set xeself to begin a thinta search for Isaho, not really expecting to find her within xe's range. Xe thought xe'd have to have to get into the Fort and sneak about the streets, testing places xe couldn't reach otherwise. This workshaft must go somewhere. Any thought of moving, though, would have to

wait until after nightfall. Xe reached out as far as xe
could and began sweeping the thinta in a circle. . . .

Xe laughed aloud as xe touched a pair of familiar
fires—the peddler and his cretinous son. He was raging
while the mallit was a bundle of sullen resentment.

Thann tracked them for a while, built up a picture of a
haphazard search by a mal who hadn't the beginnings of
an idea where to look for xe. At first that was satisfying,
but xe's complacency faded when the peddler stood still
for what felt like an eon. His rage died down until only
embers were left, overlaid by a sense of cool but intense
thought.

A moment later he was marching away, taking his son
with him.

Thann scratched the fold in xe's upper lip, puzzled by
his actions. With a sigh, xe dropped the touch and went
back to xe's search. The few clues the thinta had brought
xe were not sufficient to let xe even guess what he meant
to do.

Xe reached further and nearly fell out of the niche.

Isaho! She wasn't in the town at all. She was on one of
the ships tied up out there.

Bait! He's going to use Isaho as bait to catch me.

Thann steadied xe's breathing and drew the thinta back
into xeself; xe was afraid to touch the child more deeply
because it would distract xe from what xe had to do. If
Isaho was on a ship, xe had to get to her, but there was no
way xe could get onto that ship with these chains on xe's
arms and legs.

Xe shifted position, got the fork and spoon from xe's
trouser pocket, grimacing at the reek of xe's clothing. Xe
probably should have hidden the trousers and shirt somewhere outside, but xe hadn't thought of that, and it was
too late now.

Working by touch and using the handle of the spoon as
a lever, xe bent one of the tines back from the others so

xe had a short stiff probe. Xe set the spoon beside xe, worked the cuff on xe's left leg around so xe could get at the lock, then began trying to lift the wards. It was a simple lock, xe'd seen the key, it couldn't have more than two wards, all xe needed was patience and care . . . again and again xe thought xe had it, pushed a little too hard so the probe slipped or turned in xe's hand . . . again and again xe lost the wards . . . again and again xe took a deep breath and tried once more. . . .

Xe felt the click through xe's whole body. One ward lifted. Xe tugged at the cuff—gently—but the lock still held. The second ward surrendered more quickly now that xe had the feel in xe's hands. Xe opened the cuff and sat a moment with xe's eyes squeezed shut, xe's hands pressed hard against xe's thighs to stop the shaking, then xe went to work on the second cuff.

The leg irons made a satisfying splash when xe dropped them into the water.

The lock on the left wrist cuff came open with no fuss, but using xe's left hand to pick the last lock was frustration multiplied. That hand was stiff and awkward and lacked the delicacy of touch of the right. Again and again the probe slipped off the ward. Xe's hand started shaking and twice xe nearly dropped the fork over the edge.

After the second time near disaster, xe set the fork down at the back of the niche, moving carefully, slowly because xe's hand wouldn't quit trembling. Xe set the palms of xe's hands on the sides of the niche, cold stone, God's gift to the builder. Xe narrowed xe's mind to that, called the strength and solidity of the stone to come into xe and prayed for the calm that would let xe finish the task and swim to the boat where Isaho waited.

When all the words were gone from xe's head, when prayer was gone, xe went back to the simple rhymes xe'd taught Isaho so many years ago, the night prayers before she climbed into bed, the morning prayers before she started her day. Over and over xe said them until a vast lassitude filled xe.

Perhaps xe slept a while. It was likely xe slept because time slipped away and there were dreams—at least, xe thought there were dreams though xe couldn't remember what they were.

Too mind-dulled and limp to be afraid or even to care whether xe succeeded or not, xe took up the fork and inserted the tineprobe into the lock.

A moment later the wrist irons followed the leg irons into water.

The splash took a lot longer. Xe frowned. Time? How much time had passed? Xe scraped up a handful of the debris on the floor of the niche, dropped it. Listening to the slap of the water against the stone. Xe must have slept and while xe was dreaming, the tide had turned. It was going out. Ships went out on the tide.

Hastily xe sent the thinta searching.

Isaho was still there. But . . . oh, God, the activity around her, the mix of anxiety, anger, the dregs of a long drunk, the lassitude of too much sex, impatience, greed . . . all that urgency on and around that ship. They were getting ready to leave. Could be sailing out any time now. And—yes—the peddler was nearby. Not moving. Sense of patience and malice. Yes. Waiting for xe to come for Isaho.

Xe took several deep breaths, then dropped xeself into the water.

Thann clutched at the cross beam and gasped until the dizziness left xe and the worst of the shaking stopped. Without the suction from the receding tide, xe would have drowned in that hole. Xe whispered a blessing to God for One's care, then began making xe's way toward the ship that held Isaho.

When xe was clear of the outfall, in water marginally

cleaner, xe became aware of the stench that xe brought with xe. Though the delay put knots in all of xe's stomachs, xe backed as deeply into shadow as xe could, stripped off xe's clothing, dipped and squeezed it, rubbed it against the tarred sides of the heavy piles; xe sniffed at the tunic and trousers, repeated the washing and rubbing until xe was mostly smelling tar and fish.

Dressed again, xe swam and wriggled xe's way along, passing directly under the peddler; xe couldn't see him, thought he must be sitting on one of the bales xe'd seen scattered about the wharves. *Watching for me,* xe thought, *vumah vumay, let him watch.*

Staying in the shadow under the wharf, xe crept along beside the ship, listening to the grinding and squealing as the waves rubbed the fenders against the heavy planks.

The mooring on the far side was empty and xe got a better view as xe clung to a cross beam and examined the ship. It was a coastal steamer, one of those with the stubby masts kept for use if the engines died and the ship started drifting toward the Fence. The davits were groaning and squealing as they lifted the loading nets and swung them round, lowering cargo through one of the gaping hatches along the deck, or depositing it on the deck itself. Crewmals swarmed everywhere, guiding the nets, loading crates and bales on dollies and shoving them into stowage areas.

Thann drew several quick breaths, then jackknifed deep into the murky green water, down and down until xe was swimming below the huge twin screws. Using the ship's shadow as guide, xe kicked upward and surfaced to the slap slap of a net dangling just above her head. Blessing God for the chance, xe scrambled up the net without considering why it hung there, tumbled over the rail and in among a haphazard huddle of bales.

By the time xe'd caught xe's breath, xe realized the net was there to pin down those bales; it was a more professional equivalent of the old sail the peddler pulled over his goods. Which meant xe had to get out of there as soon as xe could, because the crewmals could be along any time to sort out the mess and get it properly stowed, the net hauled over and tied down.

Xe lowered xeself onto xe's toes and elbows and crept to the rail, then along it until xe reached a section of deck cargo that was already prepared. Xe realized why once she wriggled under the net and into the tiny open space between the outcurve of the rail and the sides of the crates. There was offworld writing in red which xe couldn't read, but scrawled over it in black paint the word DANGER, under that: Pellet rifles. Ammo. Grenades. Mines.

Xe knew then where the ship was bound. The neutral cities of Impixol. Icisel, Gajul, Yaqshowal. Where anybody could buy anything they wanted. Weapons. Girls. And anyas, xe reminded xeself.

Xe wriggled on, found a gap between odd-sized crates that was just big enough to hold xe and settled there to wait for the ship to finish loading and slip its moorings. Xe had no water, no food, xe's clothing was soaked and already xe was beginning to shiver from a chill, but xe was safe for the moment and Isaho was somewhere below xe. The rest could wait.

2. Decision

Wintshikan laid out the cards and frowned at them, then glanced irritably at the radio Luca had found in the gear of the thieves. It was sitting on one of the packsaddles a short distance off, turned as loud as it would go, blaring out tinny, static-ridden music.

Luca and Wann were dancing what had once been a sacred dance from the Great Gathers, turning it into something wild and corrupt that troubled Wintshikan, especially when she saw how entranced Zaro and Kanilli were. That was the Mating Dance. They were too young to even see that.

Zell patted her arm, whistled a soft, comforting chirrup. +The last reading said Change,+ xe signed. +What God has set going, Pixa will not stop. Read the cards, Wintashi.+

They'd left the foothills behind a little past mid-afternoon and reached this barren shore as the sun went down, the back end of a long narrow bay like a blue finger of brine. There was no fresh water, so the place was left to the wind and the sand and the long-legged brown birds that ran along that sand.

Wintshikan touched the base card. "Death again. No matter how I mix them, Death is always the base card, Zizi."

+I think it's that we aren't ready to be reborn yet.+

"It could be." She contemplated the determinants. "Cauldron, Spindle, Drum. Cauldron with Spindle, that's a plot. A plan is cooking and we're part of the stew. I don't understand the Drum being there. Rhythm, music? The plot's march? Or that God-cursed radio interfering? I don't know, Zizi. Have you any notion?"

+It will come clear later, such things always do.+

"I've no patience these days, I'll admit that. Hm. The guides. The Eye of God. A blessing. That is a comfort. The Balance. Seek the balance when the change is done. Ah, Zizi, I'm afraid when that Balance comes, it will be so strange I won't recognize it."

She gathered the cards, began wrapping them in the silk scarf, troubled eyes on the children dancing and giggling while the others snapped their fingers in time with the music from the radio.

The music stopped. A man spoke. "For all those who have suffered, we play these songs. Let the killing stop."

A woman's voice came into the sudden stillness of the

camp, strong, pure, unaccompanied, something about it
that reached under the skin.

> *"Child of the hill, child of the city*
> *Why do you march so happy to war?*
>   *happy happy happy to war*
> *Oh, Pixa upon your barren rock*
> *Do I bend my neck*
> *in feigned complicity,*
> *march at your beck*
> *to the chopping block?*
>   *chop chop the chopping block.*
> *Oh, Impix who bends and burns*
> *the heart of God in funeral urns:*
> *your factories foul, your mills.*
> *bow your head indeed*
> *and as you bleed*
> *in blessed simplicity*
> *Praise the god who yearns*
> *for your return*
>   *yearns oh yearns for your return.*
> *I hide at my back*
> *the hacking knife*
> *in fatal duplicity.*
> *I hold your head low*
> *let the blood flow.*
>   *let it flow, let it flow.*
> *From my leather jack*
> *I drink your life.*
> *So.*
> *Child of the city, child of the hill*
> *What will you do when all breath is still?*
> *What will you do when there's no one to kill?*
>   (the voice rose to the word *kill* until it was a crystal
>   knife pointed at the heart, then dropped so the next
>   words were tender, dulcet.)

What will you do when there's only you two?
What will you do?"

Luca made a face and shut off the radio. She reached
out for Wann, hugged xe tightly for a moment, then she
laughed and spun away. "Mouth music," she cried. "Let
us have mouth music and finger music and Zaro and
Kanilli will dance for us and chase the sorrow away."

In the morning the radio was playing again as they rode
along the shore of the inlet, mostly music, some news.

*"... bombardment of Khokuhl continues. The city is still
holding against the attempts of the Pixa fighters to enter and
destroy the Impix command there. Reports have come from
the far south that the declared neutrality of Yaqshowal has
for the first time been violated by artillery forces and repeated incursions by so far unidentified phelas apparently
intent on raiding the storehouses for weapons, fartalk radios
and other items of use in the war. . . ."*

It was easy going, the sand hardpacked and more or
less level; there were a few patches of scraggly brush
hardly higher than the ankle, but the rest of the green was
mostly a mix of sea grass and broadleaf weeds. The
jomayls walked steadily along, their necks curving in an
easy arc, their dark crimson eyes half shut. Luca and
Wann rode ahead, nearly out of sight, scouting for them,
Nyen and Hidan rode rearguard. Wintshikan walked along
near the middle of the line, leading the first of the packers, Zell perched on its panniers, Xaca and the children
following with the others. She tried not to listen to the radio, focused instead on the sounds of the hooves: Crunch
crunch, doin' the job, doin' the job.

"*. . . and here's a song for all young bonders, setting up families in hope and trust.*"

"*Anya Alina, oh, love of our hearts, be the true bond that closes our ring, Anya Alina, oh, star of our. . . .*"

Around midmorning the land on the right began to tilt upward. The brush was taller and thornier, there were patches of berry vines with canes so thick with thorns that they resembled saw blades. Wintshikan began to see trees again, wind-twisted nyenzas and bushy bohalas. Long-legged brown birds ran on the sand and songbirds hid among the foliage. Large white seabirds rode the winds high overhead, their raucous calls falling like stones through the blare of the music from the radio.

Luca and Wann were out of sight for a short time as the line of jomayls began to turn the end of the hills to start north again. They came galloping back. Luca slid off her mount and held up a hand to stop the others.

"There's a village about half an hour on. It backs up onto the shore, and there's a wall around it, the trunks of lekath trees with the limbs chopped off and the top ends sharpened to points. We need water, but they don't look very friendly."

Wintshikan frowned. "We're Pilgrims. Surely. . . ."

Luca shrugged. "How do they know that? If we'd trusted Old Bukha, we'd be bones for the boyals to fight over."

"There's truth in that. How much open space is there in front of that wall? Enough so all but one can wait and be safe from the guns they'll have?"

"Far as we could tell."

"Good." She took the Shawl from Zell and wrapped it round her shoulders to show she was speaking as Heka of the Remnant, *I am still that*, she thought. *For a while yet.* "Listen to what I say. The Remnant will stop out of range and line up so that the villagers can see that you are fems, anyas, and children. I am what I am and it's easy enough to see what that is. I'll do the approaching and the talking. Luca, if you see anything that bothers you, get the Remnant away. If I can talk myself loose, I'll join you. If not, so be it."

Zell tugged at her arm. +I'm going with you.+

"No, Zell. Anyas in this war attract more evil than fems and mals combined. Come with me and you may bring on trouble that wouldn't happen otherwise." A knot twisted tight around her heart as she saw the pain in her anya's eyes, but Zell knew she spoke the truth though it was a very hard truth. "If they won't give us water, at least they may tell us where to find some." She glanced at the sun. "The day's sliding away from us. We'd best get started."

There were mals on the wall, standing behind the pales, silent, stone-faced, looking down at Wintshikan as she crossed the open sand and stopped before the door. She looked up. "I am Wintshikan Heka of the Remnant of Ixis Shishi. We are Pilgrims bound for Linojin and mean harm to none. We have no water and would ask of you, give us water or tell us where to find it."

The mals looked at each other, then one of them leaned over and spoke. "That all there are of you? I don't see any mals."

"Our mals are dead. We are the Remnant of Shishim."

"Those little 'ns, they anyas, huh?"

"The littlest are femlits, but, yes, there are anyas among us. Will you give us water? Will you help us on the way to Linojin?"

"Why go on? We can give you shelter here."

"We have sworn an Obligation to visit the Grave of the Prophet and pray for our dead. Until this is done, we cannot think of our own needs."

"Vumah vumay, so be it. Follow the wall around the corner, you'll see a corral with some milkers in it. There's a well by the fence. You can get water from there. And don't worry, we won't interfere with you."

Luca stayed back, the rifle she'd taken from the thieves held visible. The anyas and the children waited with her while Nyen and Xaca led the packers over to join Wintshikan. More villagers joined the men on the wall and stood silently watching them as they worked, watering the stock and filling the skins.

As they started to leave, the man who'd spoken before raised his voice again. "There's a river about a day's ride north of here, be sure to fill up good when you get there, it's five days to Linojin from there and you won't find more. It's all salt marsh and sand. Go with God, Pilgrims. Pray for us as well as your own. And pray with us all for peace and destruction to the Fence."

As the sun went down behind the rounded hills, Luca stood on a patch of grass that grew near the top of a dune and stared out across the sea at the golden glimmer that turned copper where it pulled down red from the sunset sky.

Wintshikan joined her. "What are you thinking?"

"About that." She jabbed her thumb at the Fence. "About one of those songs that fem sang. The one that calls us puppets dancing to the jerk of Ptakkan strings. Do you think that's it, Heka? Do you think that's why we're dying?"

"I don't know. The war's gone on so long. It's hard to know why."

Luca moved her shoulders impatiently. "I can't remember when I knew what I wanted or why I was born. I've been looking at that thing out there and I think I do know.

Now. I'm going to pull it down, Heka. I don't know how, but that's what I'm going to do."

3. Song and riddle

Yseyl shifted position again, ignoring the glare from the mal sitting on the bench beside her. That bench was hard on the tailbones and she'd been sitting there since the door opened, sliding up inch by inch as one of Noxabo's aides talked to those ahead of them, arranged appointments for later, or waved the petitioner on to the next hoop to jump through before he got to see the Arbiter himself.

She'd gone first to listen to the Prophet Speaker preach. He was good, he'd gotten that crowd stirred up and seeing visions. He even won through her defenses, started her blood pounding until her mind broke through the glitter of the words and the force that shone from the man, and she remembered how much she didn't believe the things he was saying.

Still, this was what she needed, if she could just trust him—and get him to believe her.

Yseyl left the meeting and went to find Zot.

"Word is he's dumb as a rock. It's his anya that writes those things and tells him what to do. I know one of the girls that clean the Tent. Weird calling that big mess of stone a tent, but there it is. Anyway this Beritha, she says Anya Hukhu's got the teeth of a shark and a blob of iron where xe's heart should be. Only thing xe cares about is that wikiwic."

"So I should get to xe."

"No use trying unless it's somethin' big. And somethin' that's gonna make him look real good."

"It just might be."

* * *

When she went back to the Tent the next morning, there was chaos. People huddling in little groups, shocked, angry, grieved. Others clung to each other, sobbing and wailing.

Anya Hukhu was dead, the Blesséd Kuxagan was having hysterics somewhere, no mistaking that voice.

She listened, slipped in a question here, a question there, and built a picture of what had happened.

There'd been some sort of warning about assassins and Hukhu had set up a ring of anyas to screen out all strangers and two rings of armed guards, but the assassins had come through the roof somehow and gotten past the outer ring before they were discovered. Two of them were dead, offworld women they were, and why they tried it no one had a clue. The third had almost gotten to Kuxagan, but Hukhu threw xeself between them and stabbed the stranger with a poison knife at the very moment she was killing xe.

Yseyl slipped away, angry and frustrated. It seemed almost as if the Ptaks had known what she was planning and had struck to stop it. In her calmer moments she knew that couldn't be true, but the realization didn't help quiet her stomachs.

Before nightfall the city was buzzing with the news that there were three attempts at assassination, all expected, all thwarted. Six offworlders were dead, the rest had gotten away. And everything was closed down. No suppliants allowed anywhere except the petitioners in the Arbiter's Office. Noxabo wasn't there, of course; like the other targets he'd gone to ground. There was speculation about where he was, but it was all wild rumor. Those who knew weren't talking.

Another four petitioners were called into the Aides' cubicles. Yseyl slid along the bench, then thrust her feet out over the braided rush matting that covered the floor. She opened her feet into a wide vee, brought the toes tapping together. Did it again. And again. Till the mal beside her dug his elbow into her side.

"Stop that, fem. You're driving me crazy."

She scowled at him, shifted the scowl to the far wall. *Assassins. Cerex said the Ptak wanted the war to go on and on till all Imps and Pixa were dead. Until now Linojin's been out of the war. They're trying to change that. On the radio ... I need a radio, I'm missing too much just listening to people talk ... the news ... phelas attacking the neutral cities ... they want it all, the Ptaks do, that's what it is. They want it all. I've got the way ... if only someone would listen to me ... I've got the way out ... God ... I wish I believed ... I wish I could pray and feel like it meant something ... God! Any god that allows this obscenity. ...*

Three armed mals came from the back room beyond the Aides' cubicles. They stood by the door looking grim and ready for anything. She'd seen phelas like that, waiting in ambush as she used her gift to slip round them. Those mals were ready to kill anyone in this hallway, to shoot at a cross-eyed look, an unconsidered scuff of a foot.

The oldest of the Aides came out of his cubicle. "Petition time is over," he said. "Give your names to the scribe at the door. You'll be first in tomorrow."

As Yseyl stepped onto the walkway, Zot came from an alley and began walking along beside her. "No joy?"

"Scribe took down names. Aide said those'd be first in tomorrow."

"Bribe's two ounces silver to make sure your name stays on that list."

"It isn't on there now. I didn't bother." She wrinkled her nose at the crimson glow in the west. "One day wasted is more than enough. Want some dinner? I'll buy."

"Won't say no to that. Plenty of time. Mehll wants to see you, but not till seventh hour."

"Why?"

"Xe din't say."

Zot dragged the piece of bread through the gravy, popped it in her mouth. After she swallowed, she said, "Mehll doesn't like me talking to you. Xe said I should stay away from you, you're a killer."

"Xe's right."

"Who'd you kill?"

"You told me once go find a whore, I'll tell you the same."

Zot giggled. "That'd be a sight, that would." The giggles trailed to a sigh. "This place is a dead bore. Mehll says you're a thief, too. Howdya get to be one? I'm dying to get outta here."

"You wouldn't want to try my route, young Zot. I ran away and the first mal who found me was a thief. He taught me about locks and planning. He also had some peculiar tastes." She blinked, looked into the wide eyes of the child. Not innocent eyes. Zot had already seen more of the evil that people do to each other than any child should. "He was impotent, you know about that? Yes, I see you do. But he could still get those feelings when the setup was right. He liked to watch rough mals beat me and have sex with me. Sometimes two or three a night. He taught me a lot. You wanted to know who I killed. Well, he was the first. There are things a lot worse than being bored, Zot. And if you go where you don't have friends, you're going to find them. Real fast."

Zot's eyes went wide, then she smiled.

It was easy enough to read what was going through her head.

Not mo. Wouldn't happen to me. I been around, not like some dumb femlit never been out of the mountains.

Yseyl shook her head, but said nothing. Pain and loathing were the only teachers for some lessons.

Yseyl smoothed her hand across the front of her tunic; the stunrod was in place, basted to the waistband of her trousers by threads she could break with a quick jerk if she had to get it out fast. She circled the house, checking out potential ambushes; with the city in such uproar, she wasn't taking chances.

When she was satisfied, she slipped one hand under her tunic and took hold of the rod, used the other to knock on the door.

+Who?+

"Who you sent for."

Mehll took Yseyl into xe's parlor, seated her in a comfortable armchair and poured tea for her, gave her a plate with some triangles of buttered toast, all the while keeping up a stream of chatter about the assassinations and the fishboat that got blown into the Fence and the need for rain.

The old anya settled in xe's own chair. +I believe you don't have your own radio.+

"No."

+Ah ah ah. I'm not going to ask questions. And I don't want answers. What you do is your own business.+ Xe pointed to the large black receiver on the mantel above the fireplace. Xe signed, +Turn that on, will you? It's set and ready to go.+

The sound of strings filled the room, a dance tune Yseyl didn't recognize. She returned to her chair and folded her hands. "Why did you call me here? I doubt it was to listen to pretty music."

+Your name's Yseyl, isn't it. No. Don't answer that. I don't want to know. Xe snapped xe's fingers. +My curios-

ity does get away from me sometimes. Yes. I wanted you
to hear a song. It'll be on soon. They broadcast it every
day about now. I thought a while and a while about sending Zot, telling myself yes then no then yes then no, but
this assassination thing, that convinced me. Something
has to be done. I think there's a chance you'll be the one
who'll do it. In any case, at least you're new. The rest I
wouldn't trust with a week dead fish. Ah. There's the announcement. Listen.+

The singer startled Yseyl. There was no oddity to the
accent, the words might have been spoken by any mid-
range Impix or Pixa, but the quality of the voice was
alien. Offworlder. How did she come to be singing at the
Linojin station?

Yesyl found herself nodding as the cycle progressed—
and wondering how the stranger had caught her feelings
so precisely, that mixture of rage/sadness and the frustration that was not quite despair. She lifted the cup when
the "Song for Yseyl" was announced, sipped steadily at
the lukewarm liquid as the words flowed into the room.

> *"A ghost   little gray ghost*
> *reaches out her hand*
> *her fatal hand*
> *an arms dealer cries*
> *an arms dealer dies*
> *Yseyl, your tears are red*
> *Yseyl, do you weep heart's blood?*
> *A ghost   little gray ghost*
> *gazes at her land*
> *her tortured land*
> *How can I end this?*
> *Or is it endless?*
> *Yseyl, your tears are red.*
> *Yseyl, do you weep heart's blood?*
> *A ghost   little gray ghost*

> *searches the stars*
> *the cold proud stars*
> *To free her land*
> *Her anguished land.*
> *Yseyl, your tears are red.*
> *Yseyl, do you weep heart's blood?*
> *A ghost   little gray ghost*
> *Holds the key*
> *the piercing key.*
> *Who would be free?*
> *Who will follow me?*
> *Yseyl, I hear your call.*
> *Yseyl, hear me, I know it all.*
> *O ghost   little gray ghost*
> *You look the wrong way*
> *You take the wrong road*
> *Hear what I say*
> *Let me lighten your load.*
> *Look to the peaks*
> *Not to the sea.*
> *Where feet become holy*
> *There will I be.*
> *Unravel this rhyme*
> *Your heart's wish to find."*

Mehll pushed onto her feet and went to turn off the radio herself. +If I knew what that's about, I'd have to act on my knowledge. I don't want to know. We'll finish our tea, then you can leave.+

Yseyl walked to the end of the dock and stood gazing across the dark water at the Fencelight.

A short distance away Bond Sisters and Anyas of Mercy were kneeling and murmuring through shimbil after shimbil, twelve upon twelve upon twelve, in a litany of pleas to God to open the way, bring down the Fence.

She listened a moment and felt a vast impatience. If she marched over to them right now and said she could

open the way for them, that they didn't have to wait for
God to act, they'd probably drown her for impiety.

People. She scraped her hand across her eyes. Those
like Mehll, they didn't want to know. Others . . . vumah
vumay, playing by the rules had never gotten her anywhere, nor had not-doing something ever kept her safe.
The offworld woman—she said she had the answer. No
need to believe her, just bargain with her. Might be a Sunflower agent sent to fetch back the disruptor. That didn't
matter. The only thing that mattered was stopping this
misery.

*Might as well listen to her. She's standing on my road
not hers. And she wouldn't be taking the trouble if she
didn't mean to deal. Do me down if she can. Hah! They
think they're so clever these star-fliers, just because they
can get away. But they're only using what other folks
built for them . . . those arms smugglers . . . so stupid
sometimes it was almost embarrassing to do them. Look
to the peaks . . . hm . . . where feet become holy . . . probably means the Outlook where the Pilgrim Road starts . . .
I'll need food . . . gear . . . be out there a while . . . wonder if I can find her before she finds me . . . it's a thought
. . . she's a grand singer . . . it's almost worth . . . ya la,
don't you get stupid, fem . . . listen to the words she says
and forget the voice.*

She left the religious to their chant and went to the
room she rented to do some concentrated thinking.

eastward, curving away from the city. Luca and Wann
rode a short distance along the curve, then turned and

10

Wings cup the air and go where
they will. Things
volatile and unsteady change
at the puff of a breath.

Chapter 10

1. Setup

Shadith touched the test sensor and triggered the holo, then stepped back and walked in a slow circle about it, checking the smoothness of its turn, how the eyes followed her and the way the leaf-shadow flickered over and through it without obscuring the basic shape. She stopped where she'd begun the circle, said, "Speak."

The image smiled, lifted a hand. Its translucent lips moved, and sound came forth. "Because you see this, I know you are Yseyl, thief and assassin. Your face and form trigger the image. I want to make a deal with you. I can help you take the whole Fence down instead of just blowing a few holes in it. In return...."

Shadith listened critically while the speech played to a finish, ending with the date of her return, then she reset the projector. "Well, little gray ghost, it's time to lay down more bait. Can't take a chance you're somewhere else entirely. Sar! I hope Digby appreciates the beating my tailbone's going to get. They could rent out those miniskip seats to a torture museum."

2. Yaqshowal: under siege

The land around the harbor at Yaqshowal was grass from horizon to horizon, grass dotted with herds of ruminants whose thick loose skin fell from their spines in folds that shifted with every step they took as they wandered about on their own, their herdmals dead or fled. Dark red glows marked the places where carcasses roasted in huge pits to feed the Pixa phelas which had gathered there to attack the city.

Big guns boomed continually. Those belonging to the phelas were mounted on massive wagons pulled by teams of lumbering red and white skazz; smaller wagons moved with them, piled with shells almost as large as the mals loading them into the guns.

Guns inside the city answered them, the shells rarely dangerous to the phelas though, as Shadith lingered in the clouds above the city, she saw one munitions pile go up and take a gun wagon with it.

The harbor was lit with strings of naked lightbulbs; the harsh shadows they cast seemed to breed swarms of Yaqshowans shouting and shoving, waving bags of coin as they tried to buy their way onto the few ships that were tied up there.

The radio station was deserted except for a single nervous mal who twitched at every loud noise, but kept a close eye on the spools as the wire snaked past the heads, sending out a mix of music, messages, and pleas for help.

He squealed as Shadith burst in, took a look at the rifle she held, and sat where he was, sweat popping out on his temples. In the recent past his crest must have been a bright orange and green, but the hair paint was flaking off, and now it simply looked diseased. His face was thin and pinched, with a network of tiny lines across it that deepened about his eyes and mouth.

The lines deepened even further when Shadith pushed back the hood of the robe and he saw her face.

"I have some songs I want you to record and play," she said. With her free hand she dug into a belt pouch, pulled out half a dozen heavy silver coins and, one at a time, tossed them at his feet, the metallic chinks as they landed loud in the small room.

"Ah. I think I know which you mean. A sailor I met had a song wire that got rather a lot of attention." He glanced at the coins, his mouth curving in a tight, sardonic smile. "Happy to do business with you, kazi."

3. Icisel: nervous and crowded

Icisel was lit so brightly it was like day on the streets, the glare from the bulbs reaching far out into the deep placid harbor, turning the ships that thronged there into patterns of black and white. Refugees from coastal villages and from Yaqshowal were blotches of black in whatever shelter they could find, one standing watch against thieves, the rest trying to snatch a few hours of sleep before the city guard came by and moved them on.

The Nightplayers among the Iciselli walked around and over those unwelcome visitors, ignoring them with the notorious Ciselle arrogance, the same arrogance with which they ignored the war itself. Fantastically painted and decorated—what they wore looking more like sculpture than clothing—adorned with sound as well as shape and color, music trickling from song wires winding through their hair, the Nightplayers swarmed from playhouse to casino to dancehall, doing the eternal nightround. The Impix triad were all there—anya, mal, and fem—sometimes firm in the tribond, sometimes changing partners with the fluidity and fickleness of raindrops sliding down windowglass.

Shadith circled through the patchy clouds above the city, searching for a way to reach the radio station without being spotted.

The roof of the station was steeply slanted, the ridgepole a jumble of spiky metal objects whose purpose escaped her though they very effectively barred her from landing there.

She circled a last time, swore under her breath, then turned the skip toward the hideaway she'd found for herself inside a grove of thile trees growing beside the river that emptied into Cisel Harbor.

An hour before dawn the city was quieter, though not much darker. The nightround was over and only thieves and sleepers were still in the streets.

She came in low, skimming the roofs until she reached the station, then she brought the skip down and landed in an alley beside it. A quick probe told her there were only two people inside at the moment; Digby's reader found no alarm system, so she picked the lock on the back door, fed a little power into the skip, and pushed it inside.

Shadith pulled the hood up to conceal her face and tried the latch. It moved under her hand and the door to the control room opened a crack. She listened, suppressed a grin, pulled the door wide, and went in. She stopped just inside and stood looking down at a mal and fem engaged in noisy and energetic sex.

The young mal howled his completion and collapsed on top of the fem. She pushed him off, glaring at Shadith. "Stinking Godmal, what you staring at?"

Without waiting for an answer, she hauled the mal to his feet. He stood leaning against her with glazed eyes and shaky knees. The fem smiled at him, patted a trim buttock. "You go have a nice warm shower, maldoll. When you get back, we'll think of something new to pass the time."

When the mal had vanished through the door, the fem raised her arms over her head and swiveled on her toes with a dancer's grace, head thrown back, long dark hair brushing at her buttocks. "Like what you see, Brother? Want a turn in the saddle?"

Shadith chuckled. "Hardly." She pushed the hood back. "My tastes run otherwise."

"Prophet's piss, what t'hell are you?"

"A singer, kazi. With some songs to peddle."

"Now would these be them going round on pirated songwires?"

"Why don't you listen and see? You could do a few duplicates for yourself at the same time."

"What d' you want?"

"To have the songs broadcasted as frequently as possible, spread as widely as possible."

"What's in it for you?"

"My business, your profit. That's all you need to know."

"Maybe. If you are that singer."

"The proof's in the singing. You could always erase the wire."

"True. Studio three's set up. Let's hear what you have to offer."

The mal learned round the door. "Hajja. . . ."

"Go keep it warm, hon. Be with you later. This is business."

4. Dreaming Gajul

Gajul lay beside a broad river flowing into a bay shaped like a leaf with three pointed lobes—a bay so big it was almost an inland sea. Shadith circled through scattered high clouds, using her binocs to examine the city that sprawled below her, its streets serpentines of glowing polychrome against a velvet black ground and in those streets a richly gaudy throng of wanderers that never seemed to stay anywhere for more than a breath.

The Nightplayers of Gajul had a lighter, more whimsical touch than those of Icisel; there were fewer refugees, and most of those were housed in a tent city on the far side of the river where groves of maka and thile trees hid them and the Brothers of God who cared for them from the dreaming gaze of the Gajullery.

She scanned and swore at what she saw. The streets and pocket parks around the radio tower were the busiest in the whole city. The tower itself was twice as tall as the one in Linojin. It was a mass of metal rising from four elegantly curved legs, with the station itself laid like a square egg between those legs. There was no way she could slip in as she had in Icisel, not without announcing to a few hundred Nightplayers and prowling street guards that something odd was happening.

With a sigh of frustration she left the city and followed the river until she found a thile brake nestled in a wide sweeping bend; it was deserted except for birds and a scatter of small beasts.

She made camp, fixed a quick supper, and rolled up in blankets to catch some sleep before she tried again.

About three hours after midnight, she was over the city again. Gajul was quieter around the edges, but in the center where the station was, some street musicians had set up in a small park and were playing for Gajullery who'd taken a notion to dance under the stars, at least what stars were visible. It was a lovely summer night, just cool enough to be pleasant, a wandering breeze to lift and flutter ribbons and set heart-shaped maka leaves to shivering, and the dance showed every sign of lasting till dawn. The streets themselves had gained another group, no hairpaint on mal, fem, or anya, sober clothing in dark colors with long sleeves—visitors from the farms and the lesser merchants out for a night on the town. Brothers of God moved through the mix, white motes in Brownian motion.

Shadith sighed. *If ever I wanted rain*

She landed the miniskip in the fringe of the thile trees along the city side of the riverbank, hid it high up in ancient thile, strapped into a threeway crotch, invisible from the ground. Despite that, she set the shocker to stun anyone trying to steal it, checked the stunrod strapped to her arm, clipped the rifle to her belt so it hung along her leg where the robe would conceal it most of the time. Too bad she had to fool with the rifle, but the locals would snicker and ignore the rod, and she'd waste too much time waiting for them to wake up.

She slung the Brother-robe over her shoulder and dropped from limb to limb, landing with a scrape of booted feet on the knotty roots. Wrinkling her nose with disgust, she shook out the robe. It was stained and smelled of sweat, the hem she'd ripped out to get more length was stiff with dirt. She pulled it on anyway and started walking into the city.

Getting through the streets undiscovered was easier than she'd expected. Intent on their conversations or performances, Nightplayers glided around her as if she were a post in the street—something in the corner of the eye that they avoided without having to take note of it.

Street guards leaned from their kiosks and shouted quips at the Players or slumped against the back wall and drowsed; they, too, ignored her.

A silence in the center of waves of noise, she walked on and on, the radio tower her only cue in that maze of curving streets where straight lines of any length were rare and the only cues were names that meant nothing to her.

The Players, pickpockets, and cutpurses grew thicker as she got closer to the station, the guards had moved out of their kiosks and on occasion marched off a cutpurse clumsy enough to raise a howl from the victim. Except when she stepped out into the street to check direction,

Shadith kept as close to the walls as she could, walked with eyes on the pavement, hands carefully tucked into the long sleeves.

She swore under her breath when she rounded a bend and saw the station ahead—and something she hadn't noticed in her overflights, a wrought iron fence set in the spaces between the tower legs, at least six feet high with sharpened spear points on the pales.

She leaned against a garden wall and contemplated that fence, wondering once again if she should have simply coerced the tech in the Yaqshowal station into duplicating the master for her onto wire spools. She hadn't trusted his skill all that much and, from the little she'd heard, the quality of the recordings on those spools diminished rapidly with the mounting generations of copies, but she was tired and sweaty from all that walking and trying to sing after climbing over those spear points was not an appealing thought.

Why don't I forget the whole thing? Yseyl is probably still in Linojin anyway.

She followed with her eyes the upward curve of the nearest leg and the soaring spindle of the tower. This station was the most powerful on Impixol with the widest range and the biggest audience. *I should have come here first,* she told herself. *Still. . . .* She pushed away from the wall and began walking around the square, hunting for a gate. Picking a lock would be a lot easier than trying to haul herself over that fence. A lot more exposed, though. . . . She glanced at her ringchron. Around two hours till dawn. Didn't leave a lot of time.

As she walked around the second leg, a band of anyas danced past, big eyed and silent, hands busy with the flow of gesture talk like five-finger dances; they wore wide bronze neck collars with bronze chains linking them together. A one-eyed mal with a scattergun and a spiked knucklebar walked beside them, looking warily about, his single eye narrowing to an ominous slit when other Nightplayers got too close.

As she watched the group move on, she realized suddenly that she'd seen very few anyas among the Gajullery Nightplayers. There'd been two or three tribonds, but none of the flowing partner exchange. She remembered things she'd seen, things hinted at in the Ptakkan teasers. *Ah Spla! I don't care what Digby says, that Fence has got to go. Once the pressure is off at least some of this will stop.*

She moved quickly along this lesser fence and turned the corner in time to see a cloaked mal come swaying toward her. He stopped near the middle of this side, felt around under the cloak, then began to stab a key of some kind at a lock she couldn't see from where she was standing. Shadith moved quickly, quietly up behind him, reaching him as he finally managed to locate the hole in the gate's lock.

Insulated in an alcohol fog, all his attention focused on turning the key, he noticed nothing. With a grunt of satisfaction he lifted the latch and shoved at the gate, then sputtered in confusion and surprise as she caught hold of his collar and the seat of his pants and walked him inside. She tripped him, rescued the key and slammed the gate shut before he managed to get back on his feet.

"Wha ... who ... Brother? What?"

"Let's go."

He stood swaying and blinking. His crest was braided into dozens of thin plaits threaded through silver beads that clicked musically whenever he moved. The sound of her voice cut through the muzz in his head, enough for him to realize something odd was happening. "You're not. . . ."

"All things will be explained once we're inside. Aren't you late for work?"

"God!" He shuddered, struggled to pull himself together. "Rakide's go going to ki kill me. Ahhhurrr. Can't talk straight." He stared at her for a moment, then swung round and stumbled toward the station's single door.

"Just stay where you are and there won't be any problem."

The mal she'd followed in stood rubbing at his face and looking both dazed and harried. A lean, hard-faced fem taller than usual glared at her, thin lips pressed so tightly together her mouth nearly vanished, her face a net of wrinkles, dark smudges under her eyes. She sat in the com chair, earphones draped around her neck, one hand on the control panel, the other on the arm of the chair.

Shadith saw the hand on the panel start to shift, lifted the rifle. "I won't kill you, but a pellet through the wrist won't be pleasant."

"What do you want? We don't keep coin here. Stupid, there," she nodded at the mal, "he might have a stash of muth around somewhere, but I doubt there's much left. He doesn't get paid for another week."

"I'm here to give you something, not to take anything away."

"Oh, really."

"Really." With her free hand, she pushed back the cowl and smiled at the twitch of the fem's face as she registered what stood before her. "I have some songs I want to sing. They've been well received otherwhere."

"Ahhh, I begin to see. I recognize your voice now. What do you want for the master?"

"See that it gets played often and aired widely. That's all."

"You wrote them?"

"Yes."

"You have more?"

"Not to give away. Well?"

"Harl, go set up studio two. And do it right. If I lose

this because you zekked up, I'm going to skin you strip by strip. You hear me?"

The mal's greenish-gray skin went papery pale, and his eyes got a distant look.

"And if you heave in here, I'm going to use your tongue to mop it up. Get on with it."

Shadith left the station reasonably satisfied that Rakide wasn't going to spoil her exclusive acquisition of those songs by sending guards after the singer. The one broadcast had gone out, but what fussed her most was a feeling that it would be the only broadcast. From what she'd heard on her way here, Gajullery Station was given more to comedy and romantic songs and management might have something quelling to say about stronger fare. Yaqshowal Station had given them a good play, but Yaqshowal was under siege. Ciselle Station had broadcast the spool four times while she was in range—and had added several similar songs in other voices. The war was hitting them harder now with the floods of refugees and the fear that the phelas would move on them next. For the Gajullery, though, the profits from the war were flooding in, the arms dealers were here and the dealers in flesh, the harbor was crowded with the ships of the coastal traders. She'd heard a farm fem talking to a merchant tribond, saying that the rainfall had been good this year, they'd gotten three harvests already and a fourth lot was growing well, and when she finished, the merchant fem nodded with smug satisfaction as she sang the praises of her family's profits. And they were only one pair out of many Shadith had heard on her way in who mouthed talk deploring the horrors of the war, but whose eyes were shiny with satisfaction.

The complacency of the unthreatened. She heard more of it as she made her way through the crowded streets of the city, in a hurry to get away from there before dawn.

Laughter and pleasure, profit and ease, built on the bones of the dead—she'd seen these a thousand and a thousand times in her long life and longer unlife.

A wrong turn took her into the warehouses along the bay front. She ground her teeth at the delay and her own stupidity at getting so sunk in mind games that she forgot what she was about.

Hm. If I follow the bay front until I reach the river, I can follow that to the grove. And get out of here. She started walking faster, the rifle slapping uncomfortably against her leg, the ragged hem of the robe irritating her ankles.

A small figure came racing from a narrow alley between two warehouses, caromed into Shadith, and bounced off her into the wall. Two mals emerged from the alley, reached for the anya who was sitting up, shaking xe's head, dazed, but not so dazed xe couldn't shiver with fear at the sight of the mals and start scrambling away on hands and knees.

Shadith had the robe up and the rifle unclipped before they reached xe. "Back off," she said, pitching her voice as low as she could. "Now. Or lose a knee."

"That un's ours, this is Kugula's patch."

She snorted. "I don't know Kugula from that piece of crud you just stepped in. And I could care less. Back off." She watched them intently, felt the one on the right gathering himself. Cursing their stupidity, she put a pellet in his knee, swung the rifle, and squeezed the trigger again. She missed the second thug, but that was no problem because he flung himself back, scrambling for the shelter of the alley.

She darted over, picked up the anya, tossed xe over her shoulder, and took off running, driving her weary legs as fast as she could move them.

She plunged into an alley on the side away from the

water and a few moments later was thoroughly lost in the maze of littered, stinking little streets that never ran straight for more than a few strides.

When she felt she'd separated herself far enough from the shots, she slowed and looked around. Nobody in sight, no feel of watchers behind shutters. She lowered the anya to xe's feet. "All right. We seem to be clear of that lot. If you've got someplace to go to, you'd better head there, sun'll be up soon."

She started to turn, but the anya caught her sleeve, pulled her back around with a strength born of urgency. When Shadith was looking at xe, xe signed, +What are you?+ Abruptly, xe made an erase-sign, went on, +Help me.+

"It seems to me I have. And I've got other places to be."

+My daughter,+ the anya signed, xe's face twisted with grief and fear. +She's only twelve years old. They sold her. Slavers sold her to a mal old enough to be her granther. Help me get her away.+

The trouble with empathy, Shadith thought, *it doesn't let you tell yourself xe's lying. Spla! Twelve.* "Do you know where she is?"

+I know the direction. Thinta tells me.+ Xe pointed. +That way.+

Shadith followed the line of xe's arm. *Hm. That's the way I want to go. I think. Don't interfere with locals, Digby said. At least, don't get caught at it. And he laughed. And then he stopped laughing. Don't make bad vibes for the business, Shadow. Not if you mean to keep working here. Spla!* "Here, you take this." She thrust the rifle at the anya. "What's your name, by the way?"

+Thann.+ Xe took the weapon, tucked it under xe's arm to leave xe's hands free. +I do know how to use it, if you're interested. And your name?+

"Call me Shadow. And do me a favor, ignore the cues you picked up about me. I'm not supposed to be here."

+It's the least I can do, Shadow.+

"Hm. Well, let's go find your daughter."

The sun was pinking the east when they reached the house where Isaho was. It was a big house, set inside a wall ten feet high with sharpened spears along the top. There were a number of trees inside the wall, but they'd all been trimmed, no branches allowed to thrust past the spear points.

The main gate had a guardhouse with a watchmal dozing inside, but around the corner there was a small door set deep in the wall. Shadith moved into the alcove and bent to examine the lock. "Thann, give a whistle if you see company coming. Shouldn't take long, a baby could turn this thing."

Despite the care with which Shadith eased the door open, the hinges squealed as if they were in pain. She stiffened, sent her *reach* sweeping across the ground. No alarm. Either no one had heard the noise or they thought it was outside in the street. She shoved the door wide enough to let them in, shutting it as soon as Thann was through.

They were in a small court paved with flags, an open arch at the far end.

"Hm, far as I can tell, the place is still sleeping. You thin any problems waiting for us?"

+No. God watches over us.+

"Over you, perhaps. I doubt he worries about me." She pushed the hood back.

Thann stared, seemed to gather xeself. +One worries about all living creatures.+ Xe stepped away from the wall, settled the rifle under xe's arm. +Isaho is that way.+ Xe pointed toward the southern corner of the house. +On the second floor. The room at this end, the one with the balcony and all the windows.+ Xe's hands trembled, and xe stopped signing until xe had them under control again. +She is not ... I don't know ... the sense of her is so weak ... he ... he has ...+ xe's hands started shaking again.

"Right. I've got it. You stay here. Be ready to get the door open the moment you see us. We may have to get away fast."

As Shadith passed through the arch, she heard growls and the scratch-thud of running feet. She flung herself to one side, rolled up with the stunrod in her hand. The quickest of the chals collapsed with his drool on her foot, the other went down only half a step behind him. *Spla! I think I'd better go up the outside. Who knows what I'd find prowling the halls in there?*

A dusty ancient vine coiled up the side of the house, its rootlets set deep in the interstices between the courses of stone. She jumped, hung from her hands long enough to make sure it was going to hold her weight, then she half-walked, half-hauled herself to the balcony. She swung over the rail and crossed the deck in three quick steps, broke a pane of glass, reached in, and tripped the latch.

The huge room was filled with a mix of gray starlight and the tiny yellow flickers from half a dozen nightlights. Whoever he was, he didn't like the dark. She crossed to a bed big enough to hold a dozen Impix or Pixas.

A small form lay sprawled on a pile of rugs as if the mal had shoved her from the bed when he was done with her. The smell of blood mixed with sharper sweeter odors from the ointments smeared over her.

An old mal lay on his back in a tangle of silken quilts, faint snores issuing from a sagging mouth.

She looked at him a moment, sighed. *I know what I'd like to do,* she thought, *but I'm not your judge and definitely not your executioner.*

She stunned him, then looked round for the child's clothing. Nothing.

She found shirts in a chest by the door, used her beltknife to shorten the sleeves on one of them and pulled it over the comatose child's limp body. She took another two shirts, rolled them into tight cylinders and shoved them down the front of her shirt; the anya could turn them into clothing after they got young Isaho cleaned up. She pulled one of the quilts off the bed, laid Isaho on it, and tied the ends into a sling.

Using another quilt as a rope, she lowered the sling to the ground, then climbed after it.

In the courtyard Shadith set the bundle down. "I have her. She's fainted or something, but she's alive." She untied the knots, rewrapped Isaho in the quilt with her head clear, her fine hair pooled like black water, her small bare feet out the other end. "I'll carry her." She pulled her cowl forward to conceal her face, eased her arms under the quilt, and lifted Isaho as she stood up. "You walk guard, Thann, and chase off the nosy with an avert sign. One that says sickness, keep away. The streets will be filling up with dayworkers, but that should stop them from looking too hard at us." She settled Isaho, so her face was pressed against the robe and concealed from the casual viewer. "Let's go."

They moved through the winding streets at the trailing edge of Gajul, a zone of silence and emptiness about them generated by Shadith's size, the limp and apparently lifeless child cradled in her arms, the rifle tucked under the anya's arm, xe's warning gestures. No one spoke to them or tried to stop them; even the guards yawning in their kiosks only watched as they strode past.

The paved street became a dirt lane that wound for a short distance between small but intensely farmed plots of land and finally turned into the woodlands where she'd stashed the miniskip. Shadith sighed with relief when the lane cleared for a moment and she was able to move unseen into the lingering shadow under the trees.

She lowered Isaho onto the leafmold, turned to face Thann. "I'll be here a while," she said. "Until nightfall, at least. If you want to stay, that's all right. Or you can move on. I won't stop you."

Thann sank to the ground beside Isaho, letting the rifle fall from cramped arms. Xe smiled and shook xe's head, then wearily, as if xe had barely enough will left to move xe's hand, xe signed, +No. Where would we go?+

"All right. I'm heading for the mountains above Linojin. If you'd like to go with me, I can take you. It might be safer there."

The anya's fatigue-dulled eyes brightened, and xe managed a grin that gave new life to xe's thin, worn face. +We were going to Linojin before the slavers took Isaho. Thank you.+

"Ah Spla, the ways of fate." Shadith pulled off the robe with a sigh of relief, hung it on a limb stub to air out for a while. She thought about discarding it but decided not; what happened next depended too much on when Yseyl heard the song and what she did about it. She swung into the tree where she'd left the skip, got the emergency rations, the canteen, and the medkit and dropped down again.

Thann was stroking the child's face, xe's thin fingers shaking with anxiety and fatigue. Xe looked up as Shadith walked across to xe but didn't try to sign.

Shadith twisted the top off a tube of hipro paste. "Here. Eat this. Food concentrate. Doesn't look like it, but it's good for you. Think of it as paté." She gave Thann the tube and chuckled as xe eyed it dubiously. "Squeeze it in and swallow fast as you can. Believe me, you don't want to taste it. And here." She unsnapped the cup from the canteen and filled it with water, passing it across. "Wash it down with this."

As Thann followed instructions, Shadith opened the medkit and ran the scanner along Isaho's body. "Hm. Your daughter's torn up a bit, but the physical stuff isn't bad. Do I have your permission to give her something to keep away infection?"

Thann nodded, then drank hastily from the cup as the after effects of the hipro began working on xe's taste buds.

"Ordinarily, I wouldn't advise letting any offworlder give you medication, Thann." She turned the scanner over, ran the pickup long enough to suck in a few dead cells for Isaho's baseline. "But my boss sent along a kit tailored to your species. Just in case, you might say." She fed the scanner's data into the pharmacopoeia and tapped in the code for antibiotic. "He's a being who thinks of things like that. I say being because I'm not quite sure what he is these days, other than an intelligence that has made a home for itself inside a kephalos or maybe it's a system of kephaloi. This is my first assignment." A small green light came on and she pressed the spray nozzle into the bend in Isaho's elbow, activating it with a tap on the sensor. "There. That's done. And if I get caught here, it could be my last."

She set the pharmacopoeia in its slot, took up a transparent tube filled with green gel. "When we get her clean, I'll give your daughter a shot of nutrient. That'll help bring her strength up. Chances are she'll wake on her own once she feels safe again."

Thann rolled the hipro tube into a tight cylinder, dug into the leaf mold and the earth below it and buried the tube, concentrating on what xe was doing with an intensity that was a measure of xe's fear. Xe sat staring at the little heap of decaying leaves and dark brown dirt.

Shadith unbuttoned the shirt and slipped it off Isaho

She used her belt knife to start the cut, then began ripping the shirt into rags.

The sound of tearing cloth brought the anya's head up. Xe moved closer, signed, +Why?+

"I thought it would be helpful if the child woke to the smell of soap, not those oils smeared over her." Shadith wet one of the rags, squeezed out a dollop of soap and rubbed it until it lathered. She handed the rag to Isaho. "I'll do her arms and shoulders. Better, I think, if you took care of the rest."

The anya shook out the quilt and helped Shadith ease Isaho onto it. The femlit sighed deeply and moved on her own for the first time, turning onto her side, her thumb going into her mouth; she didn't suck on it, only left it there for the comfort it gave her.

"Ah," Shadith said. "That's good, baby. You've got time, lots of time now." She pulled the quilt over the femlit, tucked it in, then stood, stretched, patted a yawn. "Thann, you think you could stay awake for a couple hours?"

+Watch?+

"Yes. I need to get some sleep. Anything that worries you, wake me. There's a way we can get out of here fast, but I'd rather not use it in daylight."

Shadith woke with a collection of aches and a taste in her mouth like somebody died. It was full dark. She'd been asleep for at least eight or nine hours. "Thann? You should have waked me sooner."

The anya moved from the shadows. Xe shook xe's head. Xe's hand moved in signs Shadith had to strain to see. +No one came. And you needed the sleep. I'll rest when we're away from here.+

"Aahhhh Splaaaaa, I feel like someone's been beating me with chains. How's your daughter?"

+She still sleeps, but it seems to me she's easier.+

Shadith dug out another two tubes of hipro, held out one of them. "Get that down. If you faint from hunger, you could fall off the skip and take your daughter with you." She squeezed the paste into her throat, swallowed hastily, grabbed the canteen, and gulped down the last of the water. "Try shaking the femlit while I'm fetching the skip from the tree. It'll be safer for us all if she doesn't wake in the middle of the flight and go into a panic. Well, you don't know what I'm talking about, and how could you? Anyway, see if you can wake her."

She jumped, caught hold of the lowest limb, pulled herself up. It was an easy climber, that tree, which was the reason she'd chosen it; no point in making trouble for herself if she had to get to the skip fast.

She unhooked the straps that held it in the crotch, put the lifters on hover, and swung her leg across the front saddle. A moment later she was easing it through the mass of thin whippy twigs and oval leaves that grew at the end of the branch. She brought it round, kicked the landing struts down, and let it sink to the ground beside the quilt. She dismounted and began stowing the things she'd scattered about the campsite, rolling up the blankets, tucking the medkit away, removing all traces of her presence. Then she strolled over to the anya and stood looking down at the sleeping child.

"Thann, you're going to have to hold Isaho in your lap. I'll strap the two of you together. Hm. It's a warm night, but there'll be some wind where we are. Tell you what, I'll lift the femlit, you wrap the quilt around you and get yourself settled in back saddle. Put your feet in those stirrups there and signal me when you're as comfortable as you can get. Remember, you'll be spending six, seven hours seated because I'll not be stopping unless we absolutely have to. T'k, that's another thing. If you have to relieve yourself, you'd better do it now."

* * *

Shadith fed power to the lifters and took the miniskip up slowly. She could feel the anya's fear as the earth dropped away, but the darkness helped and the soft hum of the lifters was soothing, so xe's jags of anxiety rapidly smoothed out. She stopped the rise when they were a few feet above the tallest trees and sent the skip humming along the curve of the river, avoiding the farmlands and the ranches with their grazing stock.

When Thann's fear had simmered to a slight uneasiness, Shadith twisted her head around and smiled at the dark blotch so close behind her. "There, it's not so bad, is it? If you need something, give a whistle and we'll see what we can do, otherwise I'll keep on till near dawn."

Thann whistled a pair of notes to signify xe understood, modified the last into a soft warble that went on and on, a wordless lullaby, the anya singing in the only way xe could to xe's sleeping daughter.

Shadith began thinking about the muteness of the anyas in this species, what it meant in terms of languages and things that voiced beings never had to think about. When she read about it in Digby's file, it seemed an interesting twist on the things that life got up to and the sign language itself was fascinating, a language that could be translated to a degree but never fully into spoken words. Whistles like birdcalls for times of danger and times of need. Whistles for song like that lullaby. For the quick exchange of complex thoughts, though, anyas needed light and proximity so their gestures could be seen. Odd that the Impix had clung to the radio for the transmission of words, but had never developed or had forgotten coded transmission. Perhaps it was a reflection of the anya's role in this society, the expectation that xes would not work outside the home except as religious and in that case did not need more than the occasional letter to their kin or clans.

That lullaby was lovely, though; it really crept under the skin, so much tenderness in it that words really seemed unnecessary.

Toward dawn she slowed until the skip was barely moving, swept her mindsearch as far as she could, hunting the bite of a thinking brain.

Horizon to horizon, the world seemed empty of everything but fur and feathers. With a weary sigh she chose a clump of trees where they could camp, kicked the landing struts into place, and put the miniskip on the ground beside the river.

5. Hatching

The child's eyes were open and aware, watching Shadith as she unbuckled the straps that bound her and her anya into the seat. When Shadith reached under her to lift her from Thann's lap, she was stiff and afraid at first, then that fear suddenly vanished and she relaxed, smiling and sleepy.

Shadith shook her head and settled the child on the blanket she'd spread beside the skip.

Thann didn't move through all this; xe sat hunched over, eyes squeezed shut. Shadith touched xe's cold, clammy skin, then quickly got xe off the seat and onto the blanket beside Isaho. She snapped the quilt out, transferred xe onto that, and got out the medkit.

As she knelt beside the anya, she looked over her shoulder at Isaho. "What's wrong? Do you know?"

The femlit stared at her a moment, then she spoke with an odd and troubling calmness. "Xe's in egg. I think the babbit hatched when we were flying. Sometimes hatchlings use their eggteeth to bite before they start sucking. Thann and Mam talked about it when they didn't know I was listening. They said I did, bite, I mean, but it was just skin I got. Sometimes they bite the wrong place, and there's lots of blood."

"Oh, shays! Can I take the babbit out of the pouch? Will it drown if I don't?"

Isaho shrugged. "Mam and Thann, they didn't talk much about that."

Thann's eyes opened to crusted slits. Xe's hands moved. +Please . . . my babbit . . . please+ A hand moved down xe's body, pressed against the swollen pouch, and a gout of blood came rushing through the cloth of xe's trousers.

"Isaho, come help me. Quick." Shadith began working on the ties to the anya's trousers, the sodden cloth resisting her fingers. With an impatient exclamation, she cut the tie with her belt knife, and with Isaho's help, rolled the trousers away from the pouch.

"Your hand is smaller than mine, Isaho." Shadith spoke quickly, reached out, caught hold of the femlit's wrist. "See if you can catch the hatchling and get it out of there." Isaho tried to draw back, the smell of fear sharp in her, so Shadith put more urgency in her voice. "I have to stop the bleeding, but I don't dare while the babbit's in pouch."

Shaking, eyes squeezed almost shut, Isaho forced a hand through the pulsing sphincter of the pouch. She squeaked suddenly, snatched her hand back, a dark worm-like thing attached to it, teeth sunk in the flesh of her smallest finger; it was slightly larger than her hand, with eye bulges sealed shut and a stubby tail. Silent and determined, Isaho cuddled the anyalit against her chest and squatted, watching as Shadith worked over Thann.

"Good femlit," Shadith said. She drew on a glove, worked her hand into the pouch, watching a readout as the sensors on the fingertips sent data back. "With a little luck, we'll . . . ah, got you. Looks like it isn't as bad as I thought, Isaho. It's only a nick in a small vein. It's been leaking quite a while, that's all. I wish . . . ah, lie still, Thann. This may hurt a bit. I'm going to cauterize the wound, and I don't think I'd better give you any drugs, not if you're going to be feeding the baby. Let's see, slide the tube in . . . right, right . . . good! In position. Stay as still as you can. Wait, just a moment. Isaho, there's a bit of wood beside you . . . right, that one . . . wipe it off . . . yes, that's good . . . now, set it in your anya's mouth so xe can bite down on it . . . yes, that's right . . . get a good grip, Thann . . . bite down! Now! Good . . . I think . . . yes, that got it. Now a little blind gluing . . . what do you think about that, hm? Glued together like a nice little cabinet. Now we suck the blood out, get things neat and tidy in the nursery . . . now comes the *really* bad part, you're going to have to eat a tube of hipro every hour till you've replaced that blood and gotten your strength back. Isaho, slip the babbit back home and I'll have a look at that bite."

Isaho watched as Shadith painted antiseptic over the wound and sprayed it with faux skin. Her eyes opened wider as Shadith set the pharmacopoeia's spray nozzle against the inside of her elbow and touched the sensor. "Oh! That tickles."

"What it does is keep you from getting infection in the bite."

"Oh." She smoothed her finger across the faux skin. "Is this what you put inside Thanny?"

"No. That was something else. Does the same job, though. How are you feeling otherwise?"

Isaho's eyes went suddenly blank, then she looked away, her gaze shifting rapidly from point to point until she'd forced herself to forget the question. Only then did she turn back and smile at Shadith. "We're going to Linojin. Mam and Baba and my brother Keleen, they're waiting for us there." Her eyes flickered again, then her smile brightened like a sheet of ice concealing the turmoil in an undertow. "Did God send you to take us to Linojin?"

"I wouldn't know about that, Isaho. Do you think you could go to sleep for a while? We'll be traveling all night again."

She sensed a sudden wild burst of fear in the child, but Isaho's smile didn't falter. The femlit put out a hand, touched her knee. "Will you be sleeping, too, Messenger of God?"

"No, I have to see that Thann eats and I'll be keeping watch for strangers."

"Then I can sleep."

Shadith chuckled as Thann made a face when xe saw the tube she was holding. "I've run some water through the filtra and you can have a nice cup of hot tea once you get this down."

+Isaho?+

"Sleeping. In the beginning she woke up several times an hour to make sure I was still there watching, but she's been sleeping really well since noon. Not like before, just good healthy sleep. There. That's over for now. And here's your tea. Hang onto the mug, let me lift you up. There. You can rest your head and shoulders on my knee."

When Thann was finished, Shadith took the mug back and set it on the ground beside her. "Want more? No? Feeling like talking a while?"

+Yes. I owe you my life. Ask what you want.+

"Well, first of all, when you're in Linojin, I'd be grateful if you forget how you got there. Don't mention me, not even a hint of what I look like. Or anything about flying. Isaho told me her mother and father and brother are there. I doubt you can keep her from talking to them, so see if you can get them to keep quiet, too."

Thann sighed. +Isaho won't say anything to them, Shadow. They're dead. All of them. Her brother five years ago, her Mam and Baba just before we left Khokuhl. She saw them dead, but she won't let herself remember that.+

"Then why . . . ?"

+Because five times she started out to walk to Linojin by herself, twice she was nearly killed. I thought at least we'd be away from the war and the Anyas of Mercy have their hospital there and they know about such hurts to the soul, they might be able to heal her and bring her back to peace with God.+ Thann sighed. +And there was no place for us in Khokuhl. My clan was never big and they're mostly dead. Bazekiyl and Mandall, those were my bondmates, their cousins had their own families to care for. So there wasn't much choice about what to do.+

"I see. How's the babbit?"

+Doing well. Xe's a hungry and lively little one. I was afraid . . . not trusting God's providence enough. But One has forgiven my weakness and blessed me.+

"Hm. Good to hear. We'll reach the mountains above Linojin by daybreak tomorrow. I'll set you down beside the Pilgrim Road. Will you be strong enough to walk the last stretch, or do you want to lay up for a day and start the next morning?"

+That paste you've been feeding me is amazing. A little sleep and I can run the rest of the way.+ Xe's hands made a smile.

"Then you'd best get that sleep.' Shadith eased the anya's head down, thrust her arms under xe, and lifted xe quilt and all. "I'll tuck you in beside your daughter." She chuckled. "You can snore up a partsong together."

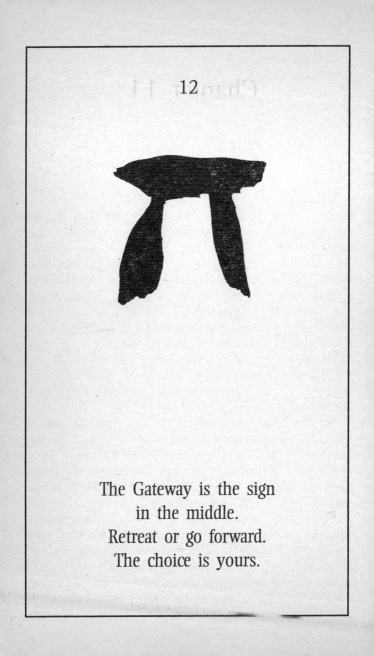

The Gateway is the sign
in the middle.
Retreat or go forward.
The choice is yours.

Chapter 11

1. Reaching Linojin

On the fourth day after leaving the village, the Shishim Remnant left sand and sawgrass behind and found a road heading north. As Wintshikan stepped onto the worn paving, she sighed with relief—at last some solid land that didn't slide away from under her feet and slip into her sandals until each step was a punishment. Never mind that she'd walked mountain trails for sixty years now; her knees hurt, and there was an ache in the place between her shoulder blades that she couldn't reach.

No more swarms of black biters that lifted off the sawgrass and drank the sweat on her arms and face, walking over her sticky skin with their tiny tickling feet until she wanted to scream.

This was open land like the Meeting Grounds. Fields with small herds of maphiks and zincos grazing under the eyes of mallits and femlits. Flocks of small dark maphabirds following the beasts and pecking at the droppings. It squeezed her heart to see those familiar things here in the lowlands she despised.

The paving was cracked, even crumbled in places, square flags of stone held together with a dark tarry substance. The jomayls' hooves click-clacked loudly on that stone. Their red eyes flickered in the sunlight, and one after the other they announced their pleasure at the footing with drawn-out nasal honks; they'd liked slogging through the sand even less than she had.

A breeze touched her face, cool air with a touch of
brine, stirring the heart-shaped leaves in a small grove of
young vevezz a short distance ahead, turning them over
so the silver sides caught the sunlight, letting them fall
again so they shimmered from pale green to silver and
back again.

Kanilli rode one of the pack jomayls, Zaro was
slumped on the back of another; she was miserable, covered with welts from the biters. The last time Wintshikan
had checked on her, she'd been running a slight fever, but
she'd become angry when Xaca wanted them to stop so
she could tend her daughter. "I hate this place," she said.
"If I have to crawl, I'll keep going."

Luca and Wann rode ahead of them, talking energeti-
cally, guiding their jomayls with the balance of their bodies, looking as wild and unconfined as the sea birds that
soared overhead.

We're not even a Remnant now, Wintshikan thought,
*not Pixa at all; we're turning into something else, and I
don't know what it is.*

Would it have been better to stay on the Round and fall
at the hands of the Imps where at least they'd know who
they were, what they were? Would it have been better to
hold more tightly to the bond with God and let One har-
vest them, set them aside to be reborn into the Company
of the Faithful? *I want things to be like they were,* she
thought, *I want to know what I'm meant to do.* Her eyes
burned with tears—which made her angry with herself,
then angry with God for allowing this. Which appalled
her so much, she tried to wipe the thought away with her
tears as she scrubbed her sleeve across her face.

Zell leaned down to stroke Wintshikan's hair. Xe was
riding a packer jomayl, but xe was all the gear it carried.
Xe's joints had suffered in the passage through the edges
of the salt marsh, and xe could no longer walk because
something had gone wrong with xe's hip. Even riding

meant endless grinding pain, but xe never complained nor would xe permit Wintshikan to hold the Remnant in camp longer than necessary. +I can rest when we reach Linojin+, xe signed. +And I'd certainly rather ride than scratch+.

By mid-afternoon the Remnant was moving through a patchwork of small farms, the land intensely tilled, some plots with vegetables, berries, and fruit trees growing together, three levels of crops ripening at the same time. There were more people working in those fields than Wintshikan had seen since the last Grand Gather.

Her heart ached again when she looked at them. They were lightly clad because it was a very warm day, so she could see that they were unarmed except for cultivators and pruning shears. Not a single rifle anywhere. No guards, no fences, no watchchals. *It isn't fair,* she thought, *it isn't right that life on the far side of the mountains should be so terrible, and here so peaceful that those folk don't care that we're strangers. No guns, no guards, no walls, yet they're calm and contented, at ease with the world. It just isn't fair. They ought to feel some kind of guilt for their good fortune, they should lower their eyes when we go past and be ashamed because they have so much while we've lost everything.*

By mid-morning on the next day there was a dark blot visible on the northern horizon. At first Wintshikan thought it was a cloud though there wasn't a wisp in the rest of the sky, but as the hours slid away, the blot turned into shining white walls and dark green foliage with the patchy browns and grays of a fishing village obscuring part of it. The coast curved closer to the road so the ocean was visible again in the west, a shattered blue so brilliant that her eyes hurt looking at it.

When they were close enough to make out the sails of the fishboats out in the bay, the road turned suddenly eastward, curving away from the city. Luca and Wann rode a short distance along the curve, then turned and came trotting back.

Luca dropped her hands on her thighs, scowled down at Wintshikan. "I don't know what to do," she said. "The closer we get, the more I don't want to go in there." She nodded at the Pilgrim Road half a mile off. "Look at them there. Walking. What're we supposed to do with these?" She dug the fingers of one hand in the roached mane of her jomayl and scratched vigorously, drawing a mooing moan of pleasure. Her face hardened as she glanced over her shoulder at the city. "Walls," she said, then shivered.

Wintshikan brushed her hand across her eyes. She'd drifted out of the habit of leadership on the difficult walk north from that village, ceding its problems and pleasures to Luca.

Zell touched her arm and tried to give her the Heka's Shawl, but she shook her head. That was done with now. It was sad, it meant that all the past was really gone now, but at the same time it was almost a relief to acknowledge the passing. She straightened her shoulders.

"Hm. I've heard they don't allow weapons inside Linojin, so—Luca, why don't you and Wann take the gear and the jomayls except the one Zell's riding to that village over there. See if you can find a place where to stay. Nyen, you and Hidan go with them, no telling what kind of thieves live there. Xaca, I want you to come with us and mind the children."

Xaca nodded, but Kanilli wasn't pleased at all with this division. "Ahee, Heka, I want to go with Luca and Wann."

"Quiet, Kanli, you help your mother take care of your cousin. I don't want to hear any more nonsense out of you." She rubbed her thumb across her chin. "I mean to see the Anyas of Mercy about Zell and about Zaro's bites. Don't know how long that will take to set up. Tell him . . .

yes, I don't like the thought of walls either. Soon as we can, we'll join you. That sound all right?"

Luca smiled, the grin that lit up her face and gave her the charm her usual sullen stone face denied her. "Sounds real good," she said. "Kanilli, you keep on whining like that and for all I care, the Heka can leave you with the Anyas of Mercy, maybe they can teach you some manners. Now, move your little butt and help Zaro down, get her up behind Zell."

Wintshikan stood a while, watching the four ride off across the open grassland, then she shook her head and started walking toward the Pilgrim Road, Xaca quiet beside her, a sulky Kanilli stumping at her side, the lead reins of the jomayl clutched in her fist.

2. The meeting

Yseyl lay stretched out on the limb of a bulky maka tree, the cinque-lobed leaves rubbing stiffly against each other in the breeze that trickled downslope from the peaks. The Outlook was some distance behind her, around the curve of the mountain, but she was still nervous about being watched and not quite recovered from the sudden appearance of that small black box that had scared the stiffening out of her bones when it popped up from behind a boulder, called her name and brought her here to listen to that . . . what did Cerex call it? hollow something. Sweet talking twisty-tongued . . . why do I bother?

The painted air folded itself up when the spiel was done and was sucked by a flat black slab with its eggchild clicked into a hole in its side. She almost couldn't see it any more, last fall's dead leaves blown across it by that same breeze that was tickling her hair.

This was the day when that offworlder was supposed to be here. She checked the setting on the stunrod for the tenth time, then went back to chewing on her lip and getting angry that the fool creature hadn't shown up and in less than an hour the sun would be going down.

The offworlder came gliding into the open, deft and silent for such a big and lumpy creature. *This one's a hunter,* Yseyl thought. *Not like Cerex and the rest. Be careful, fem. Don't give her the slightest opening. . . .*

She knelt beside the slab and did something to it; the surface went white, and there was a flow of writing across it. *Reporting that I came,* Yseyl thought. *Maybe that I'm here now?*

As the offworlder shut off the box and started to stand, Yseyl shifted the stunrod so that it pointed at her. "Stay where you are," she called. "On your knees."

"Ah." The offworlder sank back on her heels. "Mind if I say your name?"

"Do you know it?"

"I think so. Cerex said you're called Yseyl."

"How do you know him?"

"The person I work for has hired him on occasion."

"You work for an arms dealer?"

"No. Digby's . . . um . . . strongly opposed to such people. We find things for people, dig up information they can't get any other way, at least not so quickly or easily. The company is called Excavations, Limited and my boss calls himself Digby. Which is a pun but you wouldn't know it because it doesn't translate into Impix."

A whirring sound, a rasp of leaves, and a faint thud brought Yseyl's head around. A large black bird landed on a branch near her. It blinked at her, then closed its eyes and settled into a stoic silence. A moment later a second appeared, then a third. Then several smaller brown birds. Odd.

She couldn't afford the distraction, so she ignored the soft sounds as more birds arrived. "Why are you here?"

"We were hired to get the disruptor back."

"What's that?"

"Now, Yseyl, it's long past the time for playing that game. We tracked you from Marrat's Market, got confirmation from Cerex about what happened there."

"He thought no one could do that."

"Well, Cerex has never been one of Caan's brighter products. That's an interesting talent you've got. Digby collects talents. He asked me to tell you he'd be interested if you decided that you might like to work for him. Once this bit is finished, of course."

Yseyl didn't like the tone of that last comment; it was far too confident. She thought about stunning the hunter and getting out of there, but the offworlder had already tracked her from the Market and God only knew what resources she had to hand now. "You said you had a deal. Well?"

"I assume you've stashed the disruptor somewhere while you looked for a way to use it." The hunter looked toward Yseyl, amusement written on her face. "Trusting your own people about as much as you trust me. I also assume that you've about run out of patience with the people you thought might help you. You wouldn't be sitting in that tree if that weren't a fair description. This is the deal. I can help you take down the whole kis'n Fence. Wipe it out. Then you won't need someone to lead the Impix and Pixas through a hole, all you have to do is let Impix nature take its course. Within a few months ships and people would be heading out, too many of them for the Ptaks to stop. Besides, they've gotten lazy after so many centuries of penning you up. No arms, no ships, just a few fliers to ferry techs and assassins back and forth. In return, I want the disruptor. And you, of course, if you care to come back with me."

"Now, hunter, explain to me just why I should believe a word of that." She heard a soft whuff, glanced over at the black bird. It flapped its wings again, did a kind of dance on the branch. Overhead, the brown birds were flitting from branch to branch, restless but silent, not a whistle out of them. Her hand tightened on the stunrod, and she went back to watching the hunter kneeling on the dead leaves.

"I have drugs that would make a rock sing arias. I could turn your head inside out and get everything you know in less than an hour. Digby's techs have done their best to adjust them to Impix bodies, but there's an appreciable chance you'd end up dead or mindless. Having a certain degree of distaste for that kind of thing, I'd prefer to deal rather than drug."

"You'd have to catch me first. Seems to me it's you who're caught."

"Appearances are somewhat misleading, Yseyl. I gave you a clue a while back, but you overlooked it. Too bad. I see I'm going to have to illustrate my point."

The black bird darted at Yseyl, its talons struck her hand, knocked the stunrod from her grasp and slashing through the skin before it went sweeping away. At the same moment, the brown birds began mobbing her, pecking and screeching. Other black birds were stooping at her, striking her buttocks, her shoulder, pecking at her eyes, tearing her skin.

As she tried to fight them off, she lost her balance and fell from the tree.

The hunter caught her before she hit the ground, spun her around and in a couple of seconds had first her wrists then her ankles wrapped in tape that stuck to itself and wouldn't yield to the strongest pull she could manage.

Face impassive, eyes cool and patient, the hunter stood a few paces off and watched her struggle.

"Point?" she said finally.

Yseyl lay still, lids lowered to hide the rage in her eyes. "Point," she said. "Let me go."

"Not quite yet. Not till you stop thinking about how to kill me. No, I don't read minds, but what you're emoting is like print to me. You're set to come at me the minute you see a chance." She clicked her tongue against her teeth, a series of small irritated sounds. "All that means is that I'd use your own stunner on you and then have to wait around till you woke up again. Stupid waste of time."

Yseyl drew a long breath and tried to calm the roar in her blood. After a moment she said, "A clue?"

"I told you, Digby collects talents. I'm one of those."

"Ah. What are you going to do now?"

"Well, first I take care of the damage those birds did to you. Then we get back to negotiating."

While the hunter bent over a backpack, fitting the medkit into its pocket, Yseyl brought the hands the woman had freed around in front of her, smoothed her fingers along the fake skin sprayed over the wounds from the black beaks; it was as if she were a photograph and the wounds had been painted out, no pain, no give to the touch, no nothing. She reached down and tried to pull loose the tape about her ankles.

A chuckle brought her head up.

The hunter was sitting on her heels, watching her. "My name's Shadith," she said. "Call me Shadow. There's not a knife made that will cut a tangler tape. I have to key it loose."

"Do it."

"In a while. I've a strong feeling you'll listen better if you can't disappear into the mountains."

"Then give me something to listen to."

"Right. The Fence is created and kept in being by a group of satellites, ancient clunkers that have been up there since the Ptaks drove your ancestors out of the rest of Ambela. Ptaks being what they are, they do as little as possible to keep them maintained and operational. Why fiddle with something that works perfectly well with a minimum of attention?"

Yseyl grimaced. "Your idea is we go up there and do something to those satellites?" She'd kept picking at the tape but was ready to concede defeat; it was too snug to push over her feet, and she hadn't managed to loosen it to any perceptible degree.

"Simpler than that. The Ptaks do oversight from the ground, course corrections and other routine things that don't require replacing components. The ground they've chosen to do it from is here on Impixol. Secrecy, I suppose. Or convenience—in Ptak terms, at least. Or maybe it was a requirement of the tech they used way back when they set up the system. Hunh! If it ain't broke, don't mess with it. Waste of good coin. I got a fair look at the place." She grinned, the outline of the bird branded into her face jumping as the muscles moved. "Through the eyes of a bitty creature like a worm with fur."

Yseyl fought to resist the seduction of that voice, the warm rich tones that caressed the ear, the laughter that seemed to lie just below the surface. *Shadith . . . Shadow . . . that's a good name for her . . . remember she's a shadow, you can't get hold of it and it changes when the sun moves.* Shadow was doing it deliberately, Yseyl was convinced of it, using her voice to ooze behind the thinking mind. *Don't let her get you, Pixa. Keep your eyes on the cards so the trickster won't slide one in on you.* "Worm with fur? Must have been an ulho. So what are you saying?"

"Get me into that building, and I can give those satellites such a chewing over that the lot of them will have to be replaced not repaired. And the minute they go, the Fence is gone. All of it."

"What's to stop the Ptaks from doing what you said, replacing the satellites and putting the Fence back up."

"Not my business, that. Me, I'll be on to my next assignment." She grimaced. "If Digby doesn't give me the boot for getting involved with locals."

Yseyl glanced at Shadow, then looked down. She picked up a dead leaf, began breaking pieces off it, watching them fall. "Why do you need me?"

"I don't. I may find the Fence and the mindset that made it appalling, but I find lots of things appalling. I'm not about to go round setting the universe right. I'm not even sure I know what right is. I'm being lazy, you know. If I worked at it, I could probably find reasons enough to blow a dose of babble into you, go get the gadget and take off. Don't push it, Ghost. Where was I? Oh, yes. To get into the Control Center without rousing the whole base, I'll need the disruptor. Their security's laughable, but that one building's shielded and I don't have your talent for fooling scanners."

Yseyl dropped the last of the leaf, brushed her hands together. "But I could get in?"

"I expect you mean I should tell you what to do and let you go do it. If it were something simple like punching a flake in a slot, well, no problem. But from what I've seen, that equipment is so old, the software so overlaid with layer on layer of accretion, centuries of accretion, I have to be there to work my way through it. You couldn't, you don't have the training."

So very plausible, Yseyl thought, anger acid in her throat. *So very good at making lies taste sweet. If they are lies. I don't know what to think. I don't know your kind.* She plucked at the narrow white tape around her ankles. *If I could just get loose. . . .*

"Why should I trust you?" she burst out. "If I decide to go with this, I have to bring out the disruptor. All you have to do is take it and leave me with nothing but a memory of pretty words."

"I don't have to deal. Remember?" Shadow tapped the

pack resting beside her knee. "One squirt from the pharmacopoeia and you'll tell me anything I want to know."

"You keep saying that. Why don't you just do it?"

"That a challenge? All right. You'd babble, but I've a feeling you hid the gadget in a hole in the ground. You could tell me where the hole is and chances are I'd walk right over it without seeing it. I'd find it eventually, but why waste all that time? More practical for you to fetch it yourself."

Shadow twisted her face into a grimace she probably thought was comical. Yseyl found herself unable to appreciate the hunter's attempts at humor. The tape round her ankles was strangling more than bones. "If I say do your worst, what happens?"

"I give you a few minutes to think it over, then I shoot you full of goop and record the pearls that fall from your lips."

"Do we do this thing with just the two of us, or do you have friends waiting for your call?"

Shadow smiled at her. "I do my recruiting on the ground. You saw some of my troops a little while ago. No, I know you meant people. If I could guarantee everything would go by plan, the two of us could handle the job."

"Hunh. That never happens. There's always a crack you have to patch."

"You're so right. You think you could come up with say five or six people you can trust? When I say trust, I mean they won't shoot themselves in the foot, they can take orders without playing games, and they won't chatter about this once it's over."

For the first time Yseyl's doubts began to fade. She dropped her eyes to hide the glow, then swore at herself because she'd forgotten that Shadow could read every emotion that passed through her body. She felt a surge of distaste; it was almost more of an invasion than reading minds. She drew in a long breath, let it out, and looked the hunter in the eye. "I've walked alone for thirty years. I'll have to find strangers and it won't be easy. In Linojin, either people are religious and sworn to serve without arms or they've had their fill of fighting." She sighed. "But if you went where the real killers are, out among the phelas, I also doubt you'd find many interested in stopping the war."

3. The search

Zot grinned and came trotting over when Yseyl beckoned to her. "Missed you," she said. "The incomers the past week have been mostly real boring."

Yseyl led Zot around a corner to get away from the ears of the guidepack overseer, handed her half a dozen coppers. "Pay off your whip, hm? Tell her you've got a client for the next three, four days."

"Four days? Akamagali!" She rubbed the elastic tip of her nose, stared at the ground. "You know I got to be back in Hall by an hour after sundown? I stay out all night, I lose my place in the pack."

"No problem."

Zot's grin flashed again, then she whipped around the corner, was back in half a breath. "She wanted to know who and what I was gonna do, I said it was a Pilgrim I took to the Grand Yeson a couple days ago, now she wants to pray at all the shrines."

"Zot, if I was the kind to worry, I'd fuss myself about how fast and easy you lie."

Zot giggled. "Vumah vumay, you aren't, so you won't."

"True. Had breakfast?"

"Yeh. They shovel us outta bed round sunup and feed us. Usual slop."

"So you could eat some more."

"I can always eat."

"That teashop's open?"

"Yeah. And they make graaaand womsi buns, and it's still early enough they'll be hot from the oven."

Yseyl watched Zot devouring the big soft bun, a dot of the white icing on the tip of her nose. A powerful wave of affection for the femlit rolled over her, something she couldn't remember ever feeling before.

Zot pushed in the last bite, looked up, her cheeks distended like a yeph at nut-fall. "Good stuff," she said, the words muffled by the bread in her mouth. She gave the mouthful another few chews, washed it down with a gulp of tea, then sat waiting for Yseyl to tell her why she was here.

Yseyl shifted around so she was leaning against the wall, one knee crooked and resting on the booth seat; she lifted the tea bowl, took a sip, cradled it against her chest. "I've been up in the mountains for the past week. Anything interesting happen?"

"Funny you should ask. Yeh. There's a huge hoohaw going on. This femlit, s'posed to come from way over in Khokuhl, least that's what she says, me, I think she's got futhus eating her brain, anyway, she says a Messenger of God brought her here with her anya, anya's kinda sick, xe was in egg and the anyalit that hatched out, it bit her wrong and she almost went off, but the femlit says the Messenger of God saved her anya, anyway something did, but that's not what's got ol' Humble Haf running to talk to her, and the Venerable Whosit the Prophet Speaker and even ol' Noxabo went squinnying around to get the tale from the jomayl's teeth and the Anyas of Mercy are lighting candles and just about everybody's talking like they got the runs of the mouth, No, it's 'cause the femlit she says the Messenger of God told her the Fence is com ing down. Before the moon is new again, she says, the Fence will be gone. All gone."

"Folks believe her?"

"For sure. Lots of 'em. Well, most of this lot would believe anything just about. Long as someone said God said it anyway. And them that don't want it to happen, even they gettin' nervous."

"That is interesting."

"You sound like you think it's maybe true. I know. You saw something out in the mountains, din't you. Tell me, huh?"

"Zot. . . ."

"No. Tell me, or I'm going back right now." She pushed along the seat until she was perched at the very edge, her hands flat on the table, that absurd dot of icing falling away as she glared at Yseyl.

Yseyl was briefly angry, then amused. "T'k, young Zot, try that on someone who doesn't know you. I'll say this much. I think I met your femlit's Messenger Not from God."

Zot's grin threatened to split her face in half. She slid back along the bench, leaned across the table and whispered, "You gonna do it, aren't you. You gonna take down the Fence."

"Think what you want."

Zot straightened, snatched the last bun and broke off a big piece. "So. What you want me to do?"

"I need some people with guns who know how to use them. Not crazies and not types who'll use them on me."

"Yeep, that's not gonna be easy. How many?"

"Five maybe six."

"Hm. There's One-Eye Baluk, he's got a stable of face-breakers he rents out when one of the merchants wants to collect a debt or a coaster captain is after a sailor who went for a walk and forgot to come back." She scratched alongside her nose, shook her head. "They're all

dumber'n rocks. 'Sides, I think Baluk don't want things
to change, and he'd be apt to bop you on the head if he
thought you could really do something about the Fence.
Nah, you want fighters, you not gonna find them inside
Linojin." She chewed on the bun, her brows drawn down,
her eyes focused on air.

Yseyl leaned against the wall feeling peculiar. She'd
been alone since Crazy Delelan disappeared. Whenever
she was with other people, she didn't connect with them,
only used them. She was using Zot, that was the same,
but how she felt about the child, that was different. Like
the femlit was hatched from her egg, learned from her
hand. It made her queasy, as if she'd picked up some kind
of disease.

Another thought struck her suddenly and curdled the
tea in her upper stomach. If she messed up Zot's life,
she'd have to do something to make up for that. She
couldn't just walk off and say *tough* and forget about it as
she'd done before. Vumah vumay, she could, but she'd
feel like the stuff you scrape off your foot if she did.

Zot straightened, wriggled her nose. "I think maybe
hohekil who just got here would be the best place to
look. Whyn't you let me go talk to a couple people I
know. How soon you need the shooters?"

Yseyl pushed away from the wall. "Keep it easy, Zot.
No hurry." She slid along the seat, got to her feet. "No
hurry at all."

The next several days while Zot ferreted about, Yseyl
did her own looking and listening.

Pilgrims swarmed about Mercy House, waiting to see
the femlit. Slipping around the edges of the crowd, Yseyl
heard them calling for the Holy Child, heard excited, in-
coherent chatter about miracles. Fem, mal, or anya, it
didn't matter; tone, sign and fervor were the same.

Each day the excitement built. The Pilgrims walked the

streets between the House where they waited for the
Anyas to bring out the Child and the wharves where they
stared at the golden flickers of the Fence wondering aloud
if they were going to be among the blessed who got to see
the Fence come down.

In the market the merchants were ambivalent. If the
Fence vanished, none of them could figure how it would
affect them. Life in Linojin hadn't changed in generations, and they wanted it to stay like that. Maybe they
grumbled about irritations and inconveniences and the id-
iocies of the Council of Religious who ran the place, but
these were familiar irritations. Moving from the familiar
to the unknown frightened many of them.

Along the wharves there was a similar mix of feeling
with a spicing of wary skepticism and a lot of tentative
preparations. The captains of the coastal steamers kept an
eye on the Fence and each other and sent their navigators
to the Yeson's library for any information they could
scrounge about the world beyond the Fence. These mals
and fems knew what Yseyl had picked up from the hohekil who came into the city to listen to the Child. In the
villages along the coast there was impatience, irritation, a
pent up need for space that was going to explode soon,
whether the Fence came down or not. *Zot was wiser than
me. I should have thought of the villages before. Hm.
Don't need to worry about getting the word out. Soon as
the Fence goes down, the coast is going to look like a
futhu nest somebody's kicked.* She contemplated the
thought with considerable satisfaction. It made her deal-
ings with the offworlder easier to swallow.

She certainly didn't regret giving up on the Arbiter. He
drew his power from the hohekil running from the war.
This was their last hope and he controlled access to it. Let
the Fence be removed, and there was no more reason for
anyone to listen to him. *I was really stupid,* she thought,
I didn't think it through. Even Cerex knew I couldn't get

anyone actually to use the disruptor, no one important,
anyway. Politics, pah! I'm a thief, and I fall on my face
every time I forget that.

Yseyl came back to her room on the fourth day to find
Zot sitting on the bed, her biggest grin blooming as the
door opened.

Zot bounced on the mattress, so full of herself she almost took flight as she slid off it and came running toward Yseyl. "Kumba did it," she said. She caught hold of
Yseyl's hand, tugged her through the door. "He's this
mallit I knew before he got in trouble because he sorta
stole things, I mean he could wiggle into places you
wouldn't even think was places . . ." She broke off as she
reached the stairs, clattered down them and stood waiting
impatiently in the foyer for Yseyl to join her.

When they were in the street, Zot kept her voice low,
but her excitement was such the words seemed to burst
from her. ". . . but this mal who used to buy what he got,
he was cheating him, and when he got smart enough to
know what was happening, he wouldn't bring him stuff
anymore, and the mal sent a whisper round, and Kumba
got booted out from the Hall." She gulped in a breath,
looking round to make sure no one was paying attention
to them. "Anyway, we stayed friends and sometimes he
banks his stuff with me till he can find a buyer, so I
thought about him, but it took a while to find him. I told
him what you wanted and why, don't get mad, he had to
know so he'd know what to look for, but I din't tell him
who. Anyway he says there this Pixa ixis or what's left of
it, there's one old fem and her bond anya, xe's got joint
problems and don't get around too good, two femlits—
one of 'em kinda sick, she's in the Mercy hospital with
the old anya—three young fems, and two anyas. The
bunch of 'em went hohekil and just got here and already
they got trouble."

She tapped Yseyl's arm, and they turned into a narrow alley between two large hostels. "Over one of the anyas, well, you know anyas are kinda sparse on the ground these days, free anyas anyway, and even the Anyas of Mercy they got to watch themselves. This mal he started hanging round the anya, xe's living outside the wall in Fishtown, things get kinda wild there sometimes. That's where we're going now, I wanna show 'em to you. Vumah vumay, he wouldn't leave xe alone, kept offering money and other stuff and paying xe no mind when xe say back off. The mal he tried grabbing xe and xe's fembond she beat the thuv outta him, but he's kin to one of the Arbiter's guard, so he goes and gets himself some bigtime help. . . ." She grinned at the guard lolling beside the small archway, tossed him a coin and darted through, then stood dancing from foot to foot, once again waiting for Yseyl.

". . . but the rest of the ixis, even the old 'un, the Heka, they land on those fugheads so hard they crying for Mam and Baba." An unpaved path led from the arch toward a clutch of small dark structures built on stilts just beyond the dune line of the bay shore. There were a number of fishboats in various states of repair drawn up on the sand and clutches of old mals seated near them repairing nets. Other mals and fems and some children walked slowly along the shore, digging out shellfish and picking up drift the tide had left behind. The path itself was empty for the moment and Zot plunged ahead, still riding the high of an excitement that was beginning to bother Yseyl. If the child had set her hopes on coming along. . . .

"Anyway, I figure, first, these fems and anyas they're tough and they fight good, second, they jezin sure know they better be somewhere else for a while, third, from what Kumba tells me they really really hate the Fence, he says Luca, she's the fem stomped that mal, she goes out and stares at the Fence like she wants to stomp it worse'n

that mal. They got a tent on the far side of that lot there."
Zot pointed.

The Pixa hohekils lived in a series of ragged tents
pitched in the woods that grew outside Linojin's southern
wall, a stretch of brushy wasteland separating them from
the village.

Yseyl dropped her hand on Zot's shoulder. "You did
good, sounds exactly what I want. Did you set up a
meeting?"

"No. I figured you'd want to take a look at them first."

Yseyl smiled at her. "How did you get to be so smart?
Just born that way, I suppose. Never mind." She dropped
to a squat beside the path, patted a tuft of grass beside
her. "Sit yourself and tell me the rest of what you found
out about them. The more I know, the better the bargain
I can make."

Zot settled on the grass, legs crossed, hands slapping
on her knees to emphasize the points she thought were
important. "Ah-huh, so. They call themselves the Remnant of Shishim, all their mals are dead, even the little
ones. There's the Heka, her name is Wintshikan, her
anya's called Zell. Zell's the one in the Mercy hospital
with the femlit, she's called Zaro. They aren't real sick,
but traveling here was hard on 'em. Then there's a fem
called Xaca who mostly takes care of them and the other
femlit, her name's Kanilli. Then there's two sets of fem-
anya bonds, they're kinda wild. There's Luca and Wann,
Wann's the one the mal tried to go off with, and there's
Nyen and Hidan. The others were settling down well
enough, but those four, they don't really fit in the villages
and there's for sure no place for them inside Linojin." She
took a deep breath. "Kumba picked up a lot of gossip
about them, thing is they got here with a good store of
coin and a bunch of jomayls, got more coin selling all but
a couple of the jomayls, made people curious, you know,
'cause Pixas mostly don't get here with much but the

clothes on their backs and maybe a gun or two. Well, you know, femlits talk, even Pixa femlits, so word gets out. Seems there was this band of robbers on the Peddler's Trace, they'd done a lot of Pilgrims and peddlers and hohekil coming over Kakotin Pass, but the Remnant did them this time and got all their stuff. Vumah vumay, Luca and the rest of the younger ones, they kinda make folk nervous and when you put the gossip with what happened to the mal, well, like I said, better they find somewhere else to be for a while." Zot twitched her mouth and wrinkled her nose. "That's about it."

"Hm." Yseyl got to her feet. The child seemed calmer now; time to try easing her away. "Zot, I want you to point out their tent, then stay out of sight. Hush! I've got a reason. I don't want them connecting you with me. Depending on what happens when we talk, I might want you watching them. Understand?"

Zot's face lost the last of its glow and settled into its usual tough, alleyrat cynicism. "I hear you," she said and jumped up. "You want me to go ahead now so the others don't see us together."

To Yseyl those words read *I know what you're doing, it's what everybody does, use me, then shove me away like a dirty snotrag.* A fist closed round her heart and she knew, whatever it cost, she couldn't do that to the child. Zot was in this till the Fence came down. If she was hurt or killed, well, better that than another shove down the road Yseyl herself had taken. *Jish! What's happening to me? Can't even make a plan and stick to it. I don't want this . . . I can't deal with . . . that femlit . . . under my skin . . . why did I take her out of that pack . . . I know well enough . . . something about her reminded me of me . . . I just wish she'd let it go . . . let me go . . . I'm the worst choice she could have made. Until the Fence is down . . . what about after? No, I can't . . . there's no . . . I'll have to get away from here. Cerex? I could give him that call.*

Or Digby? There's no time to think about it now. I don't want to think about it. God!

She turned her shoulder to Zot and scowled at the scrubby trees, hacked about till they were half dead because of the campers' need for firewood. The tents were mostly old, patched sails passed on by coasters as part of their inkohel duty to the Yeson, turned a yellowish-gray by salt, sun, and age. Children played in the dirt outside a number of these tents, chals fought or slept by them, old fems and a very few old mals dozed or worked on this and that, leather crafts or repairing shirts and trousers that had already been repaired so often they had more darns than cloth. The breeze that wandered past was bitter with the stench of urine and hopelessness.

"Don't be silly," Yseyl said, an edge of irritation on the words. "Looking from their direction, guiding me is one thing, sitting in on the conversations is another. You take me to the camp, then you find Kumba and see if he's come up with some more possibles. I need one, preferably two more for this phela. And don't go getting ideas that I'm leaving you out. You're not a fighter, femlit, but you're small, which could be useful, and clever and God knows we do need brains somewhere."

Zot stared at her a moment longer, then she grinned and with an absurd little skipping hop, she started off along the dim footpath that went around the outside of the tent city.

The tent was set apart from the others, two jomayls beside it in a corral improvised from braided leather ropes; a femlit was in the corral with them, going over the smallest jomayl with a stiff-bristled brush. A radio sat in the dust near a fem braiding leather thongs into what looked to be a short whip. An anya was curled on a blanket beside her, reading a small, battered book. Another anya sat at xe's feet, carving a piece of wood; what xe was making Yseyl couldn't say.

She stood watching the scene, suddenly back sitting at the feet of Crazy Delelan, smelling the sweet bite of sida wood as the anya carved wheels for her toy wagon. They weren't all bad, those days; it was just that she found it too painful before this to remember the good times.

Zot's whisper broke through her rememberings, brought her back to the needs of the moment. "That one with the thongs, that's Luca. The anya with the book is Wann and the one carving is Hidan. Go get 'em." A soft giggle and a scrape of leaves, then Zot was gone, following instructions.

Yseyl swallowed, no matter how successful a thief she was, no matter how many arms dealers she'd stalked and killed, trying to persuade people to do things made her feel inadequate. She straightened her shoulders and strolled over to stand in front of Luca. "My name is Yseyl. I've got a proposition for you."

4. The final dissolution of the Remnant

Wintshikan looked up as the door opened. Luca came in, then Nyen, Wann, and Hidan.

Luca nodded to Zell, then to Zaro in the other bed. She brought her hand around and held out the case of Tale Cards. "We need you to read for us, Heka."

Wann brought Wintshikan the Heka's Shawl, setting it about her shoulders. +It's important.+

Wintshikan took the case, looked at it, looked up at Luca. "What is it?"

Luca clasped her hands behind her. "It's because you've got the sight, Heka, you always had it even when you wouldn't believe what you saw." She turned her head so she could see the others. "Well?"

Hidan and Nyen were standing with their backs against the panels. Hidan signed. +All clear. Go ahead.+

Luca nodded, fixed her eyes on Wintshikan. "Remember what I said when we saw . . . um . . . the ocean for the first time?" Her mouth twitched into a brief, taut smile. "A fem offered us a chance to redeem that pledge. I want to know is the chance real or is she pulling something for reasons I can't see."

"She?" Wintshikan slipped the cards from the case, unwrapping the silk scarf folded around them. She set the case on the bed beside Zell, spread out the scarf, sat holding the cards.

"A Pixa fem. She said she was the one in the song, the little gray ghost. I think maybe she is. You look in her eyes, and it's cold as winter and you see a hungry boyal thinking you're food." She shivered.

"You and Wann, Nyen and Hidan, you're thinking of going with her. Is Xaca?"

"No. We've talked it over, she wants to stay with Kanilli; us, we don't have daughters to worry about. I want this, Heka. You know how much."

"I know." Wintshikan murmured the blessing over the cards and shuffled them. She lifted her head. "Let it be my touch alone. I am Shishim. The last of Shishim."

With a jagged gesture, Luca called the others around her. They stood together, shoulders touching shoulders, watching as Wintshikan cut the cards and laid them out on the bed beside Zell.

Wintshikan's breath quickened as she saw the base card was no longer the black oval of formal Death, but a sign of approval. She touched the card with the tip of her forefinger. "This defines us. As you can see, it is the Fire on the Altar. This that you do, Luca, Wann, Nyen, Hidan, you do in the service of God." She moved her finger to the first of the three cards in the middle row. "These are the determinants that mark the days to come. The first card is a warning. The SkyFire. Danger, quickness, the unexpected coming at you. Be fast on your feet and never forget to look behind you. The second describes that which surrounds you. It is the Cauldron which brews both poison and health. Think well what you do. The third is the Gateway that looks forward and back. Again a choice. A turning point. I can't tell you what to do because I don't know what that choice will be. Whatever you decide, you will have my blessing and Zell's."

She touched the first card in the top row. "These are the guides to direct us to the Right Path. The Egg. Out of your actions in the days to come a new world will be born. The Balance. If I read this true, the War will end, and life will right itself at long last. It may be what I want to see, but my heart says this will happen."

She moved the remaining cards from her lap, set them on the white sheet beside Zell, and got to her feet with some difficulty, her joints protesting. Eyes blurring with tears, she hugged each of them hard, held each for a long moment before she let her or xe go. Then she stepped back. "Go with God and the blessing of Shishim."

9

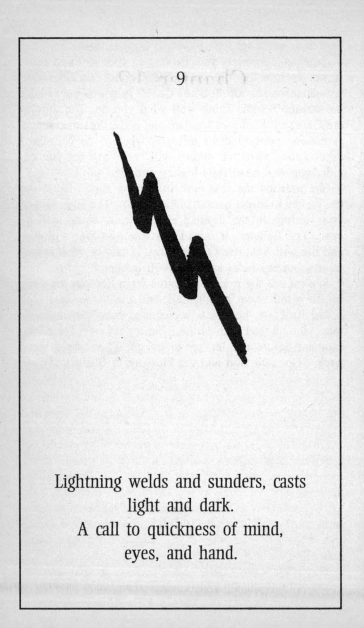

Lightning welds and sunders, casts
light and dark.
A call to quickness of mind,
eyes, and hand.

Chapter 12

1. Waiting

Shadith inspected what she'd drawn, closed her eyes, and dug into memory for more details about the Ptakkan base. She added another group of small houses to the complex beyond the Control Center, wiped at the sweat trickling from her hairline, and glanced at the sky.

The day was hot, and the air in this mountain pocket hardly moved. The sun had sunk behind the pointed tops of the conifers surrounding the meadow, and a few clouds were drifting into the ragged circle of blue overhead. No sign of Yseyl. She glanced at the locals squatting by a small fire, passing around a pan of stewed tea and talking quietly, all but young Zot who was moving restlessly about, jumping the stones in the creek on the far side of the meadow, squatting to toss pebbles at the fish that made thin wavery shadows in the clear water.

She watched Zot a moment, frowning. When she'd objected to having her involved in this business, Yseyl's face had gone dark with anger and her eyes had a glitter that said *I won't listen to this*. So she let it drop.

Zot aside, it was an odd team Yseyl had brought, two Imps and four Pixas, and it should have been too explosive to work. The only thing they shared was being hohekil.

The mals were Impix brothers from a farm outside Gajul. Khimil and Syon. After the farm was burned to the dirt and the rest of the family killed by Pixa phelas,

Khimil and Syon lived in Gajul a while, then began working their way along the coast as sailors, cutpurses, laborers, whatever it took to survive. Yseyl said they hated the war, hated the Fence so much they'd work with anyone to drop it, even Pixas, though it did help that these Pixas were fems and anyas. They were short and wiry, hunger and rage lines aging their angular, bony faces, and they were seldom still, hands busy, eyes moving continually.

Luca and Wann, Nyen and Hidan looked calmer, though that was all surface; beneath the skin there was the same anger and determination. They were more uneasy about this collaboration than the brothers, but they were also intensely focused on the goal.

Shadith began making star crosses to indicate the trees growing on the slopes leading up to the rim of the caldera, trying to get the patches in proper orientation with the settlement. It passed the time and until Yseyl got back, she had nothing to say to the team. If Yseyl bothered to return. She couldn't be sure about that; the thread of trust between the little gray ghost and her was very fragile indeed.

"What's that?"

Shadith looked up. Zot was standing beside her, hands clasped behind her back as she scowled at the drawing.

"A map. I'm trying to remember everything and set it down."

"That's where we're going?"

"Mm."

"Is that a wall, that outside line?"

"Of a kind. Do you know about volcanoes?"

Zot snorted. "I may be an orphan, but I'm not ignorant."

"Well, this is supposed to be the rim around one of them. These squiggles here, they're supposed to be trees growing on the slopes that lead up to the rim. We'll go to ground in them once we get there and wait for things to get quiet."

"Hunh." Syon had drifted over from the fire while she was talking. "What's that got to do with taking the Fence down?"

"When Yseyl gets back, I'll explain. No point in repeating myself. But if you want, I'll tell you about the map now."

His grin wiped the hardness from his face, and she realized quite suddenly how young he was. "Hoy!" he yelled, "Khimil, rest of you, come over, take a look at this."

Shadith drew her finger along the outer line. "The Ptak base sits at the bottom of this caldera like soup in the bottom of a bowl. It's near the end of the mountain range we're sitting in right now. About as far north as you can go."

Luca frowned. "How many days' travel?"

"Riding? Probably more than a month. We won't be riding, we'll be flying." She flickered her fingers in anya laughter. "Offworld machines. One-way trip is around three hours. But it'll take at least two trips to ferry you all there, so getting everyone into place ready to go will use up the afternoon and most of the night. We won't be moving on the base until. . . ." She raised her head as she heard the hum of lifters, *reached* out, relaxed as she touched Yseyl. The ghost was flying low, beneath the treetops, so Ptak cameras wouldn't catch her.

She brushed by one of the trees and brought the miniskip down on its struts. After a shake to convince herself it was steady, she shut off the lifters, dismounted, and reached for the black case strapped to the carryhopper.

Zot squealed and ran across to her. She almost but didn't quite touch Yseyl, instead she slid her hand along the bar, touched the roomy saddle, then giggled. "Looks like a broom with feet. How come it flies?"

Shadith stood. "Might as well leave the disruptor where it is, Ghost. Come join us."

2. Setting up the raid

"... do that, I'll need time and quiet to shut down the Fence generators and infect the programs. So...." She tapped the maze of small, interlocking squares. "These are the living quarters. When I was watching them a few weeks ago, the Ptaks were all inside after sundown, but you can see the houses are linked together—um, these are glass arcades and they'll be lit up like Gajul on a Feast night. A good number of the Ptaks on duty there spent half the night going from house to house, talking and partying; when they sleep, it's in bursts of two to three hours so there's usually someone awake. Which could be a problem because they don't like feeling closed in, so most of those houses are more window than wall. You'll need to remember that there are lots of eyes around. Once we reach the lake, there'll be less danger of discovery. We'll have trees and bushes for cover." She jerked her thumb at the clouds. "Radio says there's a storm front moving in. With a little luck we might have some rain up north. That'll keep the restless inside."

She touched the largest of the squares. "This is the building we have to get into. The Control Center. It's shielded and there's only one door. To get through that door, the Center's kephalos has to recognize you and you have to have a card key. T'k. Never mind all that, my tongue got behind my teeth and I couldn't see what I was saying. Shield means there's something like a cousin to the Fence around the outside and across the roof of that building. The shield can recognize who's supposed to pass through it, stop everyone else even if they have the proper key. If you touched it, it wouldn't kill you, it'd be more like someone slammed you hard with a staff and you'd be unconscious for a good while. Um, this doesn't mean they're expecting you people to attack, it's more to keep out offworld agents and spies. Ptaks are like that. Overlooking them makes them nervous."

Luca tapped her fingers on her knee, glanced from the map to Shadith's face. "You've got a way in?"

"Yseyl has. In will be easy enough. It's getting out that may be something of a problem. I already told you what I'm going to be doing, but you need to know this—the minute I start interfering with the programming, over on Ptak-K'nerol they'll know about it and they'll be on the com yelling for the base Exec to do something. Um. A com is a kind of offworld radio. No way I can block that. So we'd better be prepared to deal with aroused, frightened, angry Ptaks. And they'll have energy weapons. Unless we're sneaky and successful at it, some of us could be killed before we reach the hollow and the flier. I want you to be thinking about that. Hm. Energy weapons. . . ."

Shadith shook a dull gray rod from her sleeve, a small thing, barely longer than her hand. "You see that rock where Zot was sitting? Right. Stay back and whatever you do, don't get in front of me." She flicked the beam setting to its finest mode, touched the sensor and sliced through the stone, then clicked on the safety. "You don't think anything happened, do you? Khimil, go take a close look at that rock. Try to lift it and see what happens."

The rock fell in two pieces, the inside surfaces so smooth they shone like mirrors. The mal dropped them in his astonishment, then pushed at one of the pieces with the toe of his boot. "That thing wouldn't pay much mind to flesh and bone, would it?"

"Right. I doubt the Ptaks will use cutters like this, too much damage to their property. More likely they'll have pulsers, sweet little things that'll shake you into jelly without breaking the skin. I want you all to understand this before you commit to coming with Yseyl and me. All of you could end up very painfully and messily dead."

Syon closed his bright yellow eyes into slits, wagged his head. "Vumah vumay, it's no worse than being clubbed or shot or bored to death."

Luca nodded. "If you really do bring the Fence down, who cares what happens after."

"I care," Shadith said. "I intend to come out of this alive and intact. Look, from what Yseyl told me about you all, you're good at sliding into and out of places without getting nailed. If we have to fight, we do, but I'd certainly rather not. Now." She bent over the map. "Once we break loose, here's how I figure we get out. . . ."

3. At the target

Shadith wormed through the patch of brush that grew across the top of a long slant of scree, moving slowly so she wouldn't shake the tops of the bushes. The morning was heavily overcast, with an erratic wind blowing, wind that set the branches swaying, the thorns on them snagging in her clothes and hair. She was soaked with perspiration by the time she reached a place where she had an unobstructed view of the base a couple of miles below.

She snapped the glareshields onto the binocs, adjusted the focus, swept the field of view across the base. Nothing had changed; Ptaks wandered about, some were swimming in the lake, some working in the communal gardens, two young males in full mating plumes were doing a dance-fight while half a dozen others watched. Several times sleek female techs in white coats went into the Control Center, others came out. It was busier than before. She didn't know what that meant. Trouble?

She watched a while longer. A peaceful scene, no sign

of worry in any of the faces or bodies. Only that increasing flurry about the Center. She sighed. "Got to see what that means."

She gave the binocs to Luca with instructions on how to use them, told the others to take turns watching the base and getting familiar with the patterns of movement. "I want each of you to choose what you think is the best route to the lake; we'll run through them as soon as you've all had your shot with the binocs. Zot, stay by me and keep watch, if you see or hear anything that bothers you, slap my arm." She nodded as Yseyl raised a brow. "Yes, I'm going mindwalking for a while. There're some things I need to check."

Stretched out on a blanket, arm over her eyes, she went feeling about in the walls of the Center for a young and lively furslug. She found her mount rippling along on its double line of tiny legs, climbing a stud in the wall, and sniffing about for woodchewers. He wriggled and fussed and nearly fell before she completed her hold, clicking his teeth in extreme unhappiness as she prodded him into climbing higher, then humping along a rafter till he reached the crack she'd used for observation last time.

She gave him a quick workout, muscle against muscle, as a kind of long-distance patting, then settled him at the hole, his small bright eyes, predator sharp, sweeping the room below, his bare pink ears twitching and swiveling until they drew in the sound of Ptak speech.

". . . see what it's really like if we want more funding?"

"Vourts, what you want done with this checklist?"

"Anyone see number eight password files? I just about sifted the dust already."

Vourts adjusted her lenses, waved away the plastic covered sheet the other tech was trying to hand her. "Chitatri! That thing looks like a swarm of krees pissed all over it.

Print up a new copy and find a see-through that doesn't look like it's been here since year one."

"Where's that 'bot? There's a pile of kree shit in this drawer deep enough to drown in."

"Eight? Isn't that the one Tippa spilled the tasse of likken on at the year turn party? Ate through the cover and glued half the pages together. Should be paperwork on that somewhere around. Avo!"

" 'Bot's blown a bearing, Torml took it over to shop to see what Bijjer can do. Either wait or dump it yourself."

The young mal leaned out the door to his cubicle. "Hah?"

"You got the workup for eight?"

"Anybody remember which closet has the paper stores?"

"Number two, you gant. You think we want to haul tail feathers farther'n we have to? Parts in one, paper in two."

"Bearing? How in. . . ."

In spite of the verbal clutter, the cleanup was going quickly and efficiently enough, perhaps because the workers were limited to the techs with access to this building. By the time the Base Exec arrived, Shadith was seething with impatience. In all the chatter she still hadn't picked up any reason for this activity.

The Exec was a plump and self-important Ptak, a jowly male whose crest had a wet slickness as if he'd overdone the feather cream.

Vourts shooed the techs into a dusty, grubby line along the wall and joined them there, those anachronistic lenses glittering in the glare and doing a fair job of concealing her eyes.

The Exec nodded at them, but didn't speak as he stalked to the workstation at the end of the row. He pulled up a privacy shield and proceeded to enter his override key, three linked words in tripptakh, the broken word babble invented by parents for talking over their chil-

dren's heads. Shadith tucked the sequence into memory
and watched with amused astonishment as he called up
lists of passwords, eyes-only files, access logs, and other
artifacts of the techs' daily activities. With slow, labored
touches on the sensor board and constant consultation of
the notebook at his side, he changed the file names into
more tripptakh. When he finished, he grunted with satisfaction, logged off, and lowered the shields. He got to his
feet and snapped his fingers. As the techs broke the line
and went back to their cleaning, he wandered about the
room, kicking at debris and running his finger across surfaces, sneering at the dust he picked up.

At the door, he turned. "The Col-Kirag will be here in
two hours. Vourts, you and Ke'ik will be on duty here, go
get cleaned up. Rest of you, I want this place spotless by
the time that flier lands. And I'll expect you to be on line
with the honor guard ready for inspection. Drill Field. We
won't be making her climb ladders. For your ears only,
my sources say she's on a royal tear, some local git has
been putting out antiwar songs that are making the tourists nervous, at least they were before she blocked that
part of the feed. And that Cobben that fell over its feet
and did zip that they were supposed to—they screwed
death duties out of her and she's looking for hide to chew
on."

Shadith sat up, rubbed at her temples.

A hand touched her arm. Yseyl held out a mug of tea.
"Thought you might like this." She waited till Shadith got
down a few swallows, said, "Anything interesting?"

"Think so. We're about to be the benefactors of a bit of
luck I can brag I set up. The song that got you and the
rest of them. And a warning I slipped in." She swallowed
a gulp of tea. "Ah, that's good. It always feels like a gift
when doing the ethical thing turns out to be good tactics."

Yseyl raised her brows.

"Never mind. Just a stroke for my soul." Shadith finished the tea and set the mug beside her. "Time to concentrate on the practical. There'll be a juiced-up flier on that open ground by the lake. Very convenient. Means we don't have to head for the hollow which cuts the escape route nearly in half. And if we have a staying rain tonight, we could all get out intact."

4. Into the valley

The wind shifted and a spatter of rain caught Shadith in the face. She wiped her eyes clear and moved forward again, running bent low, two steps behind the child Zot who was ghosting along as silent as the older locals. It was a dreary night, heavily overcast, the wind erratic, sometimes there, sometimes not, the rain a weak but steady drizzle, just enough to make them all uncomfortable and the footing difficult. A grand night for sneaks, though. The Ptaks were inside where they were comfortable, warm and dry. No one would be out in this unless he had to.

She straightened when she reached the darkness under the trees at the edge of the Drill Field, took the disruptor case from Yseyl, and watched with amazement as the Pixa fem shimmered into a patch of mist and trotted toward the flier. *Little gray ghost? I was closer than I knew. Digby will skin me bald if I let this one get away. Nine dealers down the drain, so Cerex said. Didn't know what hit them. I can see why.*

Yseyl used the stunner. The field burned against Shadith's *reach*, like touching nettles it was. Twice. A sense of quick purposeful activity. Then a lull while she waited.

Shadith tapped Luca's arm, pointed.

The rain was coming down harder as Luca, Wann, and young Zot ran toward the flier, even though they lacked

Yseyl's gift, in the darkness they were only visible if the watcher knew where to look. When they reached the flier, there was a sudden flare of pale grayish light, a moonlight through clouds effect as Yseyl opened the hatch. Three dark shapes crossed the light, then it shrank and vanished as the door swung shut.

A moment later Yseyl was back. "They're in and ready," she muttered. "I gave Luca Cerex's stunrod in case there's trouble." She took the disruptor from Shadith. "Your job next."

They reached the thorn hedge without trouble. Even the nightbirds were huddling in their nests.

Bending over the cutter to shield it from the rain, Shadith shortened the blade and used millisecond bursts to slice through stems of the thornbush so they could clear a narrow path through it, angled so the cut wouldn't be easily visible from a short distance off.

When the six of them were inside the hedge, standing up to their ankles in sloppy mud, Shadith *reached* through the building. The strengthening rain hammering against her arm, she touched Hidan's shoulder. "I read two. You?" she murmured.

+Two. In the place with the big windows.+

"Right." Shadith leaned toward to Yseyl. "Third window from the end. There." She pointed at one of the storeroom windows. "Center the hole over that."

Yseyl activated the disruptor.

Because the Ptaks felt no need to provide visual clues to the shield round the Center, to the eye nothing seemed to be happening—and Shadith's *reach* only gave her a vague sense of agitation. She closed her eyes and scanned the field again. With the additional concentration she could read faint ripples in the field plane, flowing about a circular opening the size of her hand. *This is going to be a problem. When I scan, I can't see the window; when I see the window, I can't read the field.*

Hidan gasped.

Shadith swung round to face xe. +What?+ she signed, making the signs large so they'd be visible.

+A hole in nothing. I can thin it growing.+

Interesting. +Tell me when it stops growing.+ She took the climbing pole from the break-in kit she'd clipped to her belt, gave it the prescribed twist, and held it away from her as the memormel took its primary shape. When the form was stable, she set the base on the ground and waited.

+Now.+

"Is the whole window clear?" She pitched the words to carry above the hiss of the rain.

+Yes. By at least a handspan.+

+Good.+ She lifted the pole. "Hidan, warn me if this thing gets too close to the edge of the opening."

The pole touched the glass. Holding her breath she opened the jaws of the clamp on the end and began easing them toward the sill. Inch by inch, down and down until the jaws touched the wood. She glanced at Hidan.

+Still clear.+

"Good. If the pole gets less than a handwidth from the edge, stop me."

Hidan nodded.

Glancing repeatedly at the anya, she clamped the jaws on the sill, began tilting the pole downward, slowly slowly slowly—until the base end was jammed into the mud. She let out the breath she was holding, nodded her thanks to Hidan, and triggered the lockdown plate. When a hefty shove at the pole failed to move it, she wiped the rain off her face, stepped into the first half-stirrup, then went running up until she could touch the glass.

A suction cup in the center of the wide pane, four

quick slashes with the cutter, a shove, and the way was open.

Syon eased the pole into the empty storeroom, propped it in a corner and squatted beside it, a rifle across his knees, his eyes on the window.

Shadith pulled the knitted cowl over her head, smoothed it down, checked to make sure her eyes were clear. She glanced at the other hooded figures, squeezed the latch and eased the door open, slipped out into the hall and ghosted down it.

Shadith was several steps beyond the doorless arch that led into the workroom before the two techs noticed her. She stunned them, ran to Avo's office, located the keybook Vourts had used, and hurried back to the station with it.

While she leafed through the pages until she found the one she wanted, Khimil and Nyen dragged the techs away from workstations, tied their wrists and ankles, gagged and blindfolded them. Hidan stood guard at the door, sweeping round with xe's thinta, ready to whistle a warning if anyone came.

Shadith entered the Exec's override and began the tedious process of making sure none of the base cardkeys or access codes would breach the shield and open the door; the accretions were even worse than she'd suspected and tracking down all the files was a pain, though it did give her a feel for what she'd have to claw through when she began working on the satellite programming. Outside, the rain drummed against the windows, the wind wailed and whooped round the corners. Inside, Nyen and Khimil's boot heels were loud on the composition floor as they hurried about, gathering everything flammable they could find and dumping it on and around the other workstations. They spoke now and then, voices subdued.

At first all these sounds were distracting, but as Shadith

worked her way deeper into the Ptak system, they faded until she was no longer conscious of them.

5. The Holy Child

The sound of the door shutting woke Thann from troubled dreams. Xe's anyalit wriggled protest as xe sat up, so xe pushed a finger into xe's pouch for the infant to gum on. The babbit's eggteeth had fallen out and the new set wouldn't come in until the sixth month of the pouch year.

Isaho was gone, her covers thrown back, her clothes still folded on the stool at the foot of her bed. *Sleepwalking again?* Out wandering around somewhere wearing nothing but one of the starchy white nightgowns that Mercy Fisalin brought her clean each night? Thann rubbed the heel of xe's hand against xe's right eye, then the left, then drew xe's palm across xe's face, trying to wake up enough to decide what xe should do.

With a sigh, xe gave a last rub to the babbit's gums and freed xe's hand. Xe forced xeself up, pushed xe's feet into xe's sandals and pulled on the hatchry robe, fingers fumbling at the buttons that closed the neck opening. Xe couldn't count on the Mercys to notice Isaho and bring her back; they were asleep or busy at their prayers and meditations. If Isaho got outside.... Xe could thin the Pilgrims out there, hundreds of them, marching in endless circles about the House, chanting the shimbils, muttering blessings on the Holy Child. They frightened xe. The walls were too thick, and they were too far from the hospitality wing of the House for xe to hear them, but even so xe couldn't escape the terrible intensity of their yearning. If Isaho got outside and they saw her....

Xe thinta searched, touched Isaho, and started after her, as close to running as xe dared, the slap slap of xe's sandals loud and intrusive in the empty corridors. Dark corridors, lit by tiny oil lamps set a maximum distance apart.

* * *

Light flared ahead of xe.

Xe could thin Isaho coming toward xe. And Mercys. Dozens of them. As if the House were emptying itself.

Xe pressed against the wall and waited.

Isaho came round the corner, one of her hands nestling inside the Grand Mercy's. In the other she held a glass candle lamp, the flame of the candle casting odd upside down shadows on her face. Her eyes had that stony sheen that terrified Thann whenever xe saw it, and her lips were curved in a tight triumphant smile.

The other Mercys followed, two columns of them, hands gliding through the Praise Songs, the shadows they cast dancing across the walls, dancing across Thann as they swept past xe.

Xe followed them from the House and into the street.

Isaho started singing, her voice cutting through the noise from the crowd of Pilgrims. "God has told me," she sang. "God has spoken, God has promised, the Fence will fall, it falls tonight."

When xe heard that, Thann's stomachs turned to ice. Watching Isaho search faces everywhere for Mam, Baba, and Keleen after they passed through the Gate that first day was sad and troubling, and when her daughter began prophesying for the Mercys and the Pilgrims as if she were denying her grief again by using God as a shield, that was even harder to bear. But this. . . .

Xe didn't know which would be more terrible for Isaho—if the Fence stayed right where it was, or if it fell. And xe had no idea what xe could do.

The procession swept up Bond Sisters as it passed their House, sucked in more and more Pilgrims as it moved down to Progress Way. Prophet Speakers came to swell the mix as they moved past the Seminary and the Tent. Brothers poured from the Grand Yeson as they circled around it and headed down the wide avenue toward the Fish Gate and the seafront.

Thann's anyalit picked up the excitement around them and needed constant minding as xe tried to crawl out of the pouch and go scurrying up the handholds sewn into the front of the robe so xe could sit with xe's head out the neck opening and see what was happening. Xe walked with both hands pushed through the side slits in the hatchry robe so xe could catch the little wriggler and shove the questing head back past the pouch sphincter. It was a rather welcome distraction from xe's worry about Isaho, because all this activity meant the babbit was not only healthy but bright beyond xe's age.

As the procession reached the wharf, Thann tried to get closer to Isaho, but the press of the throng about her pushed xe aside. Afraid for xe's babbit, xe gave up the struggle and moved away until she came to a double bitt. Xe settled xeself with xe's legs hanging over the edge of the wharf, xe's back and side pressed against the bitts. Though xe couldn't see xe's daughter, xe could hear her as she sang the shimbil litany, the crowd of watchers answering her.

The golden glow of the Fence flickered on, constant as the beat of Thann's heart. Xe stroked the babbit's small head until xe went soft against xe's palm and withdrew into the pouch to curl up with the nipple in xe's mouth.

An hour passed.

Another.

The shimmer at the edge of the sky vanished.

Even the most fervent watchers were silent, even they didn't believe what they were seeing. They waited for the glow to come back. A soughing like the wind rising before a storm passed across the wharves as the thousands out here drew in a collective breath and held it.

Thann stared into the darkness and wondered about the offworlder who'd rescued them; it seemed a logical connection. Who else would know how to bring the Fence down?

"Praised be God, the Fence has fallen." Isaho's voice rang out, broke the spell that was holding the watchers silent.

A mal somewhere in the middle of the press shouted, "Miracle!"

More shouts.

Holy Child.

Messenger of God.

Bless us, Child.

Touch my hand.

Heal me.

Bless me.

Thann huddled against the bitts and tried to keep from being stepped on as xe watched two Brothers lift Isaho onto their shoulders.

Surrounded by Mercys and Bond Sisters and Brothers and Prophet Speakers, Isaho and the mals holding her pushed through the crowd toward the gate, chanting the Praises. Xe watched xe's daughter accept this adulation as her due, then xe leaned xe's head against the bitts, closed xe's eyes and mourned. Xe's daughter was gone; the Holy Child was a stranger with the same face.

6. Plotting the road to Change and a New Balance

Wintshikan closed her hand around Zell's as the Fence vanished. "They did it. I didn't believe they could, but they've done it."

She watched Zaro and Kanilli grab hold of Xaca's hand and the three of them join the rest of the Pixa hohekil on the beach in a wheeling, shouting, laughing dance. "I don't think my knees will hold out for that."

Zell waggled xe's hand in anya laughter.

* * *

They sat on the side of an abandoned boat and watched the celebration develop along the sands, merchants bringing out bottles of shwala and injyjy, hot meat pies, and roasted tatas. A drummer, a fiddler, and a flutemal met on the raised porch of a house a short distance off and started playing. Others were doing the same farther along the beach. Bonfires bloomed on the sand.

Wintshikan looked out to sea once again, rejoicing at the darkness at the edge of the sky—a darkness that meant the Fence was still down. She took a deep breath, let it out as she turned to her anya. "Zizi, I'm thinking that I want to stand in new mountains and watch the sun go down over land I haven't seen before."

Zell smiled. These damp lowlands hadn't been good for xe; breathing was difficult and the pain in xe's hip never left xe. +Where there's no war.+ Xe stroked xe's hand along Wintshikan's arm. +Where hate is a personal thing and not visited on strangers.+

Wintshikan sat silent as a long line of femlits, mallits and anyalits snaked past them, laughing and stomping the sand as they moved. When they were by, she said, "We'll wait a few days for Luca and the others. If they come back. If they're all right. But if we wait too long, the price may move beyond what we can pay."

+We can leave word where we're going if the time comes before they do. We should think of Zaro and Kanilli. And Xaca. The Coranthim Remnant might meld with us to make a new ixis; they've got young mals but not much coin. We've got coin.+

"Speaking of coin, I'm hungry. You?"

+I could swallow a tata or two.+ Xe used Wintshikan's arm as a brace and pushed onto xe's feet. +Ahh, Wintashi, what a night. I truly didn't think I'd live to see this.+

7. Into the wild blue....

Shadith swung the chair around, stretched, groaned, and ran her hands through her hair. "Vumah vumay, that's done." She glanced from the piles of debris to the anxious, waiting faces of the locals. "The Fence is gone."

Yseyl closed her eyes and went very still.

Hidan grinned, tucked xe's rifle under xe's arm, made a broad sweeping sign of triumph. When the sign was done, though, xe's grin shrank to a tight smile. +Ptaks been circling this place and trying to get in through the door for the past half hour.+

Shadith listened and heard through the noise of the storm a confused and muted muttering barely louder than the hum of the station behind her. A *reach* told her a crowd of wet, mean, frustrated Ptaks were milling about outside; as yet there was no organization in that mob, just a few individuals around the Exec who were focused on the codex, a few others trotting off to circle about the building, hunting, no doubt, for the place where the intruders breached security. She rubbed at her back. "They won't be getting in, I changed the ... um ... keys. You've been watching. Has anyone noticed yet that the glass is out in that storeroom window?"

+I haven't thinned many Ptaks back there, just a few who keep trotting around and around the building, I think because they're too steamed to stand still.+

Yseyl shuddered and opened her eyes. "Syon would have started shooting if they found the hole and tried to get in. Start the fire and let's go. I don't see any reason to hang about."

Shadith glanced toward the Ptak techs. Tied, gagged and blindfolded, rolled up against the wall under the windows, they wouldn't have a chance once the fire got going. They were awake now, frightened and furious. "Right, but we'll switch the order of things. Ghost, you and the others mask up and head out, I'll give you a few minutes' start before I touch off the fire."

Yseyl stopped a moment in the arch, looked back. The mask hid her face, but Shadith had no trouble reading her suspicion and speculation. A moment later she was gone.

Shadith leaned back in the chair and contemplated the Ptaks. "Listen carefully," she said. "The others will be out and clear in a few minutes. Well on their way into the mountains. You'll never find them. This is their home ground. I came into this for ethical reasons. That Fence is an abomination in the face of God, so I have destroyed it. Be warned, what I have done, I can do again. I will remove your gags before I go to join my allies. In their anger they would have left you to burn to death, but I will not. I have programmed the shield to go down and the door to open ten minutes after I leave. Yell for your people to come get you. Tell them that the kephalos has been infected and will fail five minutes after the door opens."

Shadith set the stunner to broad beam, clipped the collapsed ladderpole to her belt, and vaulted through the window. She hit the ground with a loud splash, slid across the gelatinous mud, and finally managed to scramble to her feet. Half blinded by the rain, disoriented by the slither, she dropped to a crouch, touched the triggering sensor on the stunrod, and swept the field through a wide arc. As she rose, she *reached* in a quick check of the area. No active minds anywhere close. She groped for the narrow path she'd sliced into the thorn hedge, eased through it, jumped the body of a stunned Ptak and ran for the trees.

Away from the lights and the buildings with the foliage dripping about her, the darkness was intense. The ground was soaked and slippery underfoot; though the leaves gave her some shelter, each time she brushed against a branch, it unloaded itself over her and she was wet through after her first few strides.

As she headed for the end of the lake and the Drill Field, she tried to run and scan at the same time. That was a mistake. Her foot slipped off a root she didn't notice and hit a patch of clay mud. She went down hard, her head glancing off the tree, her other knee twisting as she fell on it, the stunrod flying from her hand.

For a moment she lay there, dazed and hurting, then she heard Ptak shrieks and the splatting of feet off to one side.

She struggled up, gasping at the pain in her knee. There was no time to search for the rod and maybe no need; between the rain and the mud the Ptaks shouldn't be able to learn much from it. And they already knew an offworlder was involved. She took a step, gritted her teeth, and limped as fast as she could toward the Drill Field.

Swing that leg, plant the foot, lurch forward, over and over, grab onto branches to take at least a little weight off the knee, swing lurch splat. Confusion around her. Sound of rain hitting the leaves, rain in her face, cold and dreary, trickling down her neck. Wind. Mud. Mud. Mud.

A shout. The light brightened around her, unsteady light, wavering through the boles of the trees. *They got the door open and the draft hit the fire. For the glow to reach this far, it must be going good. Ah Spla! Ten minutes gone already?*

Step. Slide. Slither. Gasp. A gust of rain hit her in the face. Arm crooked over her eyes so she wouldn't be blinded by the downpour, she lurched another two steps and was out of the trees. She hunched her shoulders, and continued to limp toward the field she couldn't see. The rain battered at her, blew into her face until she was half drowned.

A shout. Ptaks! Close behind her. She swung awkwardly around, fumbling for the cutter at her belt. She could just make out two dim gray forms heading for her. "Ah Spla, why did there have to be two cool heads in that lot?"

She lifted the cutter, but before she could use it, she felt the aura of a stun beam going by too close and saw the Ptaks crumpling into the mud.

"Shadow, Wann said you were hurt." Yseyl's voice.

Shadith turned. "Fell and twisted my knee. My own dumb fault. Appreciate the assist."

"Ha." Yseyl moved closer. "Use my shoulder. You forget you're the only one who can fly that thing?"

Shadith managed a chuckle. "Nice to be needed."

She turned the flier in a tight circle above the caldera. "Thought you might like a look at the damage."

The roof of the Control Center collapsed at that moment in a shower of sparks; in spite of the heavy downpour the suddenly released flames leaped twenty feet into the air. The thorn hedge was smoldering and several of the closest houses were also burning.

Pressed against the window as if they couldn't get enough of the sight, the Pixas were silent, a fiercely triumphant silence. Zot clapped her hands and giggled, then she, too, went quiet, snuggling up against Yseyl.

Yseyl hesitated, set a hand on the child's shoulder. She saw Shadith watching her, stared back with angry denial, then turned her head away.

Hm, maybe Digby will have himself a ghost for hire. I don't think that relationship is going to work out. Assassin and little mother don't seem to be compatible occupations. "Right. If you seat yourselves and get comfortable, we'll be on our way. Before I take you back to the camp where we started, I want to go look at where the Fence was. Just to make sure it's really down, not an aberration in the software. Thought you might like to see that, too. Or rather, not see it."

Luca threw herself into the front seat, drawing Wann down beside her. "Yes," she said. "I want to see it. I want to see it gone."

Khimil slapped his hand hard against the side of the cabin. "Yes. I saw that cursed thing every day when we were on that coaster working our way south. Syon, remember the time the wind caught us and Cap'n Dakwe was drunker'n thuv?"

"Urr. We coulda been ashed." The young mal shivered, edged up close to Hidan, took xe's hand, and held it against his face.

Xe freed the hand, patted his shoulder, then seated herself beside Nyen.

As soon as the rest had sorted themselves into the seats, Shadith took the flier into a sweeping circle, and sent it racing west as dawn pinked the sky behind them.

8. Afterbite

"No! What we just did is one thing, you got your adventure and lived through it, but where I'm headed now, it's too dangerous." Yseyl thrust her fingers through her hair, turned her shoulder to the crouching, glowering child and stalked to the stream. She squatted, separated out a pebble from the scree on the bank, flung it at the bole of a conifer on the far side of the stream. The snap of her arm and the satisfying clunk of the pebble calmed her. She looked over her shoulder at Zot. "I won't take you, Zot. You can argue all you want."

Zot brought her head up and forward like a striking yok. "Liar! You just want to get rid of me, that's all. You think I don't know?"

"Believe what you want, it doesn't change anything." She got to her feet, dusted her hands together. "I talked to Luca. Khimil and Syon are joining their ixis and they

want you with them. You'll have a family again and you
need that."

"I don't want a family. It'll be worse than living in the
Hall, people messing you around all the time."

"I'm doing the best I can for you, Zot. You're a good
kid and smart, but you don't know me. I don't know what
you think you see, but it isn't me. And you don't know
thuv about the world I'm going into." Her voice was soft,
almost a whisper, anger putting edges on the words. "And
don't tell me you could learn. You'd get yourself killed
and maybe me, too."

Zot stared at her a moment, biting her lip to keep
it from trembling, eyes squinted to hold tears back.
Abruptly she was up and running full out, vanishing a
moment later into the shadow under the trees.

Yseyl stood where she was, anger and affection both
emptied out of her, only a vague relief left to temper the
coldness. It was done and easier than she'd expected. *Zot
will calm down once I'm gone. She'll see it's the best
thing and go along with Luca. Family. She needs family.
Not me. Not me. Not me. . . .* She shivered, drew her hand
across her face, wiping away all that nonsense, then
walked briskly across the grass to the hunter.

"Is there any reason why you need to wait longer? I
want to get out of here."

"I don't want to lift until there's enough traffic in the
air so we won't be spotted and targeted." She nodded at
the flier a few paces off, backed under the overhang of
the canopy. "Alarm's set to tell me when more fliers are
up. Shouldn't be long now."

"I don't understand, I thought. . . ."

"The Ptaks know a lot of arms dealers and those gits
sell more than weapons. I'm no gambler, Ghost. I like to
have my feet planted and know where I'm jumping. . . ."

A musical chime, a single pure note, sounded through
the open door of the flier.

The hunter came to her feet in one of those fluid swift moves that always startled Yseyl in one so large and lumpy.

"And it's time to jump," she said. "Get your gear and let's go."

15

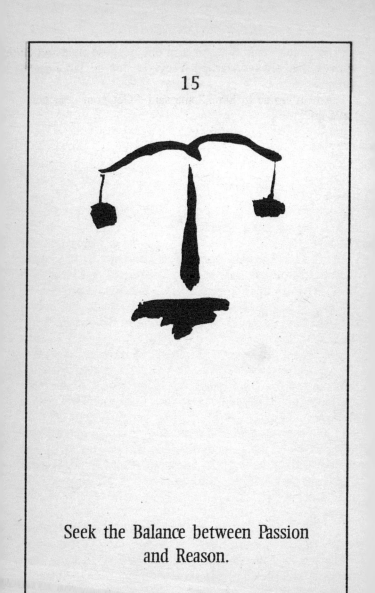

Seek the Balance between Passion
and Reason.

Chapter 13

The dawnlight was gray under the ragged trees as Luca stepped across the boundary line of the camp.

There was a loud alarm whistle and a young fem she didn't know stepped from the shadow cast by one of the tents, rifle lifted, face stony. "Stop there, or I'll shoot."

"What is this? Where's ixis Shishim?" Luca looked round. The corral was gone, and the jomayls, but two of the tents were familiar—she recognized a patch Xaca had sewn over a rip. "What happened?"

Shadowy forms were coming from the tents, spreading out behind the sentinel, then Kanilli darted forward. "Luuuucaaaa," she cried and flung herself at the fem. "You came back," she cried, the words muffled against Lucca's shirt.

Wintshikan stepped into a patch of moonlight. "It's all right, Phula, she's one of ours. Let me see you, all of you, you're all back, and who are these? Never mind, you can tell me in a minute. You did it. God's blessing on you, you did it."

Luca walked over to the leather cushion where Wintshikan was watching the celebration. She dropped to the ground and sat examining the older fem's face. Once Heka, still Heka by the rule of the Cards. Of Shicoram ixis now. "I'm not going back to the old ways."

"I know." There was sadness but acceptance in the old

fem's voice. "Those are fine young mals you brought back to us. Impix, aren't they?"

"Farmer's sons."

"Ah. That will be useful." She grinned, the years falling from her face though the wrinkles deepened. "Never thought I'd be welcoming Impix. We'll have to build like that coast village, remember? We can't make things like city Impix, but we can grow food and raise maphiks for their meat and leather. Did you know I planned to pass the Shawl to you when we reached Linojin?"

"I thought maybe you would."

"Do you mind if I don't?"

"No. Now that I understand where you're going." Luca looked at the mix out round the fire—two Remnants to blend and a pair of Impix to fit in somehow. "Everything's going to be so different, we'll need a center for a while to give us order. When the Change is finished, though . . . vumah vumay, we'll see."

The Mountain nurtures and teaches,
is cruel and kind.
Teach the right path,
discipline the heart.

Chapter 14

Thann turned and looked back a last time at the House of Mercy.

Isaho was theirs now. Xe's daughter was dead—the Isaho walking about didn't recognize xe when she saw xe. The grief of that was heavy on xe's shoulders as xe took up the pack of clothes the Anyas of Mercy had given her and walked away. Xe was more than a little frightened, but xe couldn't bear to spend another night under that roof.

Mind on the instructions the Grand Mercy's aide had given xe, xe's free hand resting in the side slit of the hatchry robe, ready to hold the anyalit inside xe's pouch, xe moved along the twisty lanes that led to Progress Way. The babbit was curled up and sleeping now, but xe was blessed or cursed with an abundance of energy and never slept for long. Xe didn't know what waited for xe in the west quarter where the hohekils were, for xe had only the few coins the Mercys had given xe, no kin, nobody to protect xe, but with so many exiles and broken families over there, maybe xe could find a place to take xe where xe could raise the anyalit in some kind of peace.

As xe left the Way and began moving into narrow lanes again, xe heard shouts, sounds of running feet.

A small compact form came round a corner, slammed into xe, knocking xe against the wall of the house beside xe. Hastily, xe thrust xe's hand farther inside the robe, pressed xe's palm against the sphincter to keep the anyalit from wriggling out.

"Oy!" A small hot hand caught hold of xe's, pulled xe away from the wall. "Run. Please."

Shouts and curses from the alley, a mal's voice, angry, vengeful and coming closer. Slap of boots on the pavement.

Still dazed by the collision, Thann let the femlit pull xe along until xe was back on Progress Way and in the shadow of the Yeson wall.

The femlit let go of xe's hand, dropped to a squat and panted, eyes sweeping over the Pilgrim throng moving past them.

Thann stroked the bulge of the babbit, relaxed when xe started suckling. Xe bent, tapped the femlit's head. When she looked up, xe signed, +Why?+

The femlit coughed, spat. "When I saw you were anya and by yourself, I couldn't leave you there. Ol' Fishbreath, he wouldn't even break stride, just scoop you up and sell you to his friend the flesh broker."

+Why was he after you? Did he want to sell you?+

"Nah. Femlits don't fetch enough to pay for the trouble of carting me there." She ran bright shrewd eyes over Thann, seemed to make up her mind about something. " 'Cause I just lifted his purse, that's why." She made a face, shrugged. "I'm not very good at it yet. How come you walking about by your lone self? Bad idea, anya."

+Because I don't have a place to be. I might ask the same of you, femlit.+

"Where's your family? How'd you get to Linojin without them?"

Thann managed a smile at the deft way the child avoided her question. +You wouldn't believe me if I told you.+

The femlit got to her feet, stood with her hands clasped

behind her, her eyes once again searching the crowd. "What I seen the last few days, bet I would. Uh-oh, Fishbreath isn't giving up. We better move on some. I know, I'll take you to the Arbiter's place. I can get you there real easy, I was a guide till a few days ago."

Thann followed her, bemused with how much xe was trusting this child. Under the surface charm, the femlit was angry and hurting for some reason, but oddly cheerful for all that. As they moved swiftly through a maze of narrow streets, a disturbing thought came to xe. *Am I making her into Isaho, what I hoped Isaho would be?*

The babbit stirred restlessly, disturbed by what xe was reading of Thann's sudden revulsion.

Xe slipped xe's hand inside the pouch, guided the babbit's mouth back to the teat, then stroked the small, strong body, bathed xe with the burst of helpless love that flooded xe.

The femlit tapped xe's arm. "There," she said and pointed to a large blocky building with black iron bars on the windows. "You go in there and somebody'll fix you up with a place to live where you won't have to be scared of the flesh mal."

Thann withdrew her hand from the pouch. +Wait. What are you going to do?+

The femlit scowled at xe. "You going to try running my life, too?"

+I thin you don't like that much. Hm, say it's curiosity. I like to know what's happening to people I've grown fond of. You know you're a charmer, so untwist that face and tell me.+

"You're sharp for an anya. They usually dumber'n rocks. All right. I'm going to keep my head down till Fishbreath's ship steams out, he works on this coast trader, then go nosing round and see what's hanging loose."

+Then you've got time to come in there with me and

show me how to work them, so they don't notice I'm not dumber than a rock. Besides, I'll tell you my story while we're waiting. If you'll tell me yours.+

The femlit eyed xe a moment, still wary, then she grinned and nodded. "You got it. My name's Zot, and I helped take the Fence down."

Thann waggled xe's hand in anya laughter. +My name is Thann, and I flew to Linojin on a broomstick with someone I think is a friend of yours, an offworld person named Shadow. This should be interesting for us both.+

Death is the end and
the beginning,
the change from which
there is no returning.

Chapter 15

Yseyl stood in the shadow of the thile tree on the crumbling cliff beside the last of the wharves along the bayfront of Lala Gemali. She slipped the carrystrap of the disruptor case from her shoulder, let the case dangle against her leg, and frowned at the flier as it plunged toward the water out near the middle of the lake. "I still think that was a mistake. You just announced we're here."

"Maybe, but when the water hits the lifters and they blow, that erases any chance the Ptaks will sniff out enough to identify me. That's more important right now than making this an easy sneak." Shadith reached for the strap. "Time to pay the bill, Ghost."

Yseyl watched the hunter settle the case against her side. "Now that you have that, tell me true. Was that job offer real or a delusion."

"Oh, it's real, all right. I get all sorts of nice bonus points if I bring you back alive and willing. As I said when we first met, Digby collects talents. Time to split. You know where to go, what to look for. See you."

As Shadith hurried along the lanes toward The Strip, she wondered if the Ghost would trust her enough to show up at the landing field. Yseyl had only come this far because she wanted to put a lot of distance between herself and that kid. Shadith sighed. *Complications. Well, I'll leave that for Digby to handle.*

The Strip was swarming with unhappy tourists, complaining in a melange of langues about having no 'bots to carry their luggage, about splitcom time booked for days ahead so they couldn't get reservations on the worldship diverted to pick up the outflow, about Ptak refusal to refund their money, about how bored they were since the screens went black. Complaining at the top of their vocal ranges until the noise was enough to shatter a stone.

Shadith moved through those conversations as she'd moved through the whispered enticements of the holoas before, savoring this cacophony a lot more than the daintier blandishments of the ads. She kept her head down and her eyes lowered to hide the fierce pleasure in them.

Yseyl drew over herself the shape she'd worn at Marrat's Market and followed Shadow into the lanes, trying to keep the map straight in her mind and her camouflage locked in place.

When she reached The Strip, the sight of Ptaks everywhere burned in her stomach and brought her near a killing rage. It was as well that the only weapon she had was the stunrod taped to her arm. She grew calmer as she picked out those complaints voiced in interlingue and began to understand the implications of taking out those satellites. Killing a few Ptaks was birdseed besides the hurt Shadow had put on them, a wound in the purse much more agonizing than a hole in the body.

Zot's face was suddenly in her mind. She shivered and jerked her thoughts away from the child. Use Shadow. Use Digby. Learn her way around the starfliers' world. Keep herself clear of all ties. When ready, call Cerex and use him. Nobody was ever going to crawl under her skin again. Never. Never. Never.

The landing field was chaos when she reached it, harried Ptaks trying and failing to keep a measure of order in the surge offworld. Yseyl chose her time, blurred past security, oriented herself, and headed for the section of the field where Shadow's ship was supposed to be. If the hunter had spoken the truth. If it was still there and waiting.

Shadow was seated in an open air lock, a stunrifle across her lap. Yseyl looked up at her. "Well?"

"Hang on a minute, I'll send the lift down for you." She got to her feet, vanished inside the lock.

When the lift reached her, Yseyl hesitated a moment, looked over her shoulder at the world she was leaving. She had a choice this time. She could walk away even now, and Shadow wouldn't stop her.

With a shiver and a touch of anger in her stomachs, she stepped onto the platform. "Take it up," she said. "Let's get out of here."

1

From the Egg all things arise.

2

The Spiral contains all within its coils.
At its heart lies the Truth.

3

In the Tribond
Cherish difference, celebrate Oneness.

Clouds cover the sun, curtains
of rain hide what is ahead.
Danger or nurture?

5

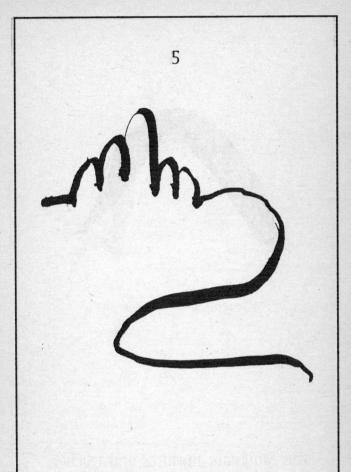

Drink deep from the Spring
that gives Life,
and from life learn Wisdom.

6

The Mountain nurtures and teaches,
is cruel and kind.
Teach the Right Path,
discipline the heart.

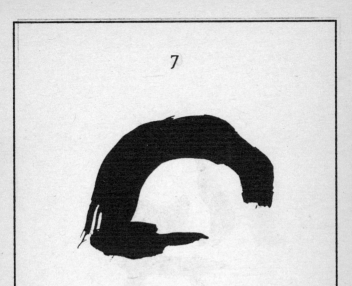

Blood is silent in darkness,
but screams for justice
when it sees the sun.

Do everything with the full passion
of your heart for by that
you serve God.

Lightning welds and sunders,
casts light and dark
A call to quickness of mind,
eye and hand.

10

Wings cup the air and go where they will.
Things volatile and unsteady
change at the puff of a breath.

11

The Trivadda is the sign of decisions.
The parting of ways
The sundering of past and present.

12

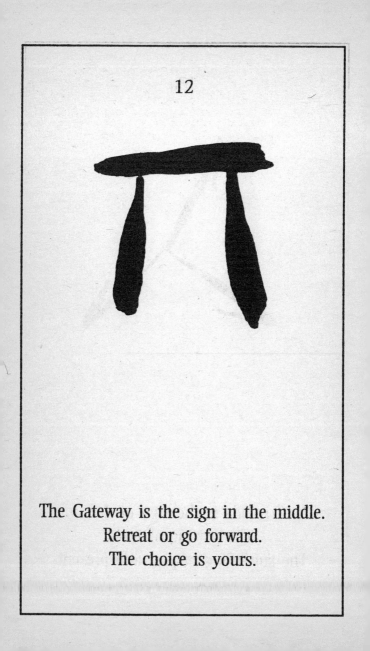

The Gateway is the sign in the middle.
Retreat or go forward.
The choice is yours.

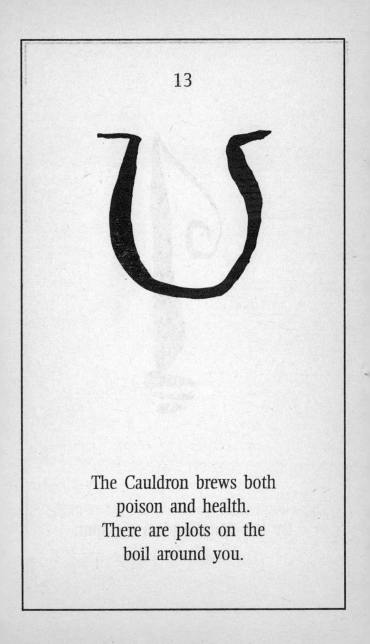

13

The Cauldron brews both
poison and health.
There are plots on the
boil around you.

By the Spindle plots are spun
for good or ill.

Seek the Balance between
passion and reason.

16

The Knot is the heart of all things hidden.
Never cut what you can untie.

The Drumbeat is a snare that lures you
from the right path.

The Wall stands in your path
and forbids passage.

19

When the Twig is Broken, Peril.
Body, mind and soul on the brink
of the Abyss.

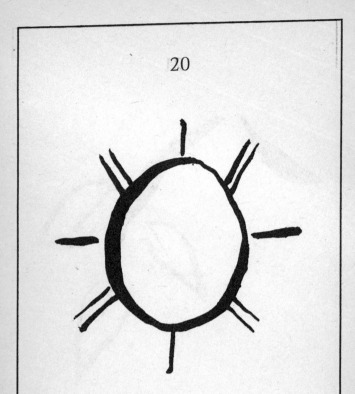

Fortune, enlightenment, joy
Such is the promise of the Sun
Danger and excess
Such is the threat of the Sun.

Study the Moon to understand
that all things change
and are eternally the same.

As the comet flares and dies
without fruit,
beware the liar and he
who swears a faithless oath.

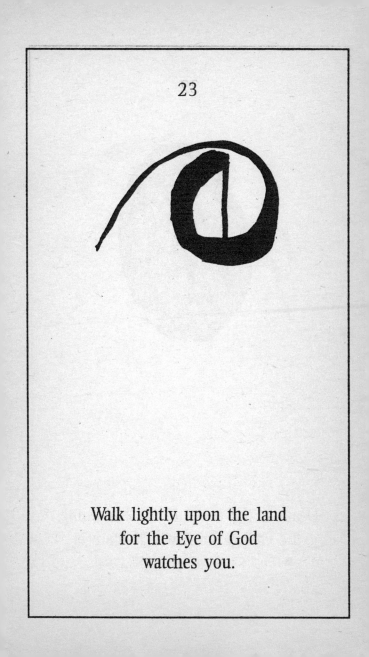

Walk lightly upon the land
for the Eye of God
watches you.

Death is the end and the beginning,
the change from which there is
no returning.

Science Fiction at Its Best

Karen Haber
☐ **WOMAN WITHOUT A SHADOW**   UE2627—$4.99
Kayla, a gifted telepath, is about to be caught in a struggle between two deadly forces determined to use any weapon to secure total victory.

Betty Anne Crawford
☐ **THE BUSHIDO INCIDENT**   UE2517—$4.99
So Pak, seeking the path of freedom, launches a mission on the starship *Bushido*. But someone is determined that neither So Pak nor the *Bushido* will ever return to Earth.

Daniel Ransom
☐ **THE FUGITIVE STARS**   UE2625—$4.99
The tail of the comet held more than just harmless space dust. It also contained the seeds of an alien invasion . . . Only one man could sense what was happening, but could he prove it before it was too late?